GUARDIAN

BOOK TWO

AbrA EbneR

Crimson Oak Publishing

Pullman, Wa 99163
Visit our website at www.CrimsonOakPublishing.com

Ebner, Abra, 1984 -
Guardian: A novel / by Abra Ebner
Edited by Christina Corlett

www.FeatherBookSeries.com

Summary: Love spans and eternity, at least for Edgar and Estella. As She fights
to figure out her past, she finds something much more. There is a whole world
of history about her and her complicated special life. Estella comes into her
own in her first great adventure, in the life she was born to live, and die for.

printed in U.S.A

1 2 3 4 5 6 7 8 9 10

To all those with loss

*Death is but the beginning,
and to fear it is trivial...*

Alone
Edgar A. Poe

From childhood's hour I have not been
As others were; I have not seen
As others saw; I could not bring
My passions from a common spring.
From the same source I have not taken
My sorrow; I could not awaken
My heart to joy at the same tone;
And all I loved, I loved alone.
Then- in my childhood, in the dawn
Of a most stormy life- was drawn
From every depth of good and ill
The mystery which binds me still:
From the torrent, or the fountain,
From the red cliff of the mountain,
From the sun that round me rolled
In its autumn tint of gold,
From the lightning in the sky
As it passed me flying by,
From the thunder and the storm,
And the cloud that took the form
(When the rest of Heaven was blue)
Of a demon in my view.

PREFACE

And though we find that the god's creations were exiled to Earth, what they never expected was the revolt that could ultimately lead to a revolution. When cast to live among the humans, forever bound to a life of sadness and torment, the two halves prevailed, defying all odds and finding each other. Despite their need to destroy all they held dear and self destruct, the breed adapted to their challenge, angering the gods and creating a reunion.

Horrified and driven by a jealous rage, the gods then set out to kill all those that defied them, finding their amusing game had turned sour. Deep in the roots of Earth they forged a dagger, strong enough to kill their creations forever. This dagger would leave nothing but empty shells of the raven, servants that would hold no heart or soul.

In their greed they ignored the simple fact that such a weapon could be used against them, their hearts too corrupt with power to understand their own demise. Among the gods creations on Earth, they searched for a worthy soul to carry the weapon and do the deed. They hunted far and wide for one so dark, that they could buy it with the promise of power and barter with his greedy instincts.

When the soul was found, they bestowed him with the dagger, outlining his task to kill and the fruitful future he was promised; a promise that they never planned to uphold. When this soul received the dagger, he turned into no more than a rat, squandering all his riches and killing all his friends, one by one.

The gods were pleased with the success of their pawn, and as the divine race deceased into legend, they had all but forgotten the game of the human Earth, leaving it to self destruct in a manner that was unstoppable. When they finally turned their attentions away from their greedy crusade and back to the Earth many decades later, the gods found that the Earth was now dying. The humans they had neglected while hunting for the pure race were now infesting the surface like a plague.

Horrified, the gods ceased their previous plans, finding that now only a few of their divine creations remained as they had slaughtered the rest. These beings that they had previously hunted were now the only beings that could save everyone. Among those left, was the first. She was the original prototype of their experiments, exponentially more potent and powerful than all the rest. She was a proven force that could not be erased, despite their evil pawn's efforts.

In this they knew they needed to recruit her, and though finding they were now locked by her wishes, they would not divulge her importance to her, keeping her power a secret and squeezing all she had left back to the Earth. Content with the new plan, the gods set it in motion, killing the evil pawn and taking collateral. This is where our story continues...

BABY STEPS

The cold granite felt like steel against my head as I lay on the top landing of the stairs, pondering my next move. I took a few calm measured breaths, allowing my eyes to stay closed. My heart was racing. I hadn't ever gotten this far, not until now. The closest I had gotten to my room was yesterday, when I finally laid one foot on the bottom step. Now here I was, at the top, my body trembling with fear and sorrow like a nervous idiot.

Slowly, I began to draw my eyelids open like a curtain at a play. I felt the granite under my sweaty palms, my arms sprawled out at my sides and my legs cascading down the stairs. I rolled my head to the right, looking at the doors to my room with sad recollection.

It had been nearly two months since I'd been back at the house, but still I could not bring myself to go back to my room and see what I feared would be a scene of sadness and loss. I had taken to sleeping on the couch in the sitting room, despite Sam's attempts to encourage me to face the facts, and move on. He didn't understand how this felt. He didn't know what sorrow was anymore, or fear. He was dead, inside and out.

I drew in a heavy breath and held it as it stung my lungs. Carefully, I rolled my head to the other side, my eyes falling on the doors to Edgar's mysterious room. His room was a place I couldn't even fathom visiting. I had never seen it, at least not in my current recollection. It still seemed like an imaginary place, a place that had never really existed.

Although I had gotten my soul back when Edgar's heart had ceased to beat, it hadn't given me all of my memory. There were certain things that slowly trickled back, like my expert knowledge for chess, and of course my heightened sense of sight, and sound, but not my memory.

I exhaled as I drew my head back to the center, staring at the gold leaf ceiling. I wrenched my tired body up as I leaned my chin into my hands and placed my feet on the top step. Dragging my fingers across my tired eyes, I heard the swift cutting of wings echoing through the large entry foyer.

My hands dropped to my lap as I looked up, seeing Henry and Isabelle circle the chandelier and dive toward me. They landed on the top step as their talons slipped, grinding across the granite like fingernails on a chalkboard. I winced at the shrill noise as they clicked their way back toward me with haste, each rubbing their head against my arm like cats often would.

In the passing months, Henry had grafted himself to me as though he were solely mine. I knew he missed Edgar. There was a glimmer in his eye that was unmistakable and sad. He now looked to me as his foster mother, and that was definitely something I could relate with.

I sighed with a heavy heart as I scratched them both on the head. This trip to my room was always destined to be a failed attempt, but I had at least gotten to the top landing. I looked up as my eyes caught the glimmer of something standing in the center of the entry. Sam was smiling at me as he stood there in angelic silence. It was frustrating that even I could not hear him moving in his soundless existence.

"Wow. Looks like you got pretty far today," he half laughed as he said it.

I wiped the sorrow from my face before he could notice, reverting back to confidence as I prepared myself to take on his sarcastic barrage of emotionless banter. "Thanks Sam." My voice was sharp, but amused.

"So why don't you just do it? Pour salt on the wound so you can move on? I know you're stronger than this, besides, you keep talking in your sleep about how uncomfortable the couch is. And frankly, you're boring." He smirked.

I pushed my brows together. "Do you watch me sleep? Come on, Sam, that's creepy."

He laughed. "Of course I watch you. It's my job. And I like being creepy. It goes well with my superhero image."

I pursed my lips and shook my head. It had taken some practice, but I was learning to hide my thoughts away from him. I had found a special room in my head that even he couldn't penetrate, and I was sure it was beginning to frustrate him. He was used to the minds of weak humans; so revealing. But I was more than human now. I was immortal, and my powers could somewhat rival his, though I still wasn't as strong. At least my intelligence and sharp intuition kept him challenged.

I narrowed my eyes. "No, I think you're trying to read my thoughts. You can't stand not knowing my every whim, can you?"

He fidgeted with his hands as he held them behind his back. His wings were entirely withdrawn into his shoulder blades to the point that you would never be able to discern him from a human, other than the fact that his skin was cold as ice and his eyes were heavily shadowed in a light mauve.

He finally smirked, snorting in a delicate manner which suggested he was guilty. "Maybe, I just like to hear your thoughts. It makes me feel alive again. Human thoughts are so boring: what to eat, what to watch on TV, what should I do to poison the Earth today. You on the other hand, your thoughts are fascinating." His eyes suddenly lit up with joy.

I narrowed my eyes even further, exhaling sharply. I pushed myself off the cold floor and stood. Henry and Isabelle trotted toward my bedroom doors, encouraging me. They stopped and looked back as though urging me to follow, but I shook my head. "Not today, guys. Tomorrow, I promise."

They both looked at me as though telling me I'd promised them that a dozen times already. Henry blinked, lowering his head as Isabelle followed suit. It made my heart break to see them that way, but what else could I do? I was a prisoner of fear.

Sam snorted. "Yeah, that's exactly what they're thinking."

I turned my gaze to Sam. I had allowed him that thought. "You can't hear what they're thinking, so stop pretending you can. You can't pull that one on me."

Sam shrugged. "True. But I can feel their emotion, and right now they seem pretty disappointed."

"Whatever," I replied tartly. "You're just upset that I can beat you at your own game. You're such a poor loser, Sam."

He chuckled. "Whatever."

I sighed as I darted across the top landing of the stairs to the shelf and grasped the Edgar Allan Poe notebook. I did it as though something was after me, but the only thing chasing me at this point was the ghosts of my past. The thick old leather felt rough between my fingers as I bounded down the stairs. It wasn't that I wanted to run away from reality. I just wasn't ready to face it.

Sam laughed again. "That was some serious Indiana Jones action there, very impressive, but you forgot to replace the idol with a bag of sand. Better watch out! An evil gremlin will likely attack!" He pointed to the stairs behind me with sarcastic humor.

I felt a sudden urge to punch him as my bare feet landed like an expert on the foyer floor, and in fact, that was just what I did. As my fist landed hard against his cold bicep, however, I felt my fingers crunch and a sharp pain pulse through my arm as though I'd punched a marble statue.

Sam looked at me with sly eyes, my punch no more than

14

a brush of a feather to him. "Whoa there missy, better be careful."

I grasped my hand as it throbbed and stung. Glowering at him, I rubbed my broken knuckles in rueful silence as I molded them back to normal in slow gentle strokes.

"I don't get why you choose to inflict pain on yourself like that, time after time. I get the point. You resent me, but get over it. I'm not leaving unless Edgar releases my bond to you." He paused as he smirked, my heart crumbling like rocks as he said his name. "And I don't see that happening anytime soon," he added, an extra twist of the dagger now stabbing at my guilty sad soul.

I growled at him. "Shut up, Sam." My hand was feeling much better as I twisted on one foot and stormed toward the kitchen, a sharp angry beat in my step.

He followed like a soundless ghost. "Oh, come on, Elly. I didn't mean it. I'm not used to being polite."

"Well then get used to it. You're acting like a monster, not an angel." His comment still stung in my heart. Any time he uttered Edgar's name it hurt as though the dagger had stabbed me instead.

"I'm trying, but it's hard to remember what feeling emotion is like. I still don't understand why you chose to get your soul back. All it does is complicate things."

I plopped down on a stool and thumped my elbows down on the copper island. "Well, try harder," I spat.

"Okay, let me make you some lunch. What would you like?" The desperation in his voice was working, and I began to feel guilty. He simply didn't know any better.

15

"How about some sympathy with a side of comfort?" I smarted.

"What's in that?"

He sounded genuinely confused, and I rolled my eyes at him. You would think he could at least smell his own sarcasm being thrown back at him.

"Just, never mind." I sighed. "Go in the upper cabinet, there should be a box of macaroni and cheese, just follow the directions."

He eyed me with an annoying smirk. I know he knew what I had been talking about, but he was a good actor. I only wished I had been so sarcastic and talented with conversation when I didn't have a soul. Maybe then I wouldn't be as miserable as I was now because I would have never come here, never met Edgar, and I could have lived on in my oblivious depressed darkness.

The box made a dull jingling sound as he tilted it out of he cabinet and the noodles shifted inside. I thought about my eggs and syrup and wished Edgar was here to make it for me; only he knew how. I was never much of a cook, and my appetite hadn't really been great, anyway. I was still sick over the loss, and I wondered if the sinking feeling of sadness would ever leave. Often they say time heals all wounds, but so far, I felt as though my wounds were still gaping, gushing sadness and blood with every painstaking moment that passed.

Sam eyed me with a knowing glare. I had allowed him the torture of that thought as well, letting him know how much I resented his attempts at filling the gap Edgar had left. Failed attempts, like eating sugar when you're starving. Sam was a great friend, but he was no Edgar.

There was an abrupt and odd look on Sam's face and I analyzed it with discretion. I had never seen a look like that before, and I almost compared it with real remorse.

I was proud of myself. Fixing Sam had become a sort of pet project, no man should forget what he died for, as he had seemed to. I knew who he used to be, based on Edgar's story of how he gave his life for a young girl he barely knew. I had never confronted him, though. I was afraid of the outcome. Afraid he wouldn't remember why he was here and become frustrated. As hard as it was to admit, I needed him. Otherwise by now, I would have already gone crazy.

Sam was watching me with nervous eyes over the top of the box as he read each direction with diligence, extracting each ingredient and measuring it as though in biology class. Sam didn't eat, either. He didn't need to. He told me he couldn't taste it, anyway. All earthly desires were stripped from him because of his duty to serve. Nothing must sidetrack him from that. But in my stubbornness, I was determined to change that idea.

He had succeeded in making a pot of water boil as it sat very close to the flames of the fire in the kitchen hearth. I was amazed, even I had never succeeded at that simple task, and my mac and cheese was rather crunchy due to that fact. He looked inwardly content with himself, as though he'd accomplished something great.

Maybe Edgar had been right when he said it was easier to be the professor than pretend to be the student. A professor led, while a student followed. It was now apparent, more than ever, that there was no one left for me to follow. I had to face the fact that stepping up to my responsibilities was evident.

I had thought about the college and wondered if Scott and Sarah were still there. It was mid-summer, so it was highly likely. It hadn't seemed right, though, to go back. What was the point beyond re-hashing hurtful memories and the doldrums of waiting? And for what? Death? Still, it hadn't escaped my thoughts and I was formulating a time to go, just not yet, not now.

Sam struggled with the packet of fake cheese sauce and I giggled in secrecy. He gave me an embarrassed and reproachful glare before tearing the pack nearly to pieces. He only managed to get about half of its contents into the pot before the rest spilled to the floor.

"Don't worry about it, Sam." I reassured him, surprised to find him upset and angry with himself. Maybe he really was becoming human again.

His face changed from embarrassment to confidence. "Pfft. What are you talking about? I'm not embarrassed."

I could see the attempt to lie crossing his face and I chuckled once, looking down at the copper counter and admiring my reflection. My eyes gleamed like small orbs of luminescent opals, reflecting in sharp rays off the copper and back at me.

"Sam?"

He looked up from the fire, his face pulled together with frustration over the result of his cooking. "Hmm?"

"What happened that day, before I was taken? What did you see?" I had never been able to ask this question, everything

18

else had come first; mostly the fact that Edgar was gone.

"I saw you being stupid," he replied in a blunt and cold manner. His amber eyes scanned my face, trying to pry into my thoughts.

"Yeah, but seriously. You saw the cat, right?" My eyes scanned his and I allowed him to see my thoughts, the blurred memory of the white cat and the vicious attack of the ravens.

His face seemed to be torn, as though he was experiencing something painful. I realized it was a look of failure, failure because he had lost me that day in the woods and had let Edgar die. It was silly that he blamed himself for that. It wasn't even his fault. But, I could see his dutiful point. He had failed at the only thing he did well: being a guardian.

"Yeah, I saw the nasty feline," he spat.

"What was it? Why was it here? Could you feel what it was thinking?" I knew how he could feel Henry and Isabelle, and I'd hoped he had felt the cat, too. He had to have noticed something.

"I felt a lot of things, Elly. There were the ravens first and foremost, but I suppose I did feel a strange muted undertone of something. It was strange, as though a mixed signal. I was certain of the fact that it wasn't normal, if you ask me." He shrugged as he pulled the soupy noodles away from the fire. I watched as he contemplated over a plate or bowl, finally settling for a bowl after the sour expression on his face recognized the contents of the pot to be closer to soup than noodles.

"But, do you think it was part of Matthew's plan? Do you think it was another strategic move in his game to lure me

19

away from Edgar and into his grasp?" My voice was laced with curiosity.

"No, I don't get that feeling. It wasn't evil. That would be the first thing I would have noticed. To me, the world is black and white, evil and safe." He pushed a plate toward me, his eyes looking at mine with observant curiosity. I could sense he felt nervous that I would judge him for his cooking skills.

"Thanks, Sam. Looks great." I smiled.

He narrowed his eyes at me and I could feel him navigating every corner of my brain, coming up empty handed. He grunted, his chest rising as he walked into the sitting room behind me. He threw his body onto the chaise lounge as the furniture yawned beneath him.

I picked at the soggy mass before me, urging my stomach to find it somewhat appetizing. I could hear Sam breathing, though I wasn't sure why he did. Being that he was dead, he really didn't need to. I suppose for the matter of fitting in, however, it made sense. For him, old habits died hard.

I had circled my life around three rooms. When I first came back it was hard for me to get past the front hall. But now, I felt comfortable being in the kitchen, sitting room and entry. Healing was a slow process and my burden to bear. I never understood how humans managed to move on, often so soon after their loss, but I guess love comes down to a choice: You can either get over it and try to be happy, or roll over and rot, all alone. Let's face it, no one likes being alone.

Sam came and went as he pleased, but it didn't seem as though he'd gone into any rooms besides the ones I had, either. I suppose it was out of respect for me, if he even possessed a shred of any. He was so rude, that it wouldn't surprise me if he'd been to every room in the house, let alone sleep in Edgar's bed. But as long as he didn't move anything, I didn't really care anymore.

I worked down another soggy and watered down load of mac and cheese before giving up. I had a new goal in mind. After throwing my bowl in the sink and grabbing the Edgar Allan notebook from where I'd set it on the counter, I tried my best to slink out of the room unnoticed. There was one place in this house I was certain would be easier to visit than my room, and I now set out on a mission to go there.

My hand grazed along the velvety wall paper as I traced toward the library. There was no real reason why I hadn't yet gone there, and I wasn't surprised to find it exactly the same. I gripped my hand around the frame of the door, feeling the familiar spot where I had dug my nails into the wood a hundred times. The memory of those last stressful days with Edgar flashed before me, and I felt the anxiety of the waiting weigh on my conscience.

I took a deep breath and stepped into the room. Sam had not followed me, but I was not so naïve to deny the fact that he knew what I was doing. Even though I had impeccable sight and hearing, he had even better. I noticed how he could watch the air before him when there was nothing there, but to him, there was always something: a particle of dust, a wisp of silk thread. He always knew, but that didn't mean he always told me about it.

I ran my hand along the thick leather of the couch, finding it cold and uninviting. The notebook of poems in my hand suddenly felt like a ton of bricks as I set it on the coffee table. I looked toward the greenhouse Edgar had built for me. A lump of guilt ached in my throat. That room was still too hard to visit, and even seeing it now was like reliving the death all over again.

As I diverted my gaze from the tables of dead plants, my sight caught the silky mahogany wood of the ladder to the second tier of the library. My breathing quickened, my body now terrified of what I knew was up there. I had tricked myself into coming here, tricked myself into my insatiable obsession with that tiny room, and the painting.

I took a deep breath, placing one hand on the middle rung. Squeezing my eyes shut, the painful memory of Edgar's hands around my waist flooded my mind. My sides began to tingle with the residual touch, and the breath was ripped from my lungs. I cursed myself for whimpering like a fool, placing my other hand on the rail. I worked to calm the burning pain in my throat, huffing through my nose in heavy breaths instead. I needed this. It had been long enough. My time for waiting was over and now it was time for a new day. Opening my eyes, I finally made my move.

ADDITIONS

I stepped onto the bottom rung and pulled myself up the ladder. I exhaled, feeling the bitter sweet pleasure of love and loss. A smile crossed my face. My memories of this place were less painful than I had originally thought, and were actually more exhilarating than expected. I pulled myself to the top, stepping onto the steel gangway with an agile hop. I wrapped one hand around the rail, the other landing on the spines of the books that were stacked against the wall.

As I walked around the familiar arch of the room, I ran my fingers along the books, as always. The even drumming was interrupted when my fingers hit a cavernous void in the stack. I paused as a memory opened up like a package in my mind, a memory of why that void was there. The thought had been one that was now buried deep beneath the trauma of that horrible day. I had forgotten all that preceded my abduction, but what had been there that day had been extremely valuable. I averted my gaze from the small arched room to my hand, halting as adrenaline ran through my veins.

I knelt on one knee until my eyes were level with the void in the books, remembering what had originally belonged there. My finger traced the tall rectangular hole as I peered to the back of the stack, but I found nothing more than the mahogany of the empty shelf staring back at me. I tilted my head to the side as I searched my mind for what had happened next. I turned to look behind me to the arched room in the corner. My mouth fell open, breath tumbling out in a gasp of disbelief. How could I have forgotten?

I stood slowly, steadying myself against the shelf. My brain raced to put the past back together. Taking a deep breath, I moved forward, placing one foot carefully before the next. I poked my head around the corner as though expecting something to jump out at me. The small candle burst to life. Sweat was now beading on my brow.

My first instinct was to look at the painting. The faces peering out at me brought on a sharp pain in my heart. I cringed, averting my gaze to the floor where something was glimmering. My sharp breathing echoed off the walls of the small space as I bent down, hooking my finger under the pages of the book that was sprawled open on the floor.

My first thought was how warm it felt, as though it had just been held. I brought it to my chest and looked toward the ceiling, feeling its strange warmth now reverberate through my soul. It felt alive, a faint heart beating from within. I cradled the book like a small child, shuffling to the armchair that was shoved into the corner. I allowed my body to sink into the soft leather, sighing as it comforted me. Placing the book on my lap, I traced the rough gold surface with my palm, feeling the embossed Italian letters mold under my touch.

Treating it with careful respect, I pulled back the cover, hearing the paper crackle as it stretched. As I opened to the first page, the familiar etched image of the raven stared out at me. My eyes fell across the Italian writing and I furrowed my brow in amazement. I began to recognize the words that had been so foreign before, translating them into English, right before my eyes, until it was finally legible. I read the same first line I had that day, finally finding some sense in the description:

In the beginning, the raven was one...

I leaned back against the cushion of the chair in shock. My newfound talent to read Italian had taken me by surprise, and I was overwhelmed by the fact that I would now be able to understand the stories in this book. I flipped through the pages with hasty hunger, remembering how the book had been half empty and unfinished. As I came across the familiar picture of the white cat entering the cave, I was surprised to see that when I turned the page, it was no longer blank.

I gasped in horror, dropping the book into my lap. The pages fanned closed and I lost my spot. I was not entirely sure about what I had just seen, but the bare glimpse had caused my heart to beat like never before. I took a deep breath as

I grabbed at the book, hungrier than before as I fanned the pages back to where the cat had been. I looked down at the page, my eyes falling on a new imprinted image that hadn't been there before.

There was a white raven in the woods, its body hunched over and its eyes screaming. A dark cloud of black ravens was diving down on her, her eyes filled with fright. The scene was far too familiar, and I felt my head surge with sudden pain. Though my mind screamed not to, my eyes could not resist the temptation to read the caption.

On this day, she was taken. The dark soul was tricked. The raven was nothing more than a shell, but the doom ahead was heavily weighted...

It was me. The white raven had been me. I ran my fingers over the detailed image, remembering the fear that had cut its way through my body. I looked to the trees that surrounded me, and to my surprise, the cat was there. Its tail had popped up from behind a log as it ran away, just as I had remembered.

I turned the page as I urged myself to fill my mind with its torturous images, but then slammed the book shut. What I had seen there I was never prepared to see again. It was the image of two ravens, one with a dagger through the other's heart. My breathing quickened and my fingers trembled on the cover of the book. My palms began to sweat, and as much as I wanted to read further, I couldn't bring my screaming mind to pull open the cover.

My eyes were squeezed shut and my breathing echoed off the walls. As I sat there, calming my nerves, I sensed I was no longer alone. As I opened my eyes, I wasn't surprised to see Sam standing before me, his figure shrouded in darkness in the cramped room.

"What are you doing?" he asked.

I kept my expression neutral, hiding my emotional turmoil. "Nothing, just reading, and trying to relax," I lied.

His eyes fluttered to the golden book in my hand. "What is that about?" he asked, clearly doing some pretending of his own.

I shrugged, trying to make it seem like it was just any old book, anything but a magical book that wrote itself.

"Looks like you're really making strides today. Good for you, champ." He looked around at the small room and winked. His back was arched in an uncomfortable manner, the ceiling too low for his large body to stand.

"Yeah, I guess so." My voice was tart and annoyed. I avoided his direct gaze, afraid he would discover my secrets.

He struggled to maneuver his body, twisting himself to face the large painting.

"Oh, hey!" Astonishment crossed his face. "Look, it's you!" He jabbed his finger at the image of me. "Oh, and look! Edgar!" He was like a small child at a candy store; no sense of mourning about him.

I winced when he said his name. "Could you please not say that?"

His eyes shot to mine, his mouth twisted in a wry smile. "Oh, yeah, sorry. I forgot that he was dead."

I exhaled sharply, my chest bones tight. He didn't forget, he was just being rude.

"Oh, but hey. Look there." Sam pointed to the couple in white. It was Margriete and... I couldn't bring myself to even think the name.

I nodded, looking away. Sam's smile vanished and an awkward silence grew between us. I found myself looking up, surprised by the sudden change. I had braced myself for another rude comment, but one never came. My eyes met his and we locked stares for a moment. The smirk was gone from his face and he was searching mine in a disconcerting way. It was as though he was finally feeling the same loss I had.

After holding the stare a moment longer than necessary, he looked away. "Sorry," he mumbled, backing out of the room and sitting on the railing. I was taken aback by the exchange. He had actually expressed a bit of repentance.

The warmth of the book in my hands pulled me back to reality. I recalled why I was still grasping it. I ran my hand over the cover again, feeling the power of the culmination of the stories inside. The book felt alive, and in some strange way, it knew everything that was happening.

I flipped through the pages mindlessly until they went blank, careful not to look at the last few images. Only about half the book was filled. I wondered if this meant that there was still more to come and more to explore. At any rate, I now had evidence that the cat was really there. If this book had deemed it so important to record, then it was surely a character that I would meet again.

Sam sighed, and I knew he was just trying to get my

attention. My gaze lifted to his and I smiled.

"Sam, can you do me a favor?" I had been meaning to do this, but my reservations to come here had stopped me. "Could you take this painting downstairs? I'd like to hang it in the library."

"What, is it too heavy for you?" he joked, now returning to his normal sarcastic self.

I gave him a reproachful glare. "Just do it, Sam."

He grinned and ducked back into the small space. Placing two pale hands on either side of the painting, he hoisted it off the wall with little effort and maneuvered it out of the space. In one swift agile movement he jumped up and over the railing, drifting to the floor below as though stepping off a small stair. I hoisted myself out of my chair and made my way to the rail. Sam stared up at me with a smug look on his face. I glowered at his disregard for human contrivances such as stairs and ladders.

"Show off," I spat.

Sam grinned, his ghost-white face almost iridescent in the light that shown through the two-story window. I noticed how the blue circles under his eyes contrasted with the sharp gold bronze of his pupils, and it sent shivers down my spine. He had a face of death, looming in my thoughts.

He leaned the painting against the couch while I made my way around the gangway and to the ladder. The book was clutched close to my chest and I felt my body begin to sweat under its heat. When I reached the ladder, I hooked it under my arm, careful to grab the rails as I had been told by Edgar a thousand times.

Halfway down, I squealed as I felt Sam's cold hands grab my waist. I instantly froze at the touch. I fought back the thoughts of Edgar, squeezing my eyes shut. Sam had managed to lift me the exact same way Edgar always had. I wriggled myself free once I was safely on the ground.

"What's your deal?" Sam chuckled, amused by my discomfort.

"Nothing," I paused, considering a mean remark but figuring there was no use wasting it. "Your hands are cold, is all."

He laughed. "Yeah, well, you feel like an inferno, so...."

I shook my head, plucking the book out from under my now sweaty arm, "Whatever."

"So where do you want this hunk of junk?" He was trying to get me pissed off, and was nearly succeeding.

I let out a shameless breath as I moved toward the middle of the room. The one thing I could always count on was that Sam would never give me any pity. That was something I truly could not handle, especially now. With a skeptical eye, I looked around the room, analyzing the possible spaces, which were admittedly few and far between with all of Edgar's clocks that were hung everywhere.

I winced at the thought of moving Edgar's beloved clocks, but really, what was the point? He wasn't here to care anymore. I was certain he would forgive me, if he ever got the chance. My heart sank at my disregard toward his things. I loved Edgar, that was never going to change, but this was necessary. It wasn't like I was remodeling because I didn't like the style. I was doing this as my first step to finding him;

a selfless act of love.

This painting was bound to be useful to me, somehow. If anything, it was a good reminder of my goal. I refused to rot here, waiting like he did. I was more proactive than that. Licking my wounds and whining about my horrible luck was never my forte.

Sam read my thoughts and began removing the clocks on the east wall, just to the left of the door that entered from the hall and right before the shelving began. There were deep faded silhouettes left as he stacked each noisy clock in a precarious pile. They were annoying anyway, like sands through the hourglass of my life, ticking away my endless existence. If I could remove everything that made me feel like sulking, rather than fighting, things here would be easier.

I grabbed the clocks and placed them into the storage chest that was also used as the coffee table. There were deep scuffs across the top where Edgar had rested his feet, and I ran my hand across them lovingly before I opened the lid. The thick wood of the clocks clanked with a hollow thud as I stacked them in their new resting place. As I shut and locked the lid, the clocks were muffled by the walls that now surrounded them. A sigh of relief escaped my lips. I caught a glimpse of Sam smirking at me.

A grumble grew in my throat. "Whatever you're about to say, save it."

He laughed then, and I knew there had been something he would have said. *What a jerk*, I thought. *Grow a heart already*. I pointed one sharp finger at the painting, instructing him, without words, to hang it and get out of my business. My mind locked onto his and I made sure to let my thoughts hiss with anger.

His eyes glimmered with satisfaction. He was enjoying the torture he was putting me through with sick elation and intent.

I began thinking of Sarah and Scott as he hoisted the painting to the wall, placing it on a hook that had already been there from one of the clocks. The thought of going down to the school to surprise them had crossed my mind today more times than I'd like to admit, and every time it did, Sam only looked at me and shook his head. For some reason, he was trying to keep me from them. Perhaps he saw how wrong it was for immortals to make friends with humans. In reality, it was just the fact that I missed the social distraction.

Though he himself had once been a human, he now regarded them as a sort of parasite, infesting and killing the Earth where he would inevitably live forever. Considering I lived most of my life among humans, as a human, I just didn't see things the same way, and I refused to throw out that part of my life. I couldn't step on the little people that got me to where I was today. Besides, they were my friends.

Sam looked over his shoulder at me, narrowing his eyes.

"Shut up," I spat with sudden fervor, sensing his need to express his disdain, yet again.

As much as I tried to keep my thoughts from him, at times it was still difficult, especially when I was daydreaming. You can't control the natural flow of thought; it's like trying to capture the wind, possible, but hard. It did have its advantages, though, and I knew that the one way to get back at Sam was to fill my thoughts with Scott and Sarah, the very humans he seemed to despise with such profoundness.

"If you hate them so much, then you don't have to come. And actually, I think I'd prefer if you didn't. You're nothing but an embarrassment, anyway. And the fact that you look dead could really creep people out." I lifted my nose into the air and crossed my arms stubbornly.

He laughed. "Sorry, sugar. Can't do that. I have to come. It's my job." I saw the troublemaker in him rising.

I growled at him. "I hate you, Sam."

He chuckled. "I know, but that's not really my problem. Blame your little lover boy."

A sudden scream rose in my throat and I let it out, shaking with anger and hate, but he didn't even wince. "Just go away!"

He shrugged and left the room, my bitter hatred refusing to muster as much as a frown from him.

My face was burning and I looked toward the heavens, cursing Edgar for binding Sam to me for all eternity. This was without a doubt some sadistic trick he had planned. But then again, I doubt he had planned on dying.

I threw myself onto the couch and glared at the painting. The warm book sat next to me and I placed my hand on the cover, allowing the feeling to calm my fury. I needed to find that cat, more than anything else. I just knew there was something there, something it possessed that would help lead me forward, to Edgar.

There was also the daunting matter of Edgar's room,

which I figured would house the largest jackpot of information. Though it was hard, I longed to know what it was like. I hated the unknown. I was addicted to the thrill of uncovering the answers I sought.

Another wise plan was to go back down to the college, and not just to see Sarah and Scott, but also break into his lab. I figured by now they'd probably gotten a new professor, but what had they done with his things? It made sense that Edgar would have planned for something like this, and would have never allowed a human to stumble upon his life and learn about our secret world in such a careless manner.

If I were to suddenly re-appear on the campus, however, I would need a plan. Perhaps I would tell them that Edgar and I had run off to be married, but then he'd died in a horrible car accident and so I was here to collect his belongings. I pondered over the idea, realizing it had serious holes, but it would have to do. I laughed to myself, wondering what everyone would think of the scandal, especially Nurse Dee.

A strange feeling of liberation overcame me, and my heart filled with warmth and purpose. Whining and pouting was not getting me anywhere, and I felt exonerated that I now had a plan. There had to be a way to find Edgar, even in death. After all, Sam was dead, but he could still be here amongst us, and this fact gave me hope. Whether I believed in ghosts, the afterlife, reincarnation, or not, this world had rendered me surprised too many times to count, and I was hoping it still had surprises left that could help save me.

It was hard to feel so in love with someone I still felt I barely knew. Though our life together was impossibly long, I had only been granted the experience of those few cherished months. I brought my hand to my neck, remembering how it felt when Edgar had touched me. The way his breath would felt on my skin, how it had been intoxicating and sweet. The way his body felt against mine was now no more than a distant memory. The electricity of our connection was undeniably pre-determined, but still so sweet and real.

I longed to learn more about Edgar. Build the memory of him in my mind until it was so rich that I could almost will him to be here. His face was still fresh on my conscience, and looking upon his countenance in the painting granted me the bittersweet pleasure of seeing his face every day. His image was a reminder of my goals and purpose. There were no other pictures of him anywhere in the house, so this was my only reference. To my deep regret, it also included Matthew.

I heard footsteps in the hall as Sam traipsed back to the library. He glared at me and I saw something glimmer in his hand. Furrowing my brow, I watched as he turned to the painting, placing his hand against the canvas. When he took his hand away, I saw that there was now a gold smiley face sticker over where Matthew stood.

"I'm tired of hearing about him," he said in an even tone.

I snorted, a little angry that he would deface my painting, but slightly amused and touched at the same time. "Sam, what…"

He shrugged and left the room just as swiftly as he came.

I shook my head, too tired to bother to remove it. I sank back into my thoughts once more.

Despite my goals, there were other things that needed to be done as well. For one, I needed to learn how to fly again. If I could only remember what it felt like, I was certain I could accomplish the feat. Edgar had told me to imagine being weightless like a feather on the wind. Every night, as I lay on the couch trying to drown out the annoying humming noises Sam made in his attempt to pretend to be sleeping, I imagined myself floating like a weightless cloud above the earth, like Edgar had done with so little effort.

Sam would be helpful in this, though I was uncertain how long I would be able to handle his sarcasm while he taught me. Despite my utter dislike for him, he was my friend, and a part of me had to love him for that, no matter what. At the end of the day, I was at least relived that I wasn't alone, and in this, I felt that I could survive the time and handle the sadness I now endured.

The couch engulfed me as I pulled the warm book into my lap, coddling it as though it were a teddy bear. Exhaustion overtook my limbs like a black wave of darkness, and I filed my list of things to do away in my mind. I rested my head against the arm of the couch, the leather creaking under my weight. I breathed in until no more breath could fill my lungs, the rich smell of the pillows laced with the sweet smell of honey, of Edgar. I stifled back my tears, telling myself that there would be no more. It was time to be strong, and my turn to suffer as he had for me for so long.

PLEASE FASTEN YOUR SEATBELTS

"Just don't get fresh with me, got it?" I placed my hands on Sam's as he gripped me under my ribcage. His body was close at my back, poised to lift us into the air.

"*Aw,*" Sam whined. "That's no fun. You don't like being groped by an angel?"

I tried to pinch his hand as hard as I could. "You wish."

A chuckle gathered in the back of his throat. "You bet I do." His voice was filled with false pretenses and sarcasm.

I knew he wasn't capable of those kinds of thoughts, but still, he liked to tease me mercilessly, often invading my privacy. He always snuck into the sitting room while I was trying to dress. I knew he felt nothing, but he was entertained by the way it made me squeal when he caught me off guard. It was clear I needed to suck up my pride and move back into my room at this point, but flight came first on my list of priorities.

"Okay, Sam. I'm ready." I exhaled and clenched my fists into a tight and determined ball.

I felt him squeeze my sides a little harder as he crouched closer to the ground. His giant wings spread out around us, fanning the air effortlessly as he took flight. I had flown with him before, but this time I had something to concentrate on. The ground below me began to melt away as we ascended. As we cut through the warm air, Sam twisted us to the left and straight up. My gaze was focused skyward, envisioning myself alone.

I closed my eyes and the wind whipped through my hair as we began flying forward. My body still felt heavy in his grasp and I struggled to obtain mental weightlessness. I wriggled as I felt his grip tighten and he began to dive back down to the Earth. This wasn't working. There was no way I could feel weightless when it was so obvious I wasn't. Sam was scanning my thoughts. He knew what I was struggling with and he felt it was time to regroup, and try it from another angle.

He hovered like a hummingbird above the grass before setting us both down. He was full of surprising elegance, and it always caught me off guard. Everything was blooming around us, and I remembered how much I had loved the outdoors. Sam released his icy grip and I rubbed my ribs as I tried to warm them back up.

"So what am I doing wrong?" I turned to face him.

His grey wings were curved behind him in a graceful arc, contrasting beautifully against the bright green grass.

"You're thinking like a human. I keep hearing a small voice in your head saying that it's wrong for you to be up there, and it's against nature to fly."

I nodded in agreement. "Yeah, I know. It's just so hard to forget my upbringing, and so I just can't act and think the way I should." I kicked the grass at my feet as it tried to reach up toward my legs.

"Yeah, well, stop acting like a vile human, then." He smirked, seeing the opportunity to make fun of me.

"They're not vile, Sam. You were one once, too." I crossed my arms and turned my back to him.

"Thank goodness I'm not anymore," he snorted.

I exhaled as I tried to control my anger and avoid a fight. I was in no mood to get into another human versus immortal debate. My arms were crossed against my chest so tight that they began to sweat. The sweet welcoming wind blew across us as we stood in the field all alone. I felt the anger in me subside as I scanned the trees, listening to their soft rustle. There had to be some sort of repressed memory for this, some sort of trigger that could make me remember my former life.

There was no doubt at this point that I was immortal, and that I could fly. I looked down at my feet, tapping my fingers against my side and chewing on my lip. A sudden and vindictive idea crossed my mind, and I whipped around to face Sam, the brilliance of it igniting my senses. His face was lined with caution. I glared, defying his instinct to protect me.

"Oh, come on, Sam. I think it's the best way." In two brisk steps I closed the distance between us. I dropped my hands to my sides and stood tall.

He was shaking his head in a way that told me he would comply because he had to, but would not assist me in any way. His eyes sparkled as the sun reflected like water off his cold skin. "You've lost your mind. That's the dumbest idea I've ever heard." He put his arms up in the air in a defensive manner.

"No, come on. You know it's a good idea. Besides, you could save me if you had to." My lips curled at the edges.

He snorted. "I can't believe you're considering jumping off waterfall, Elle. Think about what you're doing for a moment. It's insane! I doubt you're in the right state of mind." He turned away from me, not willing to give me any hope or support.

"Sam," I said his name as though begging.

He tilted his head back and turned to face me, his face twisted. "I mean, I was told you were stubborn, but not insane."

I glowered at him as I pushed past his shoulder and walked briskly in the direction of the waterfall. The first time I had ever met Sam was there. It was nostalgic, so he should feel good about this. He followed like a dark cloud behind me, and I smiled, satisfied by the fact that I had forced him into helping me.

"If you die, at least I won't have to protect you anymore, so I guess that's the upside." He chuckled as his feet cut through the grass, leaving an obvious trail behind him.

"If I die, I won't have to listen to you anymore, either. So it's a win-win for the both of us," I retorted. "You know as well as I that throwing myself off a waterfall will stir up the memory of flight in a purely instinctual way. It's an ingenious and sane idea. Admit it." I looked over my shoulder at him.

Sam shrugged. "Whatever, I still think you're a suicidal idiot." He lifted his eyebrows as he tried to portray my irrationality.

Grumbling, I picked up my pace as we walked into the trees. My stride was much faster than it had been while I was a depressed lethargic human. The hour or so it had taken me to get to the cliff the first time was easily covered in thirty minutes.

"Still thinking this was a good idea?" Sam asked as we stood with our toes just over the edge of the mossy cliff. I used to fear heights, but now it made sense not to, so I didn't. Sam was my inevitable safety net, like wearing a harness or bungee cord. As long as he was here, I would never die.

I looked over the edge to where the water crashed into the lake, erupting upward and spraying across our faces. The mist nearly froze as it touched Sam's skin, dripping in icicles from his elbows. I sighed. The drop was about fifteen hundred feet, easily, and I was content that it was perfect.

"It's a great idea," I finally replied, struggling to thwart the shaking tone to my voice. My heart was racing and I knew Sam could hear it. He eyed me with a knowing glare as he leaned over the edge, making a plan in his head to save me if he had to. The waterfall to my left gorged over the rocks, the rushing sound so loud that we had to shout to hear one another.

Sam smirked at me as he put one hand on my back and

41

nudged me forward in his attempt to jostle me, only to catch me with his other hand before I fell. My heart leapt into my throat and I tried to scream through my choked lungs. He began rolling with laughter, pointing at me in a mocking manner.

"I just wanted you to get the full effect," he yelled, his face contorted into a smug mask and his laughter choking in his throat.

"I hate you. That's not funny." I narrowed my eyes at him, angry that I had let him get away with scaring me. Though that second had struck terror through my soul, it had also readied me.

I looked over the edge as he continued to laugh. I tried not to think as I let my body lean forward. I leapt with all my might, watching with sick fascination as Sam's laugh turned to one of sudden fear and protective duty. The smirk I had shot back at him as I began to fall quickly melted away and I grasped at the reality of what I was doing.

Forcing myself to concentrate, I closed my eyes as tight as I could, forgetting my fears and focusing on the task at hand. I thought about the absence of Earth below me as I tried to forget the fact that I was falling, possibly to my death. This suicidal attempt was a confirmation of my determination in this life, my determination to come one step closer to Edgar. I breathed evenly, struggling not to think about the fact that I had only seconds to make this work.

The wind was whipping around my arms as I held them out to my sides like wings. I had never felt like this in my life, and though I only had moments to enjoy it, I could not deny the utter release. All my fears melted away and I found it was easier than ever to concentrate as the rush focused me.

My mind now found immense clarity, preparing itself for the sweet release of death. My eyes refused to open and I furrowed my brow in deeper concentration, feeling a spark of something rise in my soul, like a bright light coming from a distant memory. I concentrated on the light, watching as the rays began to spark around the edges, growing brighter.

Suddenly, my body became weightless and I felt the corners of my mouth curl into a smile. As I moved my arms, I found that the air around me felt thick. It was like water, and I felt the urge to swim through it. A forgotten instinct forced me to flap my arms, astonished by the ease with which they seemed to push through the thick air, now something I felt I could grasp.

The sensation of falling that I had experienced before had completely left me, and my nervous stomach now felt as though I were atop the seas. I was bobbing on the waves of air as my chest rose and fell, controlling the breath in my lungs. Slow, but with intrigued interest, I opened my eyes. To my surprise, I was far over the lake, and no longer falling. I shot my gaze to the left where they met Sam's amazed face as he flew along beside me.

The look in his eyes was priceless, like a tricked dog. I took a moment to absorb my sweet victory before my gaze fell to the undeniable appearance of my winged arms and feathered body. I gasped, realizing I had actually done it. I was finally a raven.

The marvel of the crisp white feathers in the sun was

unlike anything I had ever seen, even whiter than Isabelle and even sharper then Henry's. In my mind I felt myself smiling, despite the fact that my mouth had been replaced by a sharp uncomfortable beak.

"*Wow!*" I tried to yell to Sam, but instead I heard a sharp "caw," and I was taken aback, recalling too late that I could not speak.

Sam laughed. "Yeah, that was funny," he yelled back.

Oh, shut up, I thought in my mind. Luckily for me, he could read that. And I had to admit, it did make things easy.

Sam smiled. "This is crazy. I never knew you were white. I was sort of expecting black, like Edgar," he yelled.

Yeah, well, white is more feminine. I winked at him and he smirked.

It was surprising how easy flying seemed, just like riding a bike. I began to test my skills as I shifted my winged rudders, tilting my body from one side to the next as I zig-zagged through the air. The thick texture was comforting, and somehow obvious to my now enlightened memory. I had never expected it would feel so natural, so easy.

I thought about the day when the orphanage had visited the Seattle aquarium and we all got to learn how to scuba dive. It felt just like that, except free of the heavy equipment and mask. Taking a deep breath, I noted how clear the air was at this altitude, and how refreshing it suddenly seemed. The world here was untouched, and for a moment, I could understand why it was Sam felt the way he did toward humans. I could see why he didn't want to allow this world to be destroyed.

44

By now we were already over the glacier on the other side of the lake from the college. I banked to the right as I twisted around the peak, remembering how I had longed to do this as I had stood oblivious to the notion in hatchery class. I felt the wind pick me up and toss me to the left with a sharp pitch. At first I tried to fight it out of fear, but I soon found that I could manipulate myself to benefit from its strong current.

My sharp eyes caught sight of the college and I eyed Sam with a rebellious look. He gave me a rueful glare from a distance above me. I narrowed my wings and dove toward the ground, picking up speed and testing my limits.

"What do you think you're doing!" I heard him yell behind me.

What do you think? I retorted, caring nothing for the fact that I was in the form of a rare and mythical bird.

I heard a distinct growl as he found himself helpless to stop me. I dove toward the buildings and he tilted and turned away, afraid to be seen by the students that moved like small pawns across the gravel paths.

With clumsy effort, I fanned myself down onto the roof of the hatchery. My talons scraped into the tin roof with surprising ease, cutting through the metal like frosting on a gingerbread village. I struggled to gather my wings behind me as I scanned the compound, searching for a familiar face.

Based on the position of the sun overhead, I figured it was roughly noon. With anxious haste, I released my grip on the roof and lifted myself skyward and headed toward the cafeteria. I didn't have long before Sam would hunt me down, so I needed to keep moving. My wings banked toward the windows and down to the backside of the structure. I landed on a pile of crispy pine needles that were mounded on the ground next to the window of the open dining space. My body bounced and I quickly righted myself. My wings were not as useful as hands.

We had always sat to eat in the far back corner, and my sharp eyes caught sight of the familiar table. My heart leapt in excitement as I saw the silhouette of two people sitting there, engaged in vivid conversation. I hopped closer to the glass, trying not to reveal myself, though I knew at some point, someone was bound to notice.

As I approached, I gently placed my beak against the pane, looking up between the grids to the faces that sat there. My heart raced as I looked into the familiar faces of Sarah and Scott, my chest ablaze with the warmth of friendship. Forgetting my bird-like state, I began tapping on the window with my beak, attempting to get their attention.

They stopped what they were doing and looked at me, their faces filled with surprise. Sarah brought a hand to her mouth and gasped, pointing at me with her other. Now that I had their attention, I was embarrassed and realized how odd I must look to them. I began to wish that I could somehow tell them it was me. I gave them a few rapid blinks as I stepped away, looking toward the building and sky, pretending to be stunned as though I'd hit the window like a normal bird would. As anticipated, they smiled and waved like idiots, thinking I was cute.

I missed them so much, but only now did I realize how important it was to come back. I needed them. The rest of the cafeteria began to take notice, and I realized it was time to leave before I managed to cause too much commotion and reveal my existence to everyone. Falling back, my wings fanned the thick air in clumsy strokes and I lifted myself up and away from view.

Cutting to the left around the pine tree, I maneuvered toward the bird lab where I perched on the roof. My sharp eyes scanned the grounds, finding them empty. Everyone was now at lunch and I was safe to rest. I sighed with a heavy heart, remembering everything about the last year and the whirlwind direction my life had now taken.

A door under me slammed and I jumped back, startled. I heard heavy footsteps crunch on the gravel below, so I stepped forward, positioning myself on the ledge. Leaning over, I peered down onto the path to see who had created such a powerful disruption. As my eyes locked onto the figure, my mind became thick and dazed. I blinked hard, tilting my head to get a closer look at the impossible figure now storming toward the cafeteria. His every move was exactly the same, and it sent chills down my spine.

Edgar? My body began to shake from the rush of adrenaline, fear, confusion, and excitement shaking me to the core. What was this trickery?

Suddenly, I felt my body lurch as I was ripped from the roof.

"You're coming with me." I recognized Sam's voice as his cold hands clasped around me, shocking me as my body once again felt human and I was now cradled in his cold grasp.

"No, Sam!" I yelled, writhing in his arms. My feet and

hands were flailing in my attempt to get away and make him let go. "Take me back! It was Edgar!" I tried to free myself mid-air, now confident that I knew how to fly.

"You're seeing things, Elly. That's not him. I promise." His voice was laced with lies.

"Yes it was, Sam! It was him. I'd know his face anywhere!" I felt tears begin to stream down my cheeks as I struggled to get another glance, even though by now, we were far across the lake, gently banking toward home.

"Elly, please," he whispered as we dove down toward the field.

My mind blazed with hate and confusion. Why was he keeping me from him like this? Why hadn't he told me? If Edgar had been back this whole time, why didn't he find me? How could he not feel my undeniable presence? The questions streamed through my mind faster that I could rationalize and my head exploded in pain.

He set me down on the ground none too gently, causing me to stumble and fall. I could tell the searing questions had irritated Sam, his brow furrowed in his attempt to make me stop and calm down. I winced before I righted myself. With unstoppable determination and haste, I began to run toward the college, but Sam's iron cold hands clasped like handcuffs around my wrists. He halted me before I made one step, anticipating my next move. I struggled against his grip, feeling my skin tearing as I tried to pull away. Insanity took over all thought.

Sam's hand dug into my arm as he whipped me back toward him. I fell to the ground, dazed as it knocked hard against the Earth. A shadow fell over me as Sam loomed above, his wings forming a cage, prepared to grab me if I chose to run again.

"That was for your own good, Elly. I'm sorry." His feet were beside my head as the grass rustled and grew around me. His face was locked in a stone stare, his amber eyes cold and determined.

"But, Edgar," I whimpered.

"*It's not Edgar,*" he said again, thwarting my thoughts before they even had time to form.

I narrowed my eyes at him and pulled myself into a ball, feeling completely exposed and saddened. It had been him. I saw it. The cuts on my wrists from his tight grasp now bled warm liquid into the earth, the flowers drinking it with haste. My body shook with residual emotion. It made no sense! My mind screamed for an explanation, yelling out in anguish.

"It's his hologram, Elle." Sam's answer sent a hollowed bullet through my heart as I remembered what Edgar had told me all those months ago. He put one foot on my hands and pressed them into the Earth as I looked to the woods, my mind gravitating toward the college like a drunken martyr. "Do you remember? He made it last winter, and now the hologram is here forever, like an echo. It's not real. He created it thinking he'd always be here. It's just an illusion. It cannot interact with you the same way Edgar did." He paused, his voice becoming stern. "*Ever.*"

My breathing began to slow and I felt my heart sink. Just seeing Edgar's face like that, so alive, had made my heart ache. I didn't care if it was a programmed image, I needed to see it. I felt like a drug addict, the withdrawals driving me insane and making me crave its synthetic existence with an irrational feeling of emptiness.

Sam reached down and grabbed my shoulders, lifting me to my feet. I felt ashamed by my sudden animal reactions, and I looked Sam in the eyes. With all the feelings overwhelming me, I had nearly forgotten about flying and the fact that I had mastered it. I watched Sam's face and saw there was a spark of something in his eye; something resembling pity, but also understanding.

"I'm sorry it happened this way, Elle. I should have told you sooner." He smirked then, and I gave him a confused expression, since the smirk had no place in our current conversation. "But I think before we discuss it further, we should get you some clothes."

Horrified, I looked down at my body, realizing I was completely naked except for my rather tattered underwear. "How…" Edgar had been able to keep his clothes, why hadn't I? I looked at my blood stained wrists, the cuts now almost healed.

"Looks like we still have a few kinks to work out," Sam laughed. "Not that I'm not okay with this, though," he pointed toward me.

I glowered at him as I tried to wrap my arms around my chest and thighs to shield myself. "Let's just go, okay?" I snapped, hobbling to the middle of the field with as much dignity as I could muster.

OBSESSION

"Could you please go stand someplace else?" I was begging at this point.

"But I wanted to talk to you. You know I don't care. Your nudity does nothing for me. Though, I know you wish it did." Sam winked, his arms crossed against his chest as he leaned against the wall of the sitting room.

An angry lump rose in my throat. "Seriously, Sam. Please. If you don't leave, I'm going to march my way back down to that college despite your warnings."

Sam chuckled as he backed around the corner and into the hall. A sharp exhale escaped my tired lips as I wriggled into a pair of jeans and pulled a shirt over my head. Isabelle was lounging on the couch, her wings sprawled in an awkward manner and her head resting on a pile of dirty clothes. I hadn't seen Henry in a few hours, and I wondered if he had also been surprised by the hologram of Edgar.

My body shuddered as my mind flashed back to when I sat perched on the roof, seeing the ghost of my true love wandering around as though nothing had changed. The angry lump in my throat only grew as I thought about Sam's lies. He knew how important Edgar was to me, so why hadn't he told me about it?

"I didn't tell you because I was afraid you would obsess over it, instead of getting over him and moving on." Sam's voice echoed from the hall. "Really, Elle. It's just a hologram. It's not even that impressive."

I growled under my breath. "That's not really your decision to make, Sam. I don't need mental protection, too. I would appreciate it if you could just stick to making sure I don't die."

He sauntered back into the room and squeezed onto the couch next to Isabelle. "Whatever you say, but don't expect me to give you anymore advice."

"Good, I don't need it. I never did." I started cleaning up my mess of clothes and books from the floor in my destructive path of fury. "And if I want to go down there and see my human friends, I will. You're not my captor." I shoved a pile of laundry into a basket in the corner.

"Whatever. Human lover." He snorted, looking quite pleased with himself.

I stopped then, a pile of books in my hand. "Whatever happened to you anyway? I know you used to be human, so what's your problem? Why do you hate them so much?" I shoved the books onto the shelf, fighting to make them fit.

His mouth sank into a solemn line and he shrugged, at a loss of words. I had caught him off guard, his inability to hide the pain leaving him exposed and helpless. I felt a little guilty as I watched him, feeling my remark was no better than his often-piercing blows. I never wanted to do that to anyone. I shooed Isabelle off the couch as she snapped at me lethargically. Slowly easing my body down next to Sam, I concentrated on his face.

"What happened?" I urged gently, my anger now replaced by understanding.

It was surprising to see Sam at such a loss for words when he was often so witty and quick. I figured he would have given me a sharp rejoinder and that would be the end of it. I hadn't expected that he'd actually clam up. He sighed, drawing his gaze out of his lap to meet mine. I gave him a tiny smile as I reached for his hand, the cold skin making me shiver. I began rubbing it out of habit, in my attempt to make it warm.

"I died." The words were flat and cold, with no hint of sarcasm. His mouth was still a straight line, the closest I'd ever seen to a frown. "I died due to the human need for violence and hate. This is why I can't stand humans. They take life for granted, but life is so special, so amazing. There are so many things worth experiencing, things that I never will." He squeezed my hand in his. I winced, holding back the urge to pull it away as it began to go numb from the cold, amazed by the amount of feeling that now poured out of him.

"Why did it happen?" I urged, finding this rare moment

worth taking advantage of.

"Why did I save the girl you mean?" He smirked.

"Yeah." Edgar had told me he'd died protecting a girl, but I never knew the whole story so I never understood the significance.

He laughed. "Because, Elle. You should know better than anyone. I loved her. I loved her so much. Even though I was only twenty, it didn't matter. When you've found your soul-mate, you just know."

I smiled as tears welled in my eyes at the mention of soul-mates. I was a sucker for love, especially now.

He sighed. "I had already decided that we would be together forever and that she was the one. After all my mistakes with love and life, it was evident that she was someone different, someone that could change me into a better person." His eyes looked into mine with a light I'd never seen in them before. "She's still alive you know." He squeezed my hand tighter.

"She is?" I gasped, amazed by how much restraint he was showing and pain he was enduring.

"Yeah. She still thinks about me, too. But I can't let her see me. Could you imagine how shocking that would be?"

I nodded, noting the thought as something I had literally just experienced when I had seen the hologram. I also realized it would have rendered me insane. I could see his perspective: to have the one you loved right there but you could not touch them.

Sam smiled, reading my thoughts. "I didn't die that long ago you know. It was only 1962. So, that makes her sixty-six."

A look of frustration crossed his face. "I died for her. I gave up everything, and you know what she did? She moved on three months later. She got married within the year, and two years after that, she had kids."

My heart broke at the thought. "That's horrible!"

He nodded. "But, no matter how much I try to hate her, I can't. She's only human after all, weak and impressionable." He shook his head as though disagreeing with himself. "I don't think she really loves him, though. Not the way she loved me, or at least that's what she thinks about. She wonders what life could have been like if I hadn't died and if we had a life now, instead of her and that James guy." He snorted. "But, that's the way it was always meant to be. This was our fate."

I said nothing as he paused.

"The funniest thing, though, and I wish you could have been there…." He raised one eyebrow and grinned before continuing. "One day, I met James at the bar. It was his bachelor party, and I scared him so bad that he nearly left her at the altar. I wanted to make sure he was worthy enough to be with her forever."

I chuckled, "So, what did you do?"

"I threatened him, naturally. I told him that if he ever did anything to her, I'd rip him limb from limb. At first he didn't believe me, but then I took his fork in my hand and crumpled it with the slightest squeeze of my fingers. I watched him sweat, terrified beyond words. From that moment on, I knew he was convinced that I was the real deal."

I started to ask if James had ever told her about the incident, but Sam beat me to it.

"Of course, I also threatened that if he ever told her about me, I'd have to kill him. The poor guy was so scared he began puking! Poor chap. Good thing is, ever since then, he's been mostly good to her."

"Mostly? What does that mean?" I gasped, my eyes widening in anticipation.

A vindictive sneer grew from his once solemn mask. "One Christmas, he failed to get her a present. I knew this, of course, because I was always listening to their thoughts. Not that I really had to, though. She was yelling pretty loudly. Long story short, I met him out by the trash can one night when he was taking out the empty Christmas boxes. Needless to say, he ended up 'tripping over the curb and breaking his leg,' and now he believes me. He even got her a diamond the following day."

I rolled with laughter. "Sam, that's horrible!" I yelped, struggling to catch my breath. "Then what happened? Why don't you see her anymore?"

He shrugged, "It wasn't healthy. The gods are evil to do this to me, but I really didn't have a choice. I couldn't have let her get shot because then we'd be in the same situation, but with different roles. I'm happy that it's me here now, and not her. She will always be the beautiful girl she was to me. Even when I see her in her old age, all I see is the face I once loved." He sighed and looked at me with an apologetic face. "But this is why I kept the secret about Edgar's hologram. It's not healthy to obsess over something that is no longer yours."

A heavy sigh escaped my lips, and I looked into my lap. "But what's the harm? Really, it's not like I can hurt the hologram. I can't even touch him. The hologram is nothing more than a cloud of air." My attempt to justify the situation was not making me seem any less deranged.

"That's what I'm trying to say, Elle. He's not real. He's gone." He shrugged. "But it's your call, so don't say I didn't warn you." He gave me a playful punch on the shoulder. "I just don't want to be spending all my waking hours following you around while you waste your time stalking a ghost."

We both began laughing uneasily. I could see how uncomfortable it was for Sam to talk about his true love, and I suppose I could understand.

"What was her name?" I asked.

He smiled as though remembering something special. "Jill."

I watched as his eyes glazed over, and for the first time I thought I saw him experience true emotion. Feeling sorry for him was not the answer. He knew what he had done, and frankly, he didn't really seem to feel all that sorry for himself. I sighed as I sat there watching him. It felt good to know he had a soft spot, something I could use against him, as horrible as that sounds.

We had finally connected, and I no longer saw Sam as the gruff brute he had always seemed. There had been a heart once, and love, and now friendship as well. I could understand why Edgar had chosen Sam. He was a complicated mess, and so he knew I'd like it, that I would connect with him.

I leaned back into the couch, listening to the steady muffled ticking of Edgar's clocks within the chest. Their constant reminder of time falling away was ominous, yet it was different when you knew it would never end, though worse at the same time. If I never found Edgar, I'm not sure if I would be able to stay here for eternity, but I would have to be certain I searched out every possible lead. I kept the dagger from the fight in a drawer in the kitchen. I knew, that should I ever leave this life, I would leave the same way Edgar had, beside him forever.

Sam was still staring into space except his eyes were now darting about the room, his face like stone. I sat up and looked at him with a hint of alarm. Something about the way his brows were squeezed together reminded me of that day in London, when he was hunting down Matthew.

"Wha..."

Sam cut me off, putting his cold hand up to my mouth so fast that I hardly had time to object. He glared at me and I felt my heart rate begin to quicken. "Did you hear that?" He whispered, almost a hiss.

His hand was still clasped over my mouth, so I shook my head.

"Shh...Listen," he urged.

I pushed his hand away in annoyance but nonetheless closed my eyes to concentrate. My thoughts cleared as I listened carefully. He was right. There was definitely something there. It was like the siren from a fire truck, except it didn't wail in even waves. I listened to the noise intently, trying to discern its source like a taste on my tongue.

My eyes opened and I looked at Sam. "What is that?" I whispered.

Sam broke his concentration. "I think..." He paused as

though rolling the flavor of the sound around in his mouth. "I think it's a *cat*."

"A what?" I gasped, trying again to listen for the sound but our voices had cut through my narrowed senses, and I lost the moment.

He nodded. "Yeah, definitely a cat. I can hear it breathing now, too." My heart surged hard as Sam eyed me with a smirk on his face. "Well, I can't hear it now, not over *that*." He pointed to my chest.

I glowered at him. "But where is it coming from? Outside?"

Sam's grin sunk into a straight line. "No," he paused, his eyes scanning mine as though still pinpointing the location. "From upstairs."

"What!" I hissed, my cheeks now flushed and my limbs tingling. It wasn't that I was frightened exactly, but rather surprised and even excited. The last time I had seen the cat, Edgar had died, and that was certainly something to evoke fear. That kind of anxiety would make anyone's blood run cold.

Sam rose carefully from the couch, as though afraid to scare off the cat, though we were too far away for it to possibly hear us. I looked around the room frantically, my mind in a haze. I wasn't really sure if I should grab a weapon or something for the cat to play with.

"Come on, let's go." Sam stood and offered me his hand.

I grabbed it and he yanked me up, my head swimming. Not only did I not want to see the cat, I also didn't want to see either of those rooms. I felt myself grow pale as the blood drained from my face at the thought of having to put myself through what surely would be a traumatic experience. There was a tart taste on my tongue.

"You can do this, Elle. Now is not the time to become a wimp." Sam squeezed my hand, assuaging my fears.

He was right. I was being a coward. I told myself I was going to fight, and now here I was contemplating running away. I took a deep calming breath and let a sharp exhale escape my lips as I dropped Sam's hand.

He smiled at me. "Alright, let's do this."

Excitement made his eyes shine brightly. He was relishing the adventure and possible danger. For a moment I wondered if he was really a guardian angel, or if in fact he was a battle angel in sheep's clothes.

I balled my hands into fists as Sam waited for me. Taking the initiative, I pushed past him and stormed into the hall. If I died, who cared anyway? This is what I was here for, and this was my time. Besides, what if the cat ended up being sweet? Then I would have a new pet.

Sam chuckled. "Really? A pet, Elle? You're such a woman."

"Shut up," I hissed over my shoulder, narrowing my eyes.

I halted at the bottom of the stairs as the crystal chandelier shook above me, sending sharp tings of sound through my heightened senses. The cat wailed again and my heart leapt. My eyes shot to the left, toward my room, and I couldn't help but feel at least a little bit relieved. I wasn't all too excited about the idea of having to go into Edgar's room for the first time on a hunt. I had planned to spend more time with it, give it the respect it deserved.

Sam walked up beside me. "Come on, it's just a cat. This will be easy, and it's frightened. Its little heart is racing."

I looked at him with sheepish eyes before wiping the pitiful look off my face and pressing forward. I grumbled as I ascended each step, my fists clenched and ready. I felt Sam behind me and it helped me to feel brave. There was no turning back. He wouldn't let me.

My foot was poised on the top stair when the cat wailed again, drawing out the sound and ending it with a sharp upward pitch of agony. No longer feeling the need to be quiet, I made a beeline toward the doors with renewed determination. My pace slowed as I approached, my hands held defensively before me, ready to protect myself against anything that might attack. My last few steps were so silent and slow, that even the dust remained settled on the floor. My toes were now an inch from the entry.

I could see the light shine from under the door and my heart jumped again as a small shadow paced behind it. The cat was acting as though it was trapped, but I knew better than to fall for that. It seemed more likely that the cat's purpose was to make me come get it, particularly in this room. I knew better than to believe that any of this was a coincidence. Someone had either put the cat there on purpose to scare me, or the cat had somehow magically gotten in.

Taking a deep breath, I reached toward the handles. Lowering them onto the cold brass, I exhaled and pressed down, throwing doors open as the light from the room poured over me and into the hall. I shielded my eyes from the light, bringing my arm to my forehead, squinting. As my eyes adjusted to the light, my heart stopped.

THAT WAS EASY

I coughed as the dust settled from throwing open the door. I fanned my hand before my face, allowing the bright hazy room to reveal its newfound secrets. I scanned the room with frantic eyes, but there was nothing there. Small particles of dust swirled in thick clouds through the rays from the window as I walked through them, disrupting the room that had once again been unused for so long.

With small careful steps, I rolled my feet across the cold wood floor, slowly placing one foot in front of the other. I glanced over my shoulder to check if the cat had hidden itself behind the door, but was relieved that nothing was lurking there. My eyes followed the floorboards until they met the far right corner and scanned along the wall before me. I took in each familiar painting on the wall, remembering everything.

I crept to the middle of the room and stopped, turning on my heel to see Sam standing on the threshold. He was watching me with uneasy intensity. I put a finger to my lips to indicate to Sam to remain quiet while I searched for the cat. I crept forward warily, bending to scan under the blue silk chair by my bed, but saw nothing. I craned my neck to look behind the gold dressing screen only to find a pile of discarded clothes twisted on the floor.

Discouraged, I released the breath from my lungs, turning to look at Sam. I shrugged, at a loss of what to do. His gaze was still intent, his eyes like two copper pennies. He could still sense the cat's presence; therefore the threat was not yet over. I looked back toward my bed, averting my eyes from the coverings in my attempt to shield myself from the inevitable sorrow of the twin impressions.

It must be under the bed, I thought. Sam nodded in silent agreement from the door. Like I had back home with the neighborhood cats, I clicked my tongue, calling the cat from its hiding place and inviting it to show itself. I listened closely for a moment, but only the sound of my shallow breathing reached my ears. As I made a move to call again, I heard a soft scratching from under the bed and my heart leapt. I jumped back, startled, on guard just in case the animal attacked my legs.

From a safe distance, I eyed the silk bed skirt. Sure enough, a white cat trotted out from under the hem. The cat rushed toward me in a seemingly aggressive manner. There was a sudden commotion as Sam lunged from the door, grabbing the cat by the scruff and whisking it across

64

the room, holding it at arms length. He moved so fast, and I barely had time to react before the cat was gone.

"Sam!" I screeched. "It was coming to me! I doubt it is harmful. You probably scared the thing to death!"

The cat was indeed very frightened, and I noticed its claws were dug deep into Sam's white skin. Its feet were helplessly dangling as it desperately eyed the floor with frantic need. Sam did not bleed, or even feel it for that matter, so I was not concerned about him. He began to pry the cat's claws from him and I watched as his skin ripped under the cat's death grip.

The cat hissed as he tried to place it on the ground, swatting and spitting. Sam snickered at the helpless creature in his arms. "Yeah its fine, it's safe. Just needed to make sure, you know, check for fleas." And with that, he dropped it to the floor. The cat's feet absorbed the fall like mini hydraulic pumps. It shook its ruffled fur and backed away, one wary eye fixed on Sam's movements.

I glowered at Sam before clicking my tongue and crouching to the floor. I laid my hand against the floor with an open palm. The wide-eyed cat pried its gaze away from Sam and our eyes finally met. It gratefully turned and trotted toward me, its body now relaxed and happy. It rubbed up against my leg with careless charm, its throat erupting into a roll of heavy purring.

"Oh, and it's a girl," Sam added. "Filthy little feline." He was tapping his foot impatiently, making the cat jump with each tap he made.

I scratched her head and she leaned into my touch, her

eyes closed as she purred even louder. I laughed, marveling at her pure white fur and unusual eyes. I had never seen a cat like her in my life, and just as I had thought last winter, I knew it was because it was special, like Sam and I.

"Can you hear what she's thinking?" I looked up at Sam, hope filling my eyes.

He pursed his lips in thought, his eyes fixed on her head. "No…" he paused, the hesitation in his voice suggesting more. "There is something, though, but I can't really tell what it is. It's very intriguing." He was nodding now, like a philosopher in deep thought.

I kept petting her, stroking my hand over her silky fur. "Do you have something to say, girl?" I smiled down at her and she twisted her head toward me, meowing plaintively as though hoping I could understand.

"Must be a girl, listen to those vocal cords. She's so whiny and demanding." Sam's expression was filled with amusement.

"You're just jealous." I smiled at Sam, a lofty look on my face.

"Jealous of a cat?" he chortled. "Hardly. That thing can't even fly, and its body is like pudding. I'm surprised I didn't squeeze her to death just then."

I picked her up and held her in my arms. She moved around, cuddling into my grasp in a manner that was surprisingly sweet. All my fear melted away as I drew the obvious conclusion: she was harmless.

Her claws remained courteously retracted, and her eyes glowed at me as they began to fall into sleep. It was amazing how white her gaze was, almost blank except for the black slits of her pupils. As she turned toward the sun that was streaming through the window, I watched them glitter like diamonds.

She was so comfortable with me, her paws curling into my arms and her tail flicking contentedly. I looked at Sam, seeing he still had an appalled look on his face. He had been relatively okay with Isabelle and Henry, but the way he looked at the cat let me know he was never going to be so kind to her.

"What should we name her?" I asked with a merciless smile, knowing that he would hate this trivial task.

Sam scowled. "I'm not naming that thing. Don't you know, once you name them it's nearly impossible to give them away to a shelter. You'll get too attached."

I laughed. "You really think a shelter wouldn't notice the way she looks? Come on, Sam. I'm not getting rid of her."

Sam snorted. "Think about it, Elly. You don't even know the thing. What if it slashes your throat in the middle of the night or something?"

"Seriously, Sam. You think a cat scratch is going to kill me? I heal in mere seconds! That's absurd." I looked back down at the cat. "And besides, this is my house, so you'll just have to conform."

"Yeah, well, we'll see about that. Have you ever heard of cat scratch fever?" he retorted.

I glared at him. "You really think that just because some hit song says I'm going to go crazy and possibly die, I need to worry?"

His remark got choked in his throat as he began to laugh.

I looked around the room then, remembering it all. Being here wasn't as bad as I had thought, and I felt silly for shutting it away. This was who I was, and I had forgotten how important that can be. I slowly stood and walked toward the paintings as the cat rolled herself on her back in my arms. Her eyes fluttered in and out of consciousness in her insatiable feline love for twenty hours of sleep a day.

The figure of me behind the piano was easier to recognize now that I was complete again. I looked at the way I smiled, finally seeing that the smile was indeed mine. I took a deep breath and the cat cooed in my arms. She needed a name, something beautiful, but finding the right name would take time.

Sam chuckled behind me, amused by my endearing thoughts of my new pet. I looked down at her, and stroked my finger over the crown of her head. "I wonder what it is you know," I whispered to her, careful not to wake her.

A rude snort was replaced by Sam's chuckles. "Alright, this is sickening. I'm out of here."

I turned and smirked at him, content with that fact that I had finally managed to make him mad, or perhaps it was jealous? He looked at me resentfully as he glided to the doors and walked out of the room, not bothering to shut them behind him. My muscles relaxed at Sam's departure, allowing a wash of relief to trickle over me.

"As I was saying, little kitty, you and I have a lot to discuss." The cat again cooed in her sleep. I walked back across the room to my bed. A sharp breath escaped my lungs as I tried to overt my gaze from the place where I had last laid. Before I got the chance to be mournful, I rumpled the covers, washing away the memory I was not prepared to visit.

I rolled her out of my arms and into a nest of down in one gentle movement. Her body rolled onto the silk and she opened her eyes in objection. I giggled as she pulled her way back across the covers toward me, anything she could do to be near me. She seemed relieved that I was finally here, as though I was her life-force.

Something about her felt warm to me, warm like the way a hug feels, or the way Edgar had. I laid back into my pillows, the waft of Edgar's scent erupting into my nostrils and sending sweet chills down my spine. Though the cat had been a good distraction, I hadn't forgotten about what I had seen earlier today at the college. First thing tomorrow, I planned to go back down there, but this time as myself and not under the cloak of the white raven. Seeing Sarah and Scott had been beautifully intoxicating. Just the sight of their familiar faces was enough to remember that this world was all still real and alive. I didn't care if all they liked to do was play Monopoly. I now realized the simple importance of having them around, because you never knew when they could be gone forever.

Not willing to disrupt the cat any further, I snuggled down deeper into the covers. My eyes were heavy and my body was wrought with exhaustion after the sharp thrill of finding the white cat. It was so surreal that she had finally found me. She had literally fallen in my lap with little effort.

My eyes fluttered closed, tired by the strain of the bright

light from the large window. As I began to doze, dreams flooded my head in an array of colors. I was in a field, but not the field I was used to. The light from the sky was not normal sunlight, and it cast all the plants in a spectrum of dark fluorescent. I looked around but no one was there, though strangely, I did not feel alone, either. As I looked toward the overhead light, I was surprised to see that the sky had been replaced by a shroud of liquid fire.

I gasped as the rays cast by the glowing mass made my skin shimmer with an ethereal light. I touched my skin, feeling the smooth, hard surface which felt like pearl. I heard a female's voice call my name from somewhere to my right.

"Estella."

I turned toward the sound. There I saw two arched doorways, each inscribed with some sort of language I didn't recognize as human. Above the words was the image of a raven, crudely carved into the stone. I narrowed my gaze as I took in the strange inscriptions.

I slowly moved toward the doors. The air was filled with the subtle pulse of the infuriated sky overhead. I listened hard for the voice, craning my neck as I approached. My eyes darted between the two openings, unsure of which to choose when the voice returned, but this time it was Edgar's.

"Estella."

Shocked, I stepped back, shaking my head. The air around me swirled in the depths of the dream. I took a deep breath and yelled out to him, listening as the yell echoed back to me through the caves. I waited for any reply when I heard his distinct whisper, saying my name again.

"Estella."

I was now just a few feet away from the arches as I continued to listen. It was then that Edgar said my name a third time, his voice echoing from the arch to the right.

"Estella."

Suddenly, someone grabbed my hand from behind. I turned to look, but before I could see who it was, the whole scene dissipated around me. I tried to grasp onto the dream, but there was little I could do. My heart throbbed with pain, and reality returned as I came awake.

* * *

The room was now dark and the candles burst to life as soon as I opened my eyes. Startled, I looked around, forgetting that I had fallen asleep in my own bed and in my own room. My breathing was heavy as I continued to grasp onto the dream, begging it to stay and tickle me with the hope of Edgar.

I was so used to waking in the sitting room that the strange realization of comfort took me by surprise. It was dark now, and I frowned at the hour, wishing I hadn't fallen asleep because now I was wide awake and anxious.

The warm mass by my side moved, and I put my hand down to pet it. I had expected the soft fur of the cat but was surprised when I felt feathers instead. I looked down and saw Isabelle nestled next to me, her eyes closed and her face smiling. Pressing my brows together, my frantic gaze switched to the room and I scanned for the cat. I twisted my body to get up as Isabelle began squirming awake. Seeing me, she got up as well.

Finally, my gaze fell to the silk chair by the bed. The cat was perched on the cushion, her eyes glaring at Isabelle with hate, her body rigid. The sharp gurgle at my side made me look back at Isabelle in surprise. It was now apparent that there had been some sort of battle between them, a fight over who got to sleep next to me. I shrugged and smiled, a little disappointed I'd missed it.

"Yeah, it was good," Sam said, as walked into the room then. "I was rooting for the ball of feathers. It's at least good to see that she has something about her I can admire. Her fighting abilities were very impressive." He eyed the cat and snorted. "This one's a wimp, though. I'm surprised it lasted in the wild for so long."

"Sam, that's sadistic."

"What? If your bird kills the filthy cat, then at least it's not my fault," he shrugged.

The cat let an angry cry escape her jowls as she tilted her head back in emotional agony. Her gaze was sharp as her eyes darted to Sam's. Sam chuckled. The cat then jumped out of the chair, the pads of her feet slapping against the floor where she landed with a solid thump. I watched her trot to the doors and slink out, her tail swishing sassily. I turned my gaze to Sam, angry that he had scared her off.

Anxiously, I jumped off the bed to follow but then halted as she popped her head back in and looked at me. It appeared as though she was waiting for me, and following was just what she had in mind. Suddenly aware that I was making her wait,

I rushed to her side. She then trotted toward the stairs. She continued to look back at me, making sure I was following. Her tail whipped with comic leadership as she leapt down one step at a time, maneuvering her decline like an expert.

The cold marble steps were welcoming beneath my feet as I worked to keep up. She stopped at the bottom while I descended the last few, her tail raised in waiting. Arriving at her side, she then trotted into the library where she jumped onto the couch. I panted in behind her as she placed one paw on the cover of the gold book that I had left to rest on the cool leather.

I walked up to her with curious caution, my eyes scanning hers with understanding. "You want to show me something?"

She chattered in agreement. I bent down and grabbed the book out from under her paw. She curled up on the warm spot left behind by the book as though cuddling in to hear a story. I giggled and lowered myself onto the cushion beside her, flipping open the book and fanning through the pages until I got to the back.

As I had guessed, there was a new page. My jaw fell open as I scanned the etched image that was still drawing itself across the paper, fresh and not yet ready for view. I watched the deep black lines bleed and spread, twisting into recognizable shapes.

The image that was forming before me in a delicate weave was of the cat and a white raven. They sat in a field, their gazes locked as though talking without words. The cat's face was twisted into something that resembled a smile, the raven also possessing a look of happiness in its eyes.

I looked to the cat as she watched the page with a calm patience, as though finding the magic no surprise. "Did you make this happen?" I asked her softly.

She looked up at me, the pupils of her eyes narrowing and her face quite solemn.

"You did, didn't you? You're the one that keeps changing this." I watched as her pupils dilated and my eyes fell back to the image. "Is this us?" I pointed to the two figures, the ink continuing to spread like a stain.

The cat chattered again, her whiskers shaking to life with both agreement and happiness.

I chuckled. "It's amazing!" It was then that the words began to form in the small caption space at the bottom of the page, and I read each aloud as they drew across the paper.

When they finally met, they recognized each other and the future was certain.

I pressed my brows together in confusion. According to the book, I knew the cat, but I could not will my memory to remember her. I looked back down at her soft white fur, laying my hand on her back and closing my eyes. Who are you? My mind whispered, but nothing whispered back.

"I wish I knew who you were. I want to help," I said aloud. My eyes opened and I looked deeply into hers. She blinked softly, discouraged with my lack of memory. Her back arched.

She sat up and walked toward me, crawling into my lap, a gentle purr erupting from her chest. Her paws were kneading my leg as she consoled me for my misperception into her heart, and into her identity.

"I'm sorry, girl. I just don't know you. My memory of my life before is lost." I felt my heart sink. I was discouraged by this interaction and my chest erupted with an angry heat.

She released one pained meow, feeling my own frustration and agreeing that she, too, felt lost. I placed my hand on her head and sighed with a heavy heart. I allowed the book to sit on my knees, the ink still curling in a few last embellishments. She rolled in my lap, rubbing her face against my leg with love, finding nothing more that could console the moment.

Sam poked his head into the room. "Are you hungry? I think I could manage a tuna fish sandwich."

The cat perked up, forgetting our moment of bonding as she pushed off my legs and leapt over the book where she ran to Sam's feet. She rubbed up against his leg, her body arching around his ankle in a bold show of both hunger and emotion. My jaw fell open in surprise, pride filling my heart as I wished I'd had the same gall.

"Oh, yuck," Sam pretended to gag, kicking the cat away from his leg and backing into the hall. Despite the less than subtle shrug-off, she was insistent to following him, her will for tuna too strong to deny.

I laughed. "You said the magic word, Sam. Tuna."

A sour look crossed his face, and I could tell he would never say the word again. He backed his way into the kitchen as she followed, jumping onto the stool behind the bar and sitting very demurely. I followed and sat in the second stool beside her, watching Sam.

Sam reached into the cabinet for a can of tuna with a begrudged grunt of irritation. He rummaged through the utensil drawer. I assumed he was searching for the can-opener, but coming up empty handed. I watched in amusement as he placed a bowl before him, unfazed by the trivial setback of not finding the opener. His hands grasped both sides of the slender can and applied pressure. The can snapped in half with a crack, the sharp edge of the aluminum barely denting his skin as it sliced across it.

The tuna burst into the bowl, and the cat's eyes dilated with greed and obsession as tuna flavored water spattered across the counter. I laughed and grabbed a chunk from the bowl, placing it on the counter before her. Daintily, she tilted her head and licked at the savory treat. Her table manners were impeccable. She chewed in an entranced show of gluttony, her eyes dazed.

Sam watched with a disgusted look of annoyance. "This is ridiculous. Feeding a filthy cat from the table is not proper." His eyes flashed with unmistakable jealousy. "You are aware they bury their poop in dirt, right? Not to mention walk all over it first. If I were you, I'd be protecting my flower beds."

"Sam, just get over it. She's staying. Besides, the flower beds could use the fertilizer." I smiled sweetly at his grimace of disgust.

He sighed, mumbling something inaudible under his breath as he mixed the tuna with a bit of mayonnaise. He then slopped it between two pieces of bread. "Here," he shoved the soppy sandwich toward me.

I grabbed it with a smile as his hand touched mine,

shocking me with its icy feel. Since our conversation about his life, things between us had seemed awkward. He had exposed his weaknesses and was now doing all he could to make up for it by being tough and closed off.

"Sorry," he noticed me jump, and I swear, if he could, he would be blushing from his faltering show of vulnerability.

GHOST

I rummaged through my closet in desperation as I searched for another pair of boots. I had lost the previous pair somewhere in the forests of England, and I cursed myself for being so careless. Those particular boots had been so incredibly comfortable, that I scarcely believed I could let them go. I guess in my own defense, however, I was in no state to remember material things at the time.

My heart was pounding with excitement. Today was the day I would see Edgar. Well, at least his ghost. Just knowing that my eyes would be able to trace the subtle lines of his face was good enough for me. I only wish I could touch him as well. I wish I could feel the way I had before, when an undeniable love had filled my soul.

The cat was curled in a pile of fresh comforters on my bed. Sam had helped me to change the sheets before I fell asleep last night. He had agreed it was probably best to get past the sad memories and begin moving forward. Isabelle was clawing into the back of the silk chair, her eyes slanted with anger as she watched the cat. Her gaze never broke. Isabelle had spent every moment she could watching her, stalking the cat's every move.

With an overwhelming sigh of relief, I fell out of the closet with a pair of black boots hiding in hand. I let out a cry of triumph and stood, holding the boots above my head in victory before sitting on the edge of the bed. I shoved my feet into them, pulling each on with excitement. I laced them tight.

They were made of soft suede and looked new, despite the worn heel. I ran my hand down the length of them, the musky smell of the hide filling my nostrils. The good part was they weren't too heavy, and would make the hike easier than it had been with the large, modern boots I'd bought when I moved here. It was also nice because it was summer, and I certainly did not want to wear fur boots.

Triumphantly I stood, smoothing my grey t-shirt over my jeans. There was an elastic head band in my pocket and I snapped it over my neck and up my forehead, pressing my silky hair back and away from my face. I looked at myself in the antique mirror, the angel-gilding around the edges of the glass beginning to flake away. My skin was perfectly radiant, and with one quick finishing touch, I grabbed at some powder that sat on my vanity, splashing my face and arms with a light coat to hide the obvious pearly effect.

I clapped my hands together contentedly, happy that I had achieved a believable human appearance, plain and normal. I walked toward the door as Isabelle leapt from the chair and glided to my shoulder. The cat stretched its back lazily before leaping to the floor and trotting to my side. As I descended the stairs, Sam emerged from the library. I noticed Henry was perched on his shoulder, and it took me by surprise. Sam looked uncomfortable and awkward, as though embracing Henry's companionship had brought warmth to his soul, something he didn't know how to deal with.

"Wow, you look hideous," he choked out, meaning to be hurtful.

"Gee, thanks. You really know the way to a woman's heart." I breezed by him, barely acknowledging his presence. He was struggling with this new, softer side of his identity.

He glanced at both Isabelle and the cat. "You look like a parade."

I pointed to Henry. "You look like you're coming around to my way of life."

He grunted. "Whatever, he just seemed a little lonely. What, with you and your two favorite pets. You were leaving him to the dogs." He crossed his arms defensively.

"Whatever. I was not! Henry had the choice to hang out with me if he wanted." His accusing remark had struck a chord, making me feel bad. Perhaps I had been a bit neglectful.

Sam snorted. "Yeah, whatever. So, where do you think you're going?" He knew, and I could see he was going to try and stop me.

"It's none of your business," I replied bluntly.

Sam eyed me with mixed emotion.

I raised one eyebrow. "But you're free to join me, if you

dare."

He grumbled angrily. I could see he wanted to go, but he was still fighting with his hatred for humanity. "Maybe I'll just watch."

I laughed, knowing he had given in. "Good for you, Sam. I'm glad to see you embracing civilization."

His eyes narrowed as he gave me a playful tap on the shoulder.

I smiled at him and walked toward the door. The cat was at my heels. "You stay here," I said with regret as she looked at Isabelle. Isabelle gave the cat a smug look. "You, too, Isabelle. You can't go with me on this trip." She clicked her tongue and snapped at my ear.

Sam shrugged repeatedly in an attempt to make Henry get off his shoulder. It was clear he still hadn't gotten up the nerve to touch him just yet.

"Are you about ready?" I was stifling a giggle as Sam continued to shake his body, but Henry refused to let go as he balanced himself with his wings.

I walked up to Sam with a frown, trying to grab Henry as Sam continued thrashing. I grabbed Henry's wings and pulled him from Sam's shirt as he clawed at it with desperation. "It's okay, Henry." I cradled him in my arms as he snapped his beak toward Sam. I gave him a kiss on the head. "Sam can't be broken in one day, my dear. Have patience."

Henry took a deep breath and exhaled as the feathers on his chest relaxed into defeat.

Sam let out one last violent shiver as though shaking off the smell. "Let's just go, okay?" He gave me a reproachful glare.

I dropped Henry to the ground, but he spread his wings and flew up to the top banister of the stairs instead. I walked to the door but Sam beat me to it, grabbing the handle and opening it for me.

"Oh, look who's the gentleman now," I teased.

He smiled. "After you, *witch*."

A chuckle gurgled in my throat as the warm summer air met my face. The comment didn't hurt because it was true. I was proud to be a witch. I heard him shut the door behind us as I walked down the front steps and into the meadow with little hesitation. It all disappeared behind me. I had done this so many times now, it seemed normal for my palatial mansion to fade into thin air.

"So, are you going to come with me the whole time, or are you going to back out at the first sight of human life?" I looked back at Sam as we stepped through the tall grass. The way it hooked around me in its everlasting love was at this point borderline annoying, and I looked forward to the gravel paths of the college.

Sam watched me fight with the vegetation in amusement. "I'll probably keep a safe and healthy distance. Heaven forbid I should catch a common cold."

I laughed at his absurdity. "They're not that bad, Sam. Really."

He shrugged. "No, I suppose not, but I'd rather just move on from them. There is so much life, or rather after-life, to live. I can't waste it pining over someone I'll never have."

I nodded, my brows furrowed in frustration. "Are you

saying I'm wasting my time?"

I looked back at his face again, his wings now protruding from his sides. "Perhaps," he considered the statement some more before continuing. "You should just move on. Someday they will be gone and you'll be back to square one, saddened by the inevitable loss due to the human cycle of life. It's an unnecessary pain you can avoid now, before you get too attached."

"Move on to what? It's not like the world is heavily populated with my kind. I'm almost a hundred percent certain I am the last one. Besides, I'm already too attached." The heat of the thick summer air was beginning to make me warm and I felt a bead of sweat form on my brow. "I'd rather live decades with friends as they grow old than spend it sad, avoiding life."

I looked back toward the woods as two cold arms hooked under mine and whipped me skyward.

"I'm not about to trudge through the woods like a human," Sam yelled into my ear. "That would take hours."

He swung me in his grasp with little effort, hooking one arm under my knees and the other behind my back. I squealed, not feeling so much frightened as taken off guard. The gentle fanning motion that his large wings created as we cut through the air was much different than my quick, sharp raven strokes had been. I liked it. His body was like having the air conditioner on full blast while riding in a car, and I couldn't deny that this was a much better idea than walking.

I had thought about flying down to the college myself, but then I remembered that I would likely end up naked, and that wasn't going earn me any Brownie points with Sarah. I knew she wasn't exactly excited about Scott and I being friends, but how could she really mind when it was me who had brought them together? Besides, I had no control over the way Scott looked at me; that was his fault.

We glided in silence over the expanse of forest that separated my home from the college, the air changing from warm to hot depending on the various atmospheric pockets we whipped through. As the trees thinned, I could just make out the few log structures that were scattered below, standing solid on the bank of the milky blue lake.

My heart raced as we approached, the trip was a lot shorter than I had expected. The advantage of taking the time to hike here on foot was that I would have had more time to think. Even if it was a mere thirty minutes at my heightened pace, it was still time to prepare. Sam just rejected any form of human activity, no matter what the reason, and it had foiled my detailed plans.

Sam banked hard into the forest surrounding the school, landing in a thick grove of trees and ferns that shielded us from any curious gazes. He touched down on the forest floor softly. His grip relaxed and I set my feet on the spongy, moss-covered ground. There was no trail in sight.

"You could have at least set me somewhere where I could actually walk my way out," I grumbled under my breath, straightening my shirt and warming the skin where Sam had held me.

He took a deep, dramatic breath. I narrowed my eyes at him, knowing he used the simple unnecessary act of breathing as a precursor to a horrid comment. "Just think about what you're doing, Elly. Edgar is dead. You won't get him back. Even if you could, you really shouldn't be thinking that way. Always expect the worst from life."

I looked at him in disgust. "Sam, if you have nothing to look forward to, and nothing to hope for, then why is life even worth living?"

His eyes glimmered with a melancholy sadness and his mouth settled into a straight line. "I was just saying there are things to hope for. I think they should be more realistic things, tangible things."

He was getting at something, but I didn't quite understand what that was. I couldn't imagine that he'd have the gall to tell me to move on, and to whom? I was suddenly curious just what it was that he hoped for and what had kept him going for so long.

As far as I could tell, he had nothing other than the simple task of protecting me. But then I often wondered what his end of the bargain was? What had Edgar said to make him take this task? Surely there was something, some reward when it's all over. Surely he won't have to serve as an angel forever, hating the life I led, hating everything.

Sam's mouth curled at the corners and I glared at his obvious acknowledgement of my thoughts. If there was one thing I was looking forward to with Scott and Sarah, it was that they respected the privacy of my mind.

"I'll be waiting here when you're done." Sam retracted the full length of his wings into his back and folded his arms across his chest, hunkering down for the boring wait.

"Thanks, Sam. I won't be long." I gently squeezed his

shoulder before I turned and walked down the hill through the heavy brush, my eyes focusing on every possible obstruction that could make me trip and give Sam the gratification of laughing at me.

As the woods began to thin, I quickly recognized where I was. I was entering from the east side, through the cluster of greenhouses. As I passed the glowing green buildings, I peered through the wavy glass, noticing how the plants there seemed unfazed by my presence, unable to smell or feel me through the barrier of the walls. I dropped down onto the path and the grasses around it reached toward me, almost in a way that seemed like they were welcoming me back.

There were no students anywhere in sight, and I looked to the sky in an attempt to judge the time. The sun was about three quarters of the way through its cycle and I deduced that classes must already be over for the day. I slowed on the path, realizing how horrible a friend I'd really been. I didn't even know where Scott or Sarah had lived in my short time here.

I pursed my lips, feeling suddenly frustrated. Tapping my fingers against my hips as I thought, I finally remembered that I had at least known where the infirmary was. The intoxicating hospitality of Miss Dee could help out in this type of situation. I always pictured her having a detailed chart of every student in her need to create order. She would know where to find them.

I picked up my pace, the path now dropping down through the grass toward the lower buildings. Ducking into the walkway that was shielded by the overhanging roofs of the buildings on either side, I noticed how the sound seemed to change, how my footsteps now echoed off the wood siding that surrounded me.

It was a strange sensation to hear the echo of my own footsteps. Ever since last fall, when I had moved out to the large expanse of silence, I had forgotten what it was like to hear myself walk. I had been so used to the reverberation of the city that the sudden peace had shocked me. In Seattle, I felt caged, bottled between the looming buildings and hard concrete where no sound was absorbed by the soft earth, rumbling in your head as a painful reminder of your infinitesimal existence in this life.

It was true what Sam had said about the humans destroying what beauty there was left in this world, and I now found myself coveting the tree huggers and animal activists of this race. Saving the beauty in this world was something I had taken for granted in my selfish need to find myself. Now it was evident that things needed to change, and the mysteries of the world returned so they can breed life amongst the gloom.

Scott and Sarah were not vile humans, but the last of their kind that still understood what it meant to value life, and the true privileges they have been given. They were aware of themselves and their world, aware of the footprints they left and the power they had to change it. Sam was right to hate the other humans, the selfish murderers and greedy corporate presidents, all here to exploit what the Earth gave freely to all human kind. Yet there must be a reasonable solution, a way to change them before it was too late.

I exhaled and shook my head, realizing such thoughts

were overshadowing my reasons for being here. It was time to focus on the task at hand, to be the Elle everyone here remembered, invisible and strange. My feet crunched against the gravel until at last I reached the familiar red door with the small white cross painted in the middle. I knocked once, listening as the singing voice of my past reverberated through the heavy steel.

"Come in!"

I pushed down on the handle as I took a deep breath, preparing myself for whatever lay ahead.

As the outside light flooded the dim space, Miss Dee turned in her chair. Her body was plumper than it had been the year before and I giggled to myself, remembering the doughnuts Scott and Sarah had always stolen from her. You would think that with her doughnuts always running off, she would have lost the weight, but this was clearly not the case.

"Oh, Miss!" she cried. I saw the recognition of my face flood her beady eyes, her cheeks flushing merrily.

"Hi!" I sang back to her, the light glittering off her collection of bottles. I smiled. It had never occurred to me until now just how hard it had always been to smile in my time here, both mentally and physically. Every day in this past life of darkness had been such a battle, such a struggle to survive.

"Oh my, it's like seeing a ghost, dear! What brings you back? Has another session with Professor Edgar gone bad?" A cheerful chuckle rumbled in her chest as she laughed at her cleverness. "Here to settle a score now, are we?"

I cringed at her reference to Edgar. "Oh..." I paused to

gather my thoughts. "Well, I'm just back for a visit. I came to see Scott, you know… Nothing quite that dramatic."

She chuckled. "Oh, you fox! I always knew you and Scott had a thing for each other. But I should warn you, I believe he's seeing someone, and actually I think he's engaged." She pursed her lips in a half smile, mocking me with her loving thoughts. "Sarah, I believe her name is." Her brows were fixed in a painful manner, her half moon glasses teetering on the end of her nose as she chewed on her nails, still perplexed.

I quickly rolled my eyes as she looked away. Scott was engaged? I grunted. That was fast. But I suppose someone like him has to lock it down before the girl realizes how useless he really is, not to mention how inherently clumsy.

"Oh, yeah, I knew that. That's why I came, to congratulate them on their engagement, of course!" I was laying the cheeriness on like cold peanut butter, and playing the part of a caring friend.

She pressed her chin into the roll of her neck, looking even more like a chubby cherub. "Oh, aren't you the thoughtful one." She coated her remark with a swift wink.

I stifled back the sour taste in my throat. Being this upbeat was exhausting, not to mention a full time freak show. "I was just curious if you knew where they had perhaps moved to?"

She smiled as she turned back to her desk, pulling a huge pink ledger out of the drawer and slapping it down with a loud thump, the bottles shaking under the thunderous weight. I flinched. The cover of the ledger was adorned with purple hearts and swirls, and I stifled a laugh, my notions about the detailed list confirmed. She flipped it open and trailed one plump finger down the page, mumbling Scott's name under her breath as she searched.

"Oh!" she exclaimed and I lurched back, my body readying itself for attack out of pure instinct. "Here it is! Yes, yes. Cabin twelve."

I snorted. "Cabin twelve?"

Miss Dee turned and gave me a grave nod. "I suppose they swooped it right out from under you!"

A sweet smile stretched its way across my cheeks. I turned to leave, my mind now unable to handle another moment in her intoxicatingly sweet presence. "Well, thanks Miss Dee. I'll be sure to visit again!" And with that I made a mental note to avoid the entire vicinity.

"Oh, that would be lovely, miss." She pressed her brows together and brought her finger to her chin in thought. "Let me just say you look different, more grown up, or *something*."

I chuckled under my breath. "Well, it has been a whole year, and you know how we young adults grow, like weeds," I hissed for dramatic effect, thinking of my magical talents.

She nodded, her face still twisted in thought. "Hmm... Well, did you ever find out about your arm? It still perplexes me. I have never had someone heal quite that fast." She was trying to make the conversation linger but it only irritated me further.

I turned and twisted back toward her, knowing there was at least one thing that could easily distract her from her prying question. "Oh, Miss Dee. Let me have just one last hug before I go. It's just so nice to see you!" I smiled brightly.

She popped right out of her chair, forgetting her question as though it had been wiped clean from the chalkboard. "Oh, I'd love one!" She skipped over to me in a surprisingly light-footed manner and squeezed me so hard, I actually wondered if she could break my rib.

As I pulled back, her eyes were glazed over with love and happiness. I backed away, my brilliant face still mesmerizing her with joy. I gave a little wave and made a quick move to grab the handle of the door and back my way down the stoop, exhaling with relief as I turned and the door shut behind me. I leaned back against the cool steel, my hand still on the handle as I looked at my shoes in utter disbelief. She was so happy that it was sickening.

"Excuse me."

I jumped, bringing my hand to my chest. I looked up in the direction of the voice, my heart racing from the sudden break of silence.

"Excuse me, hi." His gaze focused on mine.

I blinked hard, my voice choking in my throat and my whole body now teeming with warmth and fear.

"Is Miss Dee in?"

I swallowed hard, his blue-grey eyes piercing into my soul, the ghost before me still struggling to register in my thoughts.

"Uh…" I was stammering hard.

Edgar stood patiently, his face unchanged and his mouth set in a steady concentrated line. He didn't even flinch as he looked at me. Obviously, he did not recognize me, and I now realized how strange it must have been for Edgar when I had come back into his life. It was as though I were staring into the same oblivious face, the same lost expression that I had once possessed.

"Uh...Yeah." My lungs began to sting as I refused to breathe.

He gave me a sharp, satisfied nod. "Well, may I get by?"

I suddenly noticed that I was still barricading the door like an idiot, my arms sprawled between the two jams. I struggled to remain standing. "Oh, sorry," I breathed as I moved aside, stumbling off the stoop.

Edgar's ghost made a quick movement to catch me before halting himself, his programming telling him not to touch anyone.

I caught my hand against the wall before making a complete fool of myself and falling to the ground. A vine from under the building began to curl up toward me in its attempt to break my fall, but I quickly stepped in front of it, trying to hide its reaction.

"Are you all right, Miss?" His eyebrows rose in concern and my heart melted.

I waved him away. "Oh, yeah. I'm okay." I wanted to run into his arms. I wanted to feel his grasp, feel the love. But here I was without him, nothing more than a glimmer in his eyes and just another face in the crowd.

He turned and walked into the office without another word, his casual demeanor cold and shocking. My mind was screaming the words I longed to tell him, the words I wish I could utter again, but as the door shut, my eyes welled with tears and my voice remained silent.

I inhaled one shaky breath, trying to decide what to do next. Leaning against the building, my knees shook uncontrollably and my heart throbbed. I finally blinked, and the tears I struggled to hide poured down my cheeks. My chest began to heave as I sobbed. I allowed myself this small moment, this chance to feel the reality of it all before stopping myself.

I wiped my eyes and furrowed my brow, angry that I could be so weak. A sharp exhale escaped my trembling lips and I forced my body away from the wall, my legs struggling under the weight. I pushed myself forward. There was no telling how long it would be before Edgar came out of that room, and I was certain that I didn't want to be here to witness it. That was all the proof I needed for today.

As I lumbered slowly down the path and into the opening in the center of the complex, I found myself disappointed. Of course I hadn't expected his ghost to remember me. How could it? It was just a hologram, a figment of dust and air. It had no heart, no mind, and no soul. But there was a part of me that hoped the search was over and he would finally come home. As I put my hand to my chest, expecting to feel that familiar burn of love, instead I felt nothing. I couldn't feel him the way I used to, and in this I knew he was gone from this world.

I forced my legs up the hill toward my old cabin. I dried my eyes some more. If one thing was true, seeing his face as though he were alive only further fueled my urges to find him. This was not a question of moving on, it was moving forward. Forward to him and to the answers I needed.

LOVE AND MARRIAGE

I leaned in to listen to the muffled voices and laughter behind the familiar pine door. Lifting my hand, I rapped it eagerly against the wood, remembering how it had felt to hear that noise from the other side when Scott had relentlessly come every morning before class.

The voices hushed, and I heard a scramble of feet on the floorboards. I exhaled and rolled my eyes, hoping I wasn't breaking up some sort of private moment. My heart raced. What was I going to say to them? What would be my excuse for abandoning them like I had?

As my thoughts raced, the door flew open and a gust of wind rustled through my hair.

Scott stared at me wide eyed, his jaw gaping. "No way!" he yelped, throwing his hands in the air like a rag doll.

He ran toward me, hugging me with a force I never

thought he could posses. I grunted as he depressed the air from my lungs.

"Elle!" he yelled again, his voice piercing my ears as his chin rested on my shoulder, his arms like a vice around my whole body.

I looked over his shoulder and into the room. Sarah's mouth was gaping in the same manner Scott's had, her eyes glittering with what looked like tears. A feeling of embarrassment overcame me, and I made a quick move to smile in my attempt to ease the tension.

Her gaze broke as she finally spoke. "It's like seeing a ghost!" she screeched.

I rolled my eyes. "That seems to be happening a lot lately," I mumbled under my breath. Thankfully, neither of them heard me.

Scott pulled me away from him, his hands clasped around my shoulders. He examined my face. I pursed my lips, feeling like an ant under a microscope.

"Gosh, you look different, Elle, but still the same. How are you?" Scott's voice cracked, the sound comforting me somehow. He hadn't changed at all.

"Oh, I'm okay. I heard some interesting news, though." I wrenched myself away from Scott as politely as possible and I closed the gap between Sarah and I in just two steps. My hand grasped her left one, and I pulled it to my face to examine the jewels.

Sarah blushed, and I heard Scott's nervous laughter behind me.

"Oh, it's beautiful!" I gasped, taking in the small diamond

solitaire that was delicately perched atop Sarah's ring finger. I turned my gaze to Scott. "You did a good job." I winked at him with a genuine look of happiness crossing my face.

His cheeks were a deep shade of crimson, and his ears as red as ever.

"So, have you set a date?" I turned my gaze back to Sarah as I searched her eyes. The question was a typical one, but seemed to fit in the awkward moment.

She smiled. "The end of the summer."

My grin was beginning to hurt my face. "Oh, that's perfect!" I dropped her hand as I stepped back. The three of us formed a triangle in the tiny space.

I looked around the room, a flood of memories rushing back to me. One memory, however, was more vivid than the rest: the night Edgar had slept over. The image of him carelessly lounging on the rug crossed my mind, and I forced back the tears.

"So, where have you been?" Scott's voice finally cut the awkward silence.

I backed myself against the window sill. "Well, I had to leave, you know. Things were getting complicated." I looked down at my nervous hands, willing them to quit shaking.

Scott chuckled slightly. "Professor Edgar, wasn't it?"

I winced at the name. "Er…" I struggled to come up with another reason, but I couldn't find one, "Yeah."

A whole-hearted laugh erupted from Scott, and he had to work hard to calm himself. "Have you seen him yet?"

I snorted. "I guess you could say that."

Sarah snickered to herself, afraid to offend me. "I think

you two would make a cute couple."

I pinched myself to keep the rude comments from leaving my mouth, raising my eyebrows in acknowledgement instead. "Yeah, that's funny," I snorted again.

"So then, you're back?" Scott's voice sounded excited.

I shrugged. "I suppose you can say that."

They both looked at me with confused expressions.

My smile sunk to a frown and I knew I couldn't lie anymore. "Hey listen," I paused as I pushed myself away from the window, "If I told you something, would you try to believe me?"

Sarah and Scott looked at each other as though they knew what was coming next, as though they had speculated over me for some time now. "Yeah, sure, Elle. You're one of our best friends."

I smiled at the kind words. "Thanks."

Scott took one step toward me. "What's on your mind?"

"Well, I want to tell you what really happened. But I need you guys to try to understand, to try to believe it despite how incredible it sounds. You must trust me. I need you to trust me."

Scott looked intrigued. I could see he'd been waiting months for something exciting to happen in his small world.

"Sit down." I motioned both of them to my old bed, their bed.

As they settled in, I took a deep breath, thinking about where to start. "So Scott, do you remember when I first met you? I said I had a thing with nature, and you dubbed me 'Mother Nature'?" I smiled at the title, finding it still slightly silly, but appropriately true.

He shrugged, his eyes narrowing at me. "Yeah." He paused as he rolled something around in his memory. "I've been meaning to ask you about that." He brought one finger up to his cheek, his attempt at thinking looking painful.

I laughed. "Yeah, well, your assumptions are probably true, so let's go with that."

His eyebrows shot up in amazement. "So, the grass…"

"Yes." I cut him off. "But it's not just that. Edgar was an important player in it, too. Very important," my voice trailed off.

Both their mouths hung open in amazement as I continued. "I'm not human, so to speak." I winced, my face crinkling up as I anticipated their reactions. I let out a sharp exhale. I was struggling to find the right words, to say what needed to be said.

Scott gave me a blank stare while Sarah seemed to react to the fact, making an attempt to understand. "What do you mean?" Sarah's sharp, confused voice rang like a bell in my ears.

"So, okay…." I began to pace the room. "Scott, you remember when I got that really deep cut and there was all that blood and it would have probably taken weeks, if not months, before it would really heal?"

Scott nodded.

"Good. Well, I was completely healed the next day. My body is not like yours." I didn't look at them as I said this. I just needed to get it all out. "I am over a thousand years old, and so is Edgar. We are different from you, but somehow the same. We are a hybrid of your kind, created after you, but a better model. Think of it like a car." I paused to take a deep breath. "Edgar and I were made by the gods in pairs." I winced again, knowing how ridiculous this all sounded. "I guess you could say that Edgar and I are soul-mates, much like you two." I gave them both a sweet smile, hoping that if I related somehow, they would try harder to understand.

Looking back to my feet, I continued. "We were punished for being too perfect, too beautiful. Our bodies were forced apart, exiled to Earth like pawns in a giant game of chess." I heard a soft snort come from Scott, and my eyes met his, blazing as I kept a straight face. "I'm not joking."

His face went cold, and I knew he had noticed the terrifying look in my eyes, so like Edgar's.

"I'm not certain of my purpose here, yet, but there were more of our kind. Last year, one still lived, an evil one. His name was Matthew, and he killed Edgar." It came out of my mouth like a cold wind, filling the air with doom.

"But..." Scott was shaking his head. "But professor is here. He's not dead."

"That's not him," my voice was blunt as though still trying to convince myself that he was not real. "That's just his ghost, of sorts. If you were so bold as to touch him, you would see what I mean."

Scott gave me a grave nod. "Yeah, I've seen it. Someone tried to touch him last spring, or rather, punch him." He smirked. "But it was strange. We've all been trying to figure it out."

I glared at him. "This is a secret between us three, though, got it?"

I must have had a terrifying look on my face because he immediately nodded; his eyes wide and his body stiff.

"He died protecting me. So I guess you could say you were right about the whole Edgar and me thing. I did love him." I looked at them, content enough with what I'd told them.

"So…" Scott looked thoroughly confused. "So then, what are you?"

I crinkled my brow. Even I didn't know exactly what I was. "A Wiccan, of sorts. It's a hybrid, though," I replied. It was the only thing that really made sense in the human language. It still sounded corny saying it, but it worked.

Scott and Sarah both raised their eyebrows, agreeing in unison, their confusion somehow resolved. I had expected them to act a little more horrified about the whole situation, but here they were, just fine with the whole thing, at least seemingly so. That had always been Scott's style, somehow unfazed and strangely accepting.

"Cool," he chortled. "We know a *Wiccan*." He gently hit Sarah on the shoulder with the back of his hand.

"*A hybrid…*" I tried to correct, but I don't think they bothered to hear me. They were too shocked to care about details.

Sarah nodded. "Now I'm even plainer than before." She began to pout.

I rolled my eyes while they exchanged a sickening moment of baby talk and cooing. I only hoped Edgar and I hadn't been so irritating, but then again, we were always alone, so I guess it didn't matter if we were like that.

Scott's voice faltered, his gaze falling back on me as I stood with my arms knotted across my chest.

"So, wait. You live here? Where?" The look on his face was innocent, but something about it made me feel ashamed, as though living here was a horrible thing.

"In the woods," I replied frankly. I was prepared to answer with truth and dignity.

"Cool! So like, you live in a cave or something?" He was smiling now.

I snorted. "Hardly. I'll show you some day." I gave him a wink.

He nodded.

Sarah had a sweet smile on her face. "So, can you do anything cool? Besides this plant thing Scott told me about?"

I saw Scott blush. He must have discussed the matter with her in his frustration.

I crinkled my nose. "Oh, yeah. I can do this one really cool thing, but I'm sort of new at it."

"Do it!" Sarah squealed, clapping her hands like a child.

I couldn't help but smile. These were my friends, true friends. I could see they would love me no matter what. I took a deep breath. "Well, it's sort of complicated. I haven't really been able to work out all the kinks." I narrowed my eyes, thinking of how embarrassed I was when I'd found myself completely naked.

Sarah shrugged. "That's okay. We won't judge."

My chest fell as I let out a heavy breath, a half laugh escaping with it. "Okay, but I'm going to need you guys to look away at one point, got it? I won't really be able to talk, so let's say I'll sort of just yell at you."

They tilted their heads in unison, both confused, but their curiosity was too great to let it bother them. They nodded slowly.

"Okay. Come stand over here by the door." I ushered them up.

They shot off the bed with such excitement that it was difficult to see them move in the distance between us. In a flash, they were right next to me.

"Stand right here." I walked to the other side of the bed, figuring I would have some sort of privacy should this whole thing go horribly wrong.

I remembered how amazing I had thought it was when Edgar had done this for the first time, but the best part was knowing that someday I would, too. There was a certain smug pride inside me over the fact that I was finally special, finally unique in a way that wasn't depressing.

They watched as I closed my eyes and began to concentrate, as I had at the waterfall. I pictured myself falling, pictured the way the air whipped past my arms and filled me with the feeling of freedom. I put my arms out to my sides. Edgar had never been this dramatic, but then again, changing was much more natural to him because he did it all the time.

I took a deep breath, feeling the air around me grow thick. There was a sudden and overwhelming feeling of drowning and then I began to swim. I felt my wings cut through the air, now flying.

I heard unanimous gasps and I opened my sharp eyes,

quickly cutting left before hitting the wall behind them. Relieved that I had escaped possible injury, I soared in a tight circle back toward the bed where I landed in a soft pile of covers. My body was still clumsy as they tangled around me. Struggling without the use of arms, I righted myself in a manner that was far from graceful.

Sarah was chuckling under her breath, but I really couldn't blame her. It was obvious that I was new at this, and I was certain I had made a complete fool of myself.

"That's amazing!" Scott's eyes were larger than normal.

Sarah walked toward me. "You're so beautiful! You're practically glowing!" She couldn't resist ruffling the feathers on my head.

As she continued to scratch, I fought back the urge to snap at her, giving in to the undeniable fact that being loved like a pet felt good. It wasn't until Sarah started clucking at me that I finally broke away from her, things having gone too far. Scott was still staring, his fascination with me even stronger than before.

Twisting my head to the side, I tugged one feather from under my wing. I severed it from my body and dropped it to the bed. I then turned back and let out a shrill 'caw,' warning them to look away while I attempted to change back. They both turned and dutifully faced the wall.

I jumped in place, fanning the feathers on my wings and shaking. The coat of feathers shrugged off and before I knew it, I was half sprawled across the bed, the rest of my body scraping across the floor. I had managed to keep most of my undergarments intact, but there was still an unfortunate pile of clothes strewn behind the bed.

I fumbled with my jeans and t-shirt, thankful that it was summer and I didn't have much fabric to fight with. My cheeks were flushed as I finally cleared my throat and they both turned back around to face me. Their expressions were still enchanted by what they had seen, enchanted by me. I felt smug.

"So, I suppose you're really not lying about what you said. You really are a Wiccan." Scott was smiling.

I laughed, not willing to correct his title for me, yet again. He could keep it. I had given up. "Yeah, it's still sort of unbelievable, but I guess I'll get used to it. You see, I don't remember my life before, only my life for the past eighteen, or I suppose nineteen, years. But I will always look like I do now, forever."

Sarah's eyes went wide. "You are so lucky."

I snorted. "I don't know if I would consider that lucky. I have to watch all the people around me die." I paused, thinking of Sam. "Or at least most of them."

They didn't even flinch at my comment. "So, Edgar is dead? But I thought you were supposed to live forever?"

I shrugged. "In theory. I don't really have a medical manual or history book about my kind, so everything is a mystery. But right now, Edgar is dead from this world, and I don't know if he's coming back. No one else ever has, except me. But it is that fact that still gives me hope."

Scott pressed his brows together. "So then, it makes sense that you're here for a reason. Someone brought you back to do something."

I nodded. "I think you're right. These are the things I need to find out."

"Can we help?" Scott gave me an anxious look.

My gaze flitted from Sarah's face to his. I didn't intend to drag anyone else into my grief, or my obsession.

"Please?" Sarah pleaded. I could tell she genuinely wanted to help.

I couldn't let them down. I'd probably been the most exciting thing they'd seen all year. Their classes taught subjects that were predictable, about things that had already been scientifically examined down to every chromosome. I, on the other hand, was still a mystery. The feather I had plucked still lay on the bed and I reached to pick it up.

"Here," I handed the feather to them. "Be careful with it. It's sharp. But maybe you could look into it. See what I'm made of."

Scott's face lit up and he smiled. The truth was I really didn't think it was safe to involve them beyond finding out my science. If I ever lost them, or put them in harm's way, I knew I could never forgive myself, and forever is a long time to feel guilty about it. It still amazed me that they were so accepting, but I hadn't really expected anything less. This was how they had always been. I had always taken their friendships for granted, but I was going to change that.

My eyes scanned the room, my mind remembering the space as though it was a distant memory, a life that had only been lived in a dream. Each element was fuzzy and clotted. For the most part, everything was the same, except more lived-in. The small kitchen was a mess, and I noticed a box of

Twinkies was hidden behind the toaster.

A smile crept across my face as I remembered my past and tears gathered in my eye. I had dreamed of a day when I would finally find peace. Though this feeling of completion continues to leave me with an empty heart, it's the journey I shall never forget. From my humbled beginnings to now, from the many lost mothers I've had and the one that never existed. I will always deem myself lucky.

A feeling of realization crept over me. I continued to take in the memories of my past and I remembered that there was one thing I had left behind. It was something big, and something now useless to me. I walked to the kitchenette where I knelt down beside the small fridge. I reached my hand into the tight gap between the cabinet and fished out the thick envelope Heidi had given me the day I had left my foster home. As I stood, I twisted the envelope in my grasp and blew off the dust. My hands grazed across the indentations where Heidi had once held it with love and pride.

"Wow, what's that?" Sarah's voice came from across the room.

I turned to look at her with happy eyes, her face still bewildered from the events of the day. I placed one hand on my knee and pressed myself up off the floor and approached her. "Here, a wedding gift." I smiled.

Sarah's eyes grew even more confused as she let out a small giggle. "You kept it here? But how did you know?"

I laughed, her statement innocent and sweet.

I pressed it toward her as she gingerly took the envelope from my hands, her lips parted. "What is it?"

A sharp breath escaped my lips. "Actually, I'm really not sure. I never looked myself. But I know now that it was always meant for you."

She smiled and her eyes came alive with an awareness of life. "Thanks."

Scott eyed the envelope with a strange recognition, knowing the contents were something far too generous. We stood there for a moment and I realized they were both too polite to open it in front of me. It made no matter. Though I never knew what the envelope contained, it was no longer mine to know at this point. Either way, its contents could do little to change my life in the way Heidi had hoped, because fate had already done so. I knew that. Had she known of this passing of the gift, she would only be proud of me for finding someone I care enough about to give it to.

I swallowed hard. "Well, I should probably get going, but I'll be back soon." I walked into both their arms as they wrapped me in a hug. "In the mean time, look into that feather." I stepped back and patted them both on the shoulder. Scott winced away from my touch as I patted him a bit too hard.

"Your secret is safe with us." Sarah smiled. "It's so cool! You're a Wiccan!" she was jumping up and down, clapping her hands.

I grimaced, the title still not quite right, but at least something they could relate with. "Thanks. I just had to tell someone, and I promise there's still much more to show you." With that I winked and walked out the door.

DUST

I trudged my way back up the hill as I heard the undeniable screech of excitement erupt from the cabin. I knew it was either the fact that they had opened the envelope I had handed them, or that they were truly that excited about my existence. I stepped one foot into the shelter of the trees, and Sam's voice was suddenly right next to me.

I jumped and grabbed my chest, giving him a reproachful glare.

"Why did you do that? Don't you know they're human?" He was panting as though he had just run a long distance.

"Do what?" My voice was innocent.

"You just outed yourself to the weakest minds in the world! You can't trust that they won't tell anyone. If this gets out, there will be a witch hunt for sure!" His voice was low and full of doom.

"Oh, seriously, Sam, this isn't the 1800's. If they told anyone, it's more likely they'd be carted off to the psyche ward than start a witch hunt." I laughed under my breath.

He threw his hands in the air, unable to accept why I'd open up to a human.

I glared harder at him. "You know what the difference between you and me is?"

Sam shook his head.

"I actually posses the ability to trust someone, whereas you deny any sort of friendship or love." I swatted at a fly that had landed on my arm.

He snorted. "Whatever, but you just signed your death certificate, honey."

I glowered at him. "They're fine, Sam. And don't ever call me honey."

He laughed as we walked through the trees. "You're such a sucker for weakness. It's disgusting."

"You're disgusting," I retorted.

He frowned. "I beg to differ. I'm actually very clean." He opened his jacket toward me, baring his strong pale chest. "See. Take a whiff. It's like a newborn baby."

I looked at him with mock revulsion.

His wings suddenly sprung from his back and I rolled my eyes, bracing myself for what was to come. Despite my attempts to resist him, he scooped me from the forest floor and we shot skyward.

"You know I was enjoying the walk," I said as he held me against his frigid chest.

He smirked. "Yeah, well I'm enjoying the excuse to make

you touch me."

I wriggled in his grasp, disgusted by his lecherous advances. Though I knew, or at least hoped he was joking, it was still enough to drive me mad with anger. "You're a pig," I spat at him.

He laughed. "Oh, just take it easy, princess. You'll live. I'm not that bad. You're hurting my feelings."

The smug look on his face suggested that there were no feelings to hurt, so it really didn't matter how vile I was to him. We soared over the trees as they flashed below in a blur of green and brown. Having Sam was like having your own dragon, or Pegasus, except I'd hope if I'd had one of those, they wouldn't talk.

Sam looked down at me. "Dragons are dangerous, and a Pegasus is too aloof and ditsy. You may as well have a cricket to ride. Trust me."

I laughed. "Yeah, right. Like those even exist." There was no way I'd believe that.

His eyebrows shot up. "Did you ever think I would exist?"

I pressed my brows together. Of course, I had believed in angels, but he had a point. I never really thought I'd end up being friends with one. It had always been a human fairy tale that angels could exist amongst us, invisible and kind. Though my thoughts on their personality were tragically skewed, the stories had at least been true. I guess there was a lot of truth to fairy tales and stories these days, so the truth was, there was no truth.

The field was soon visible over the canopy of the forest

and I sighed with relief. I needed a rest. The day had been hard enough and the way Edgar's ghost had stared right through me was eerie. I was nothing more than a worthless human to him.

Sam dove down into the opening, but instead of setting us down, he skimmed the grass. We flew furiously through the meadow and I winced. The familiar watery wall appeared before us, just as it had the day Edgar and I had gone out on the snowmobile. I turned my head, burying it in Sam's chest and I felt as we crashed through it, the rippling cracking around us like glass and water.

I felt as Sam protectively tucked his body around me, the crash of metal and glass shattering all around us. We slammed hard against what I supposed was the back wall of the garage. I grunted as the breath was knocked from my lungs.

As Sam released his arms from around me, I moved to punch him in the stomach but resisted, figuring I wasn't up for the pain.

"Why did you do that?" I yelled instead, his hands cuffing me as I struggled against his confines. Anger boiled in my heart, the type of anger that drives even the sanest men into a murderous rage.

He laughed. "I always meant to destroy that thing."

I looked over his shoulder at the mass of green metal that was balled up around him and smashed into the wall, as though it were nothing more than soft foil. "Sam! That was my car!"

"You'll get over it." He pushed me out of the wreck of metal and away from him. "It's not like you were using it."

"I hate you!" I screamed, my face now hot with fury. "Why do you insist on doing this to me all the time?" His childish attitude toward life was reckless.

He shrugged. "I just like to pull your chain, Elly. Take a chill pill." He put his hand up to my face as a smirk curled across his milky cheeks. His eyes glimmered like amber marbles.

I struggled to understand what he really meant by his comments. I grumbled at him, the sound echoing off the walls of the long garage. My emotions were useless against his infuriating mask of confidence, and I wiped the look of sadness from my face. I walked to the hunk of metal, my Datsun completely unrecognizable except for the fake wood steering wheel and the green paint that was chipped from the rust and grime.

None of Edgar's cars had been touched by the incident. I was at least thankful for that. I traced my hand along the glossy black of the Hummer my car had been parked next to. I exhaled sharply at the touch. It was the first thing of Edgar's I had touched since being back, besides the clocks, but that was different. Edgar had kept every one of his cars in immaculate condition, not even a speck of dirt in the tire.

Sam stood. "At least he had better taste." He pointed to the black Camaro that had been parked on the other side of my car, now gleaming in the reflection of the Hummer.

"I don't really care to hear your opinions right now. I'd rather you just leave, before I really lose it." I pointed to the door, my eyes looking away from him, stinging with the pain of my memories.

He snorted lightly, his feet crumpling through the pile of debris and marching down the long garage toward the door.

I exhaled as I turned back and looked at the scraps of metal, my heart sinking as I took in the mess that was my past. I gingerly stepped around the twisted pieces of rubber and glass, leaving it behind as a reminder of what it had been. I made my way into the house, eyeing each of Edgar's cars as I passed, each a ghost, just as he was.

The cat popped out from behind the Mercedes as I walked toward the door and I jumped back, startled by her pure white fur in contrast to the shiny blackness of the cars. Her feet were treading with extreme delicacy, almost as if aware of the sacred things contained within this room.

"Hey there, girl." I knelt down and ran my hand along her back, her voice erupting into thunderous purrs. Her silvery eyes followed me as she rubbed against my touch, glimmering with a life I hadn't noticed in the meek air of the house.

I furrowed my brow. "What are you?" I whispered. "Who are you?" She meowed then, staring at me as though I'd hit a chord. Something about her was so different, so unique. She meowed again, her teeth bared. She let her voice trail off into a howl, reverberating off the cars and ringing back into my ears. I stood up, a little taken back by her sudden show of understanding. She turned to walk into the house then, and I followed.

After shutting the door behind me, I walked toward the kitchen, my feet dragging across the granite of the entry hall, my body tight from the crashing fear that had racked my muscles. I looked up to the top of the stairs, the cat following

113

my gaze. She darted up the steps easily. I whistled to her as she sat on the top landing, curling her tail around her body and her eyes stubbornly fixed.

"Kitty, kitty. Come here." I patted my leg but she didn't budge, her eyes now narrowed with sleep. I took a deep breath and approached the steps, my pace quiet and steady. I glanced around for any sign of Sam but I didn't see him. The air was still and the hall empty.

Exhaling, I mounted the steps, steadily climbing toward my room. As I reached the top of the landing, I knelt and traced my finger across the cat's milky white head and down the length of her nose. She watched me before she stood and darted toward the door into Edgar's room. She let out a sharp meow, almost like a command, and pawed at the crack in the jamb. I sighed, realizing I knew all along where she had been going. I tightened my hands into fists at my sides, forcing myself to face my demons as I stepped forward.

Dragging my feet across the floor, I slowly approached. The cat watched intensely, coaching me along the way. I placed my hand on the cold brass handle, thinking that the last person to touch this had been Edgar. I gripped it harder and looked down at my feet, the cat's silver eyes flashing at me, waiting for me to open the door.

It was obvious she could have done this on her own. After all, she had seemed to move about the house with ease, door or no door. She was like a ghost herself. She had waited for me, though, sensing this place was mine alone to face.

I pressed down on the handle, pushing with force as the jamb refused to let the door budge. It was almost as if time had sealed it for all eternity. My nerves faltered and I found myself discouraged. Finding no other logical action, I took a deep breath and threw my shoulder against the door, dust raining down on me as it finally gave. I rubbed my arm, noticing a dent I had now made in the wood. A gust of stale air gently blew across my face, the smell like old paper and library books.

I peeked through the small opening, the cat thrusting her head through the crack and twisting it around. She was alert, hunting for prey, but what? In the small area I allowed myself to view, I could see a large stack of books. Cobwebs clung to them with time, time greater than that since Edgar's death, indicating he rarely touched them. A dim light was cast upon them, the dust floating through the rays and tickling my nose.

I sneezed then, the cat looking up at me with alarm. "Sorry," I whispered, her interrupted gaze diverting back to the room.

My mind screamed to go further, but my muscles refused to move. I was just able to make out the decorative corner of a large canvas on the wall. The frame was a deep rich gold, which contrasted with the black wallpaper. Finding courage, I pressed against the door, but something blocked it from behind. I pressed again, this time harder, but still, the door did not give. The cat looked up at me, her eyes questioning.

I shrugged. "I'm not sure, girl. I think it's blocked."

She meowed in agreement. The crack was not quite wide enough to allow her entry, and I found myself again peering into the room's depths. My mind was alive with interest and curiosity; I had to go further. For whatever reason, Edgar had tried to stop me, and had tried to keep me from knowing what was in here. He should have known better, though. I was never the type to shrug it off. Besides, I had the perfect ogre of a man to help me.

As soon as the words crossed my mind, I sensed the presence of someone behind me. I spun on my heel. My breath was ripped from my lungs, but before a scream could escape my mouth, it was muffled by Sam's cold, dead hand. He had been spying on me. I cringed, horrified that I needed him.

"Shh…" His face was right next to mine, his eyes piercing. My heart leaped in my chest, terrified by his strange, ghostly presence and the knowledge of his crippling strength holding me at bay. Despite all that I knew about Sam, there was still a side of him that I did not yet understand. There was a side of fury and hate, a side Matthew had hidden so well.

The cat let out a sharp hiss, her ears flattening on her head, threatening him.

Sam laughed and stepped back, his demeanor changing from that of chaos to order. "I totally got you. You looked as though you'd seen death!"

I didn't give him the satisfaction of a reply. "Could you please help me? If it's not asking too much," I snapped.

His face grew serious and the cat relaxed back, now sitting quietly on the floor.

He smiled, running his hand through his already messy hair.

"Sure thing, toots." A half smile snaked across his face.

116

I glared at him.

He pushed past me, nearly stepping on the cat. She scooted out of the way, her fur fluffed and agitated. He pushed against the door with his fingers splayed. The door opened with ease. Another gust of sealed air fell across me.

"Well, then." He clapped his hands together, as though he'd just finished a hard day's work. "There you are, damsel in distress."

I tilted my head. "Oh, please."

He nodded. "Yeah, you're right. I suppose you're more 'in distress' than you are a 'damsel'."

To my surprise he stepped back, allowing me my space to explore. It was the first time he hadn't overstepped his boundaries, and I relished in the moment, figuring this may be the only one. He leaned against the hall wall, crossing his arms against his chest. His wings were completely hidden behind his back. I glanced at his face with emotionless thought, my mind spinning with the task at hand.

The cat stood at my side, staring into the dark space, watching as the dust fell around us.

"I'll be here if you need me." Sam added as I looked straight ahead, my gaze fixed on no point in particular.

I took a deep breath while I still stood outside the door, more to keep myself from ingesting the dusty air inside than from fear. I walked in, the towering stack of books now at my side. The cat followed me, her paws leaving a delicate trail of paw prints behind her. I watched in amazement, her tracks disappearing as she walked, much as mine had in the snow last winter. I took a note of it: another clue.

The black walls were scattered with paintings, each hung in a careless manner. The darkened shades of paint told me he had enjoyed a different sort of art than I. One in particular was a scene of extreme violence, and I felt a strange tightening in my chest. I now realized how dark and angry Edgar's mind was, vindictive and hungry for death. The dark shades of the paintings melted into the darkness of the wallpaper, the only nothing relief were heavy gold frames.

I ran my hand across the cover of a book that was in another stack beside me. Dante was scripted in deep gold through the heavy leather. The binding was tied in an ancient manner, suggesting he had had it for some time. The image of Edgar in my mind had always been dark, but to now be surrounded by his life, his secret life, it felt so much darker.

My heart began to race, realizing that the life I knew with Edgar had been so reserved. He had held himself at bay out of his affection for me, and hid anything that would give away his anger from the entire world. As I glanced at each subsequent painting, I realized they were all twisted into scenes of pain and anguish, except for one. As I approached, the light blues seemed to glow in contrast with the rest of the room. I stood back, seeing it was in the exact center of the wall, framed all around by chaos.

The face that stared out at me was my own, sweet and innocent. My eyes glowed with happiness, and suddenly, all the previous feelings of fear and confusion faded away. Amongst all the darkness, the light of love was undeniable, and I now saw why he did what he did and how he could resist his urge to kill and fight. He had been my love, my protector, my guardian, and his whole existence revolved around me and my renewing breaths of life.

The cat meowed, looking at the same thing as I. "That's right, kitty. That was me."

My eyes diverted from the paintings to a large oak desk shoved against the wall. I followed a path that had been carved through the hoards of books, and I found myself balancing over trinkets from seemingly all walks of life. Piles upon piles of crumpled pieces of paper lined the walls, smeared with thick, black ink. There was a large wood chair shoved to the side of the space, and I dusted off the seat, coughing as I sat down.

The cat jumped into my lap, putting her front paws on the desk and scanning the things it contained. There was a notebook shoved to the side and I slid it toward us. Opening it, the spine creaked and dust slid from the cover, collecting in a thin mound beside it. The pages were scratched with furious bits of notes, things about weather and time, life and thought. There didn't seem to be any real order to the notes, just moments of opinion. I turned the pages, looking at each scribble and attempting to decipher the mess of words.

Where is she?

I ran my fingers across the heavy ink, written over and over on a number of pages. It had seemed as though he had gotten a taste of life without me, but disliked everything about it.

MATTHEW

Was written in large print across two of the pages, a murderous reminder of his hate and anger. If Edgar had known he was still alive, I wondered what had kept him from hunting Matthew down. He had the power to prevent the events that had now unfolded, but for whatever reason, he hadn't. There was a part of me that questioned if he had battled between his hate for Matthew, and also his brotherly duty.

I closed the book, finding his writings cold and terrifying. I looked back at the desk itself. There were three drawers set into the back frame and I reached for the first, pulling it open and looking inside. There was a vial of ink and a few pen tips that had been shoved inside, a few cracked and useless.

I slid the drawer back and moved to the next, slightly larger than the first. I pulled it open with two hands, furrowing my brow as the drawer stuck for a brief moment as it dragged across the warped wood. There was a sudden chromatic glitter of colors that shown from within, and I squinted as my eyes adjusted to the light. I reached toward the contents, grabbing a cold handful and bringing it closer to my face.

The cat meowed in a feverish manner.

"Jewels?" I asked, to no one in particular. The cat put her paw on my wrist, lifting her body to look at them as her eyes reflected their beauty. I rolled them around on my palm, my mind racing to comprehend the gravity of the objects value and why he had simply discarded them in a desk drawer as though nothing but trash.

There were rough cuts, cushion cuts, and marquise, all glinting in the dim light, clear and strong. As I bent forward to place the jewels back in the overflowing drawer, my eyes caught the tip of something organic amongst the collection of colorful gems. With my other hand, I grabbed the corner of a brown piece of paper that peeked between two rocks, carefully pulling it from the beautiful pile that had concealed it. I rolled the jewels from my other hand back into the drawer, my curiosity now fixed on the small wad of brown paper, no longer finding the rubies and emeralds nearly as distracting as the curious package.

The cat crawled onto the desk as I sat back, my eyes scanning the roughly tied paper. I gingerly unrolled the parcel, now delicate with age, and nearly translucent. There was a jingling as the contents came loose in my grasp, sliding into my palm as I cradled it.

The cat's snaking tail ceased to move as her sharp eyes fixated on the contents. My breath caught in my throat, my brows pressing together as I tried to swallow past the sudden lump lodged there. There in the folds of my hand laid two rings, both glowing with ethereal life and beauty.

One was slightly larger than the other, its pure blackness like infinite night, a hint of blue glowing from the edges. It seemed to be forged from an iron ore of some sort, completely unscathed and pristine, stronger than anything I'd ever seen on this planet. As I touched the ring and moved it aside, it seemed to yawn against my hand, its temperature changing from hot to cold and back again.

The other was a pearly crystal blue, carved from an

opal rock into a seamless ring of both air and fire. The colors caught my eye, sparkling back at me as though it was filled with the lake itself, churning with the fury of a thundercloud on a sunlit afternoon.

As I looked away from the rings in my hand, my attention fell on the paper that was clasped in the other. I looked at it closely, finding the faded marks that had been carefully scribed across it familiar. My heart faltered as I turned the page right side up and began to read...

October 20, 1048

Today was beautiful, and Edgar and I finally gave in to the traditions of this world, and were married. Everyone was here, all dressed in blue, as I had requested. We were married on the highest mountain, in the crisp air of the heavens, and away from any life but our own. I will cherish this union for eternity, a symbol of why we are here and our purpose in this life...

I gasped, rolling the rings in the palm of my other hand as I realized their purpose. As I looked back at them they both became warm, much like the gold book had. These rings were alive somehow, even after Edgar's death, like a vessel for our soul.

They clanked against each other as I continued to rattle them about, the metallic song suggesting their strength and their everlasting love. Splaying my palm before me, I plucked the opal ring from my grasp, placing the black one on the desk. Touching the wood, dust blew out from around it as though it were breathing.

The cat stepped away from the black ring and lifted her paw, frightened by its life. I slide the warm opal onto my finger, finding it oddly comforting and soft. It fit perfectly, like a part of me. I exhaled, releasing a breath I did not know I was holding.

We had been married. We had been bound in this life by more than our souls, but by our hearts as well, promising each other a life that was everlasting. I had always suspected that this had been true, but I'd never found the nerve to ask.

The page in my hand was one that had been ripped from my journal, a memory that had been stolen from my life. He had been protecting me from this truth, giving our new life time to develop, time we would never have. I flattened the page on the desk and delicately pulled at the corners, a memory I wasn't willing to lose.

I looked at the page more closely, noticing that there had been something scribbled on the back that was now transferring to the front. I flipped the page over, examining the written scratches.

The ring is still alive, therefore she must be as well. She must be. I have to find her...

I gasped again. Edgar's ring. It, too, was alive. If he was right, then that meant Edgar was still out there somewhere.

The same place I had been, perhaps, and the same darkness and despair of lost memory and sleep. I stood with such force that the chair toppled out from under me, my heart rate surging with certainty.

Sam stormed in then, sensing my distress, but halting just inside the door, his eyes searching mine for answers.

I faltered for a moment, measuring my ability to stand, steadying myself on the desk as my hand trembled under my weight.

"He's not dead, Sam. He's not dead."

BEST FRIENDS

I slid the warm metal onto the cold chain, noting the quality of the material as goose bumps erupted across my body. I swept the clasp back and around my neck, fastening it before tracing my fingers across the chain and back to the ring, feeling the warmth as it fell against my chest.

This was all the life that was left of Edgar, the only breaths I now felt. I looked at myself in the mirror, my eyes catching the glimmer of the opal ring on my finger. I recalled the moment I had received it, and I remembered the feel. One year ago, I would have never imagined this life, but now it was all I knew and all I had known.

I rose from my vanity chair, my room now properly dusted to reveal grandeur I hadn't imagined before. The cat was sprawled across the cool wood floor, her tail snaking slowly across her body. She was purring to herself, satisfied with her now comfortable life, though locked away from her true identity.

Isabelle's nails dug into the wood of the bed frame, her jealousy emanating from her angry eyes. I walked toward Isabelle and scooped her into my arms. She nestled down, her talons curling as she enjoyed the embrace, her eyes happy and loved. She cooed quietly, her feathers fluffing as I ran my hand across her brow. I turned and looked down at the cat, now sitting in the middle of the floor, watching us. The look on her face did not suggest jealousy, but rather a sense of loss and longing.

I set Isabelle back on the bed and marched toward the door, the cat trotting up behind me. As I entered into the hall, I was just in time to see Henry dive across the entry and through the door to Edgar's room, now permanently cracked open. I slowly approached the room, the once crushed feeling in my heart now replaced by hope.

The large door creaked with a heavy yawn as I pushed it open and the light from the hall flooded the space. My eyes were locked on the paintings, their gruesome content a frightening reminder of this world's evil past and present. I allowed myself to scan each piece with a respect I hadn't before, among them the works of Francisco Goya and Caravaggio.

Finding I couldn't take anymore, I looked away, my gaze turning toward the room itself. The black walls made the space feel infinite, but also cold. I gingerly walked between the stacks of books, my body breaking through cobwebs that had managed to cling themselves to the dust.

Edgar's bed was much like mine, draped from the ceiling by thick velvety yards of fabric and a gold frame. The fabric was also a deep black, and I was envious that it hid away more light than mine, allowing him an infinite night.

The cat ran up from behind me and across the room, jumping into the desk chair that was beside the bed. I followed her and bravely sat myself amongst the lavish covers, all twisted in a feverish manner by Edgar's angry sleep. I took a deep breath as I ran my hand across the fabric, imagining it was still warm, as though he had just been there.

I leaned back into the indent he had left, allowing it to cradle my body with a false sense of security. As I looked up to the top of the canopied bed, I saw a large mural that had been painted above. I snorted to myself, realizing the mural looked a lot like those of the Sistine chapel and it didn't escape my thoughts that it was likely painted by Michelangelo himself. Typical Edgar.

The clouds were stormy yet pink, as though at sunset, twisting their way around the arms and feet of five angels. I smirked, picturing Sam as one of them, clothed in his leather coat and sneakers and playing a harp. I imagined the mural coming alive, heavenly music playing in the background.

I put my hands behind my head, reveling in the peace and the closeness I felt to Edgar. I took a deep cleansing breath. My eyes fell to another painting that hung on the wall directly before me. I squinted through the flying dust and dim light, trying to make out the large waves of paint and canvas.

As the scene unfolded, I saw there was a large window, the drape pulled back by the delicate hand of a woman whose head was turned to face that of another, whispering in her ear. The familiar smirk of the second girl was undoubtedly mine, but my eyes were hooded as I leaned forward into a bout of laughter. I smiled, the happiness bitter sweet and full of true joy and life.

As I continued to ponder the scene, my mind suggested a scenario. Perhaps the first girl was telling me a joke, or rather poking fun at whatever was outside. For dramatic effect, I pictured it to be Sam, unaware of our voyeuristic ponderings.

I smiled, finally finding comedy in Edgar's world, and a sense of family and friendship. I continued to smile, scanning the humored eyes of my friend, the familiar silvery glow and the oyster grey of her dress like that of someone I had loved dearly. It was then I remembered that it was Margriete, and my smile grew deeper.

I jumped as the cat leapt from the chair onto my stomach, turning to face the painting as I was. I placed my hand on her back as my smile began to fade and my eyes became wide. She let out a plaintive meow and looked at me, her eyes confirming my sudden realization.

I gasped, covering my mouth with my other hand. I took in the eerie silhouette of the cat next to the face of Margriete.

"No," I whispered to myself, denying the possibility, despite the proof before me. "No way, no." I sat up, my mind racing.

The cat rode in my lap as I pulled myself against the headboard. "You can't be," I gasped again.

The cat blinked her silvery eyes like dimes in the dim light of the room, the same soft oval as those in the painting.

I grabbed the cat's face between my hands, her whiskers scrunching through my fingers. "Are you…" I paused, my mind still a blur of sudden realization. "Margriete?" A laugh escaped my lips as I said it, the absurdity of the notion bordering on insanity, but it was too eerie to deny.

My laughing ceased as the cat howled in pain, prying its head from my grasp. She began to hiss and moan, her nails now digging deep into my thighs. She looked at me, terror crossing her face as she darted her eyes about the room. I watched in horror as she began to writhe before me, possessed by the devil itself.

I silenced a scream with my hand. Her hair began to shed, her body bubbling like a boiling pot of water. Henry flew out of a dark corner where he must have been hiding and he landed next to me, his wings spread in a protective manner as he regarded the cat that was now curled up in my lap. She breathed heavily as her body continued to tremble and twist.

"Sam!" I screamed, trying to put my hands on the cat in an attempt to calm her, to help her somehow.

The sounds of heavy flapping was audible from the doorway as Sam cut through the front hall and dove into the room, his large body crashing through a pile of books and sliding across the floor. He looked at me with frantic eyes. The cat's ears flattened against her head, her hatred for Sam still thick despite her assured pain.

"The cat, Sam! Something is wrong!" I was breathing hard, my gaze darting between Sam, Henry, and the cat.

Sam was by my side in two large strides, books and papers flying everywhere in his wake. He grabbed my arm and rolled me out from under the cat. Regaining my balance beside the bed, her body began to grow.

"What happened, Elle. What did you do?" Sam held me in

his arms as we both watched in horror.

"I…" I paused, my voice choking in my throat. The cat was now changing faster than before. "I just…said…Margriete."

He tilted his head in confusion. A blank look crossed his eyes. "You said what?"

"Margriete," I pleaded. "I just thought… the eyes!" I pointed to the painting.

Sam followed my hand, letting go of me and rushing to where the cat was now twisting in the sheets, no longer resembling a cat, but rather a deformed lion.

"Elle, help me. Grab one of her limbs." Sam ushered me forward with his hand, finally showing concern for the animal rather than hatred.

I rushed to the bed, my eyes trying to discern where a limb was at this point. I grabbed a large deformed paw, pressing it hard against the sheets. My eyes refused to blink. Her claws thrashed at me, her movements wild and flagrant, controlled by something other than herself, like a dark evil that had lived inside her. Suddenly, her claws fell out and something began to press through what little fur was left, something bare and soft.

"Sam! Sam, look!" I grabbed his attention away from the restraints he had on her and he looked to where I was. All the fur had gone now, like a scab being torn away, revealing the fresh pink skin of a human.

Sam laughed then and let go.

I looked at him with alarm. "What are you laughing at? This isn't funny!" I spat.

As soon as the words left my lips it all ceased and the

last bit of fur fell away. She writhed one last time as she coiled into herself like a baby, her breathing heavy. I stared in bewilderment, now seeing a woman lying naked among the debris of her former self, terrified and cold.

"See, she's fine." His smile was smug.

My mouth fell open as I scanned the being before me, the human figure. Her face was sheltered in her hands, the dim light of the room harsh against her young skin. As her breathing slowed, she peeked from behind her hand, trying to lift her body but failing as she fell back against the bed. I knelt down beside her and her eyes met mine, glittering with the same light as before.

I put my hand out and placed it on her back. "Margriete?"

She whimpered then, and I knew I had been right.

RE-ADJUSTMENT

I pressed a cup of water into Margriete's cold hand, her body still trembling with shock and fear. Her grateful eyes watched me, her hair stringy and white as it cascaded down the robe I had given her.

"I just can't believe it." I looked at Sam. "It's really her."

Sam shrugged. "I've seen a lot of weird things in my life, but this is definitely a first," he chortled under his breath. "Always something new with this job," he added.

I looked back at Margriete. She hastily sipped at the cup, her hands clumsy as she grappled at the porcelain. It had been decades since she had hands, and you could see that now.

"I'm just happy she's not a nasty cat anymore." Sam laughed, his eyes scanning Margriete and reading her thoughts. "And she is also," he pointed at her.

She nodded toward me, her speech lost after being silent for so long, trapped in the body of a feline. Sam had been unable to hear her thoughts while she was animal, but now, it had all become clear. He was acting as my interpreter.

Sam looked at me, excitement lacing his thoughts. "It's fascinating, isn't it? What if there were more like her. What if there is? Do you know what this could mean? There could be more of your kind, Elle! Much more!"

Margriete frantically pawed at Sam's arm, her frightened eyes scanning his.

"No." He shook his head. "Except that one," he replied.

Margriete let out a heavy exhale of relief.

"Except what one?" I asked feverishly, now pawing his other arm.

He laughed. "This is sort of nice, two women grappling at my sleeve."

Margriete and I both gave him a disgusted look and leaned away.

Sam laughed again. "Well, darn." He looked at me. "She asked about Matthew."

"Oh," I replied, looking away from her with shame.

Margriete grabbed my arm then, shaking her head with a despaired look.

Sam sighed. "She say's that you shouldn't be ashamed. She is happy to see him gone."

I nodded toward her. "I'm sorry, Margriete. I really am."

She shook her head again and smiled, opening her mouth as she tried to speak but still unable to find the words.

Sam crossed his arms and rolled his eyes. "She wants me to tell you that you're her best friend, and she always loved you and Edgar more than she could ever love Matthew," he said grudgingly before looking at Margriete. "No more of that lovey-dovey stuff, though. That was it." He lifted one finger, shaking it in her direction with a warning glare.

She giggled.

"Oh, geez." Sam stood and his heels dug across the floor in loathing. "I can't handle this. I'm out of here." He threw his hands in the air and marched out of the room.

I looked at Margriete with an alarmed face. She gave me a mischievous smile, suggesting she had told him things to get him to leave, knowing Sam's discomfort toward human emotion.

I laughed, curious about what she had said to make him leave.

Sam popped his head back into the room, glaring at me with disapproval. "She told me she was thankful for me, and would love me like a brother for all her life," he spat, noticeably discomforted by the situation. He spun on his heel, storming off with quiet anger.

I turned my gaze back to Margriete, someone I felt I barely knew and yet seemed to know like a sister. She smiled and an elated emotion crossed her face.

I smiled back. "I don't remember much about you, other than what Edgar told me." I paused, thinking of what to say. "I wish I knew what had happened. I wish I remembered so that I would know what to do." I sighed. "Sometimes, I feel so disconnected from everything, as though my mind is still struggling to comprehend that it was all true."

Margriete nodded, crossing her legs on the couch and pulling a blanket over them. She took a deep breath and furrowed her brow, forcing her mouth into various shapes.

"I..." her hand went to her throat where she felt for her voice as it crackled across her weak vocal cords. "I... can..." she paused, trying to clear her throat, straining as she pressed for the words. "I can help."

I smiled. "I hope so," I whispered, patting her on the arm. "You should be back to normal soon. I just wish you could tell me more." I rolled my eyes. "Without him around," I pointed in the general direction of the kitchen, knowing that Sam had probably heard my thoughts on the matter.

"Tell...me...what happened." Margriete winced on the last word.

I took a deep breath. "You mean, after that day in the woods when I followed you?"

She nodded.

I let out a sharp laugh. "Well, I wish you wouldn't have made me chase you." I raised my eyebrows at her.

She shrugged, her face twisted into an innocent grimace.

I snorted. "Don't act so innocent." I shook my head.

Her face now looked shocked and affronted.

I laughed, putting my hand on hers. "I was just kidding!"

Margriete exhaled in relief, grabbing her heart for dramatic effect. "I... should...have guessed," she paused to swallow. "Jokester." A smile crept across her face.

I giggled. "So, do I seem the same? You know, as I used to be?"

She nodded, her eyes bulged and serious.

"Really? So, then I don't seem at all different? Because

you do know how I ended up leaving this life, right?" My eyes searched hers, wondering what she could know about what had happened.

She rolled her eyes, craning her neck to prepare for speech. She was getting better at an incredible rate. "I saw it...happen." Her eyes became grave. "I know where...you went...I had been there."

I paused, my heart rate surging with the thought. "You knew where I was, while I was dead?" My mind rested in a selfish place, a place where I could find Edgar.

She shook her head no, but then became flustered and shook her head yes. "Yes, but no...You weren't ever... dead..."

"What do you mean?" I shot back before she was able to finish.

"You... were caged..." She took a deep breath and closed her eyes. "Asleep." She scooted closer to me, and I could see she was attempting to be secretive. With Sam nearby, however, it was no use. Her voice was hoarse as it left her lips. "You can only die... if you are stabbed by the dagger of the gods, which Matthew had... stolen." She swallowed hard. "But... I really believe it was bestowed to him by the gods themselves... another move in their game... against us."

I looked at her in astonishment. Her speech was nearly normal other than the occasional drag of hesitation in her throat. "The dagger," I whispered. "But..." my face twisted. "I have it."

She gasped at my words, coughing as the breath tickled her throat. "You do?"

I gave her a solemn nod.

Excitement filled her eyes. "If you have it, then we can use that against them."

"Against who?" I asked, finding the story now lost within her choppy words.

She narrowed her eyes at me, confused by my comment. "You don't know?"

I shook my head.

"Edgar must not have told you." She coughed hard, clearing her throat.

I winced.

She continued, "The gods..."

I cut her off. "I know about the gods, and how we got here, but I never knew about the dagger."

She shook her head. "But do you know about how the gods made the dagger, and what it does?"

I shrugged.

She smiled to herself, content with the secret knowledge she possessed. "Well the dagger kills us. But, it can also kill them. It's said that whoever rids the Earth of our kind, is then worthy enough to challenge for a seat among the gods. The gods are threatened by us, because, though they created our kind, they made us better than themselves. They're jealous, and scared."

I blinked a few times as I processed this new information. "But how did Matthew get it?" My voice was now a low murmur, to match hers.

"They gave it to him, because they knew he had enough rage and hate to kill us all, but was also weak enough

that he would never win over them. He was set up to fail."
Margriete sighed, and a small smile crept across her face.
"Matthew wasn't always how you know him today. He was
once handsome and kind, and he loved me so much. There
was never a glimmer of evil in his beautiful, silvery eyes, not
until…" Her face changed suddenly. "I remember the day, the
hushed voices from the room below me. I knew, but no one
ever believed me. Except you, Elle. You always did."

I watched as her eyes began to well with tears.

"You believed me. But Edgar silenced you rather
quickly."

The ring on my chest suddenly breathed hard against
my skin, reacting to the comment in a negative fashion.

"When I found out what was going on, I went to the gods.
It took me months to find where they hid, and to you, I was
already dead. It pained me to do that, but I knew I had to. It
was my fault that I had allowed my other half to become so
naive and gullible. I knew it was my job to fix it." A violent
coughing spasm silenced her.

I handed her another cup of water that was sitting on the
coffee table.

She took a long sip, allowing it to trickle down her throat.
"But the gods laughed at my feeble attempts, and cursed me to
roam the Earth as a cat until the day someone cared enough
to utter my name, as you did. I am forever stripped of my
ability to fly, and the life of the raven has left me. In the form
of a cat, they knew that Matthew would eventually find me,
knowing he hadn't yet taken my soul. As time dragged on, I
think he gave up." She set the cup back on the table. "All of it,

it was all a sick game."

I looked into my hands. "No wonder I hate Monopoly," I whispered under my breath, remembering Scott and Sarah.

She laughed, hearing what I had said.

I smiled. "But now that we have the dagger, we have the power, right? And all that is left is you and I?"

She shook her head. "I'm not sure. Like I said, I think Edgar survived. For whatever reason, I think they'd keep him alive. After all, he would be the last male half."

I grabbed the ring in my hand, twisting the warm metal through my fingers.

Margriete continued to speak, her voice changing from gruff, to nearly melodic. "I'm not sure what their motives are. I always believed it was to rid us from this Earth, but now, I don't see the rationality in that. We have the dagger, but it's no use to us if we kill them. Perhaps there's a way to bargain with them. If it's true that whoever holds the dagger has a rightful chance on the throne of the gods, I'm sure they're not going to want to have that falling into the wrong hands. There are many creatures that roam this Earth, creatures that aren't natural here. The gods have allowed too much vulnerability, and I'm sure they're nervous that we've got it. Perhaps...."

She trailed off, her eyes glazing over in revelation. I sat up straight as an arrow, anxious to hear what she had to say.

"That's exactly what it is!" she gasped. "They want you to bring it back to them. They know you have it, so they've taken Edgar as collateral."

My heart leapt. Yes! It made sense. I suddenly couldn't help but hold back my happiness, and I gave her a huge hug, squeezing the breath from her lungs. She winced under my grasp and I let go of her.

I slapped my hands against the leather of the couch. "So all we have to do is bring it to them!" I yelped with excitement.

She snorted and rolled her eyes, mocking me. "It's not that easy. Getting there is a whole other story. It's not like you can walk up to the god's front doorstep and ring the doorbell, or catch the next bus at the station. If that were true, could you imagine how many religions would fight over that property, over that bus?"

I laughed. "Well, then where is it?" I furrowed my brow.

She shrugged. "Jerusalem."

I laughed. "Yeah, right. You're joking."

She smiled. "Yeah okay, you're right. I was joking."

I gave her a playful punch on the arm and we both rolled back in laughter.

She caught her breath before going on. "It's everywhere, Elle." She put her hands in the air and waved them around like a hippy at a Santana concert. "But the hard part is your mind creates it. Whatever your deepest fears, whatever your darkest memories are, will be shown to you there. You have to be strong for this, and you have to be prepared to see things from your past, all things, even if your mind can't remember." She shuddered, recalling her own experience. "And you have to expect that in their defense, they will play on all those weaknesses. They will use all the things that could ever drive you mad, scared, and even suicidal."

I exhaled. "I can do this. We have to."

Margriete grasped my hand. "They will stop at nothing

140

to destroy you before you reach them, to get the dagger from you before having to give up Edgar." Her eyes were stormy and hard. "And after all, they will assume we are coming to challenge them. They are hoping to lure you in and kill you, certainly not allow you to get Edgar back. I'm sure they intend to dispose of him once the dagger is back safely in their grasp."

I looked at her with a stern glare. "Edgar is a part of me, and I can't live without him. I owe this to him, to us. What is life without that?"

Margriete's eyes fell, and I saw that my words had hurt her.

"I'm sorry." My gaze sank into sadness. "I didn't mean it like that."

She sighed. "Don't be sorry. It's my burden to bear. Matthew once gave me the love I deserved, and that is enough to serve me through to the end. I must sacrifice my happiness because of the choices I have made." She turned and looked to the painting of us on the wall, enjoying the afternoon, eternally. "I have those memories to hold on to, and living long enough to remember them is all I'll ever need. But if I were you, and my love needed saving, I wouldn't hesitate, Elle." She grasped my hand even tighter.

"Well then." I stood and took a step toward the door, noticing that Sam had been standing there, for who knows how long.

"I smell adventure," he said gleefully.

I sighed. "What makes you think you're invited?"

He laughed. "What makes you think I'd let you girls go

141

alone?"

We all laughed as I nodded. "Fine."

Margriete made a move to get up but the blanket twisted around her feet. She began to fall to the floor, but suddenly, in a flash of light, she changed. Her four paws hit the wood with a soft thud, gracefully unscathed as the blanket fell around her.

I yelped, pulling my hand to my mouth as I drew in a terrified breath, watching in horror. Margriete looked up at me with her feline eyes, meowing with a hint of disdain. I continued to hold my breath as she blinked, her body suddenly writhing as it did before, but much quicker this time.

She breathed hard as she finally changed, laying on the ground in her human form, naked and shaking. Sam had a lecherous smile on his face and I slapped his arm, rushing to her side and wrapping a blanket around her.

"That's going to take getting used to," she breathed.

I helped her off the floor. "I think you and I have the same problems to work on."

She leaned her weight on me as I walked her toward Sam. He scooped her into his strong grasp.

"Take her up to my bed, where she can rest." I squeezed her arm one last time.

Margriete gave me a tired smile. "Thanks, Elle, for bringing me back. I knew you of all people would see through to me."

"Of course, you are my family." The words stung my heart and I realized this life was worth the trouble, and worth the eighteen years I'd spent in sorrow and pain. As Sam walked away, I felt a warmth come back to my heart, and a love I had been missing. I clenched my fists, finding my path now clear and my mind ready.

THE PLAN

"Who's cat?" Scott leaned away from Margriete as she sat on the log beside us, her tail flicking back and forth and the moss growing under her like a blanket of soft green wool.

"Oh, just a friend," I said lightly, not drawing too much attention to the fact that she was an utterly perfect animal, with unearthly eyes and similar talents to mine.

Sarah stared at her with fascination, her gaze never faltering except for the occasional glance toward the trees where Isabelle and Henry both hid. The two hawks were watchful over Margriete, still uncertain of whom she really was.

"She's so different. Where did you find her?" Sarah reached out to pet her on the head. Margriete shied away and gave Sarah a narrowed grimace.

I laughed. "At the pound."

Margriete turned and hissed at me, causing Sarah to laugh.

I picked at the moss that had also grown around me, the log budding with leaves despite the fact that it had been dead for a long time.

Margriete continued to eye me with disdain. I smirked.

"So," I tried to divert their attention away from Margriete and get back to the matter at hand. I had given Scott one of my feathers in an attempt to learn more about myself, and it was what I was here to do. "Scott, did you find anything?"

Scott's eyes got wide. "Oh, yeah." He nodded fervently as he dug through his bag, retrieving a crumpled pile of notes. "You weren't lying. I found traces of metal in the DNA. Your feathers act as protection. Armor, just as you suggested," he paused and looked at the leaf that was now opening up beside us. "Your blood work was normal, except for one thing. Quite literally, your platelets seem suspended in space. You're not aging."

He touched the leaf as though afraid it would bite. "And then there's this issue." He plucked the leaf from the log and examined it. "I haven't really figured this out yet, other than you seem to secrete a vitamin rich gas. It's completely odorless, but acts much like a pheromone, attracting and stimulating all that surrounds you." He looked me in the eyes, clearly telling me that his previous attraction last year had been a scientific reaction, not necessarily love.

I nodded. "I knew I wouldn't age, but it's so odd, as though everything inside me froze when I became what I am. And the gas, I suppose I'd always had that, though it never seemed to work on people around me, or rather it did, and it completely freaked them out."

145

Sarah nodded along with me as she continued to attempt to pet Margriete. I didn't blame her, Margriete was gorgeous, but I could see how degrading it was for Margriete as well.

"If you stay this way, you'll be eighteen forever," he gasped.

I snorted. "Well, that's the plan."

"You're so lucky," Sarah whispered under her breath. She furrowed her brow and looked at the blanket of moss below Margriete. "Is she…"

I laughed then, cutting her off. "Yes," I said flatly.

"Oh." Sarah leaned away from her, suddenly realizing her error.

"Trust me. Living forever is bound to get old at some point. In my opinion, it can't be all that fun," I added.

Sarah looked at me closely before changing the subject. "So you really lived in the past? That's phenomenal. You probably saw so much!"

Shrugging, I thought about all the things I didn't remember. "Yeah, well, most things I don't even remember. My life isn't quite that glamorous. You make it seem like a dream, but really, I think I'd rather be like you, oblivious to this whole world I'm in." I winked at Margriete, feeling that she was one of the few who truly understood what it was like.

Sarah's face fell into a frown. "I'm not that oblivious. I understand what's happening."

I grabbed her hand in apology. "I didn't mean it like that. I meant that you get to live, whereas I have to suffer."

She nodded, her spirit rising as she realized my point. It

was true that though Sarah cared about this world, she didn't have to worry about living in it forever.

I ran my foot over the gravel path as students began to emerge for breakfast. They eyed me with wary recognition, some giving me looks of disgust, others watching with shameless curiosity. My heart began to pick up, my nerves taking over as I suddenly felt how different I was. Last year at this time, I had been just another face, but now, I was much more.

Margriete hopped down from the log and walked toward the middle of the path, antagonizing the fearful students and rolling around on the gravel, causing the weeds to thrive around her. She was used to being inhuman, used to the stares and judgments. It wasn't as though I hadn't been subjected to this before, but never from an angle of authority and responsibility. I put my hand to my chest, feeling the once empty space where my soul now thrived. They were our children, our future, and it was then that I felt the burden of my existence tug at my soul.

"So what will you do now?" Scott cut through the silence.

I shrugged and tilted my head, my eyes still fixed on my feet. "I have to find Edgar, and I suppose, try to put things right."

"So, you really think he's still alive?" Sarah's face was twisted with confusion.

"Yeah, I'm positive." I grabbed the ring that lay around my neck, a breath surrounding it and tickling my fingers. "There's a possibility that he's still out there somewhere. A friend of mine believes she knows where, so I'll be leaving for a while."

"A friend?" Sarah tilted her head.

I looked her squarely in the eyes before looking pointedly at Margriete.

"Oh…" Sarah nodded, still confused by Margriete in her cat form, but coming around to the fact that she was like me, and could change.

"I wanted to come and say goodbye. I'm not sure what will happen, but there's a possibility that this could be the last time I ever see you." My eyes fell back to my lap.

Scott put his hand on my back. "No, Elle. I know we will see you again. This isn't goodbye." He smiled and gave me a wink.

I felt warmth grow in my heart. Despite my leaving, it was good to have friends that had confidence in me, that knew I would return as I intended.

Margriete jumped into my lap then, her eyes searching mine with a sudden frantic urgency. I creased my brow as I looked at her, but she looked away and up the path. I followed her gaze, my heart stopping as Edgar's ghost strode toward us, his gait confident and powerful. Margriete turned to watch me, her claws digging through my jeans and piercing into my skin. She hadn't yet seen the ghost, and I was certain that she now felt the way I had. She was surprised and frightened by the hologram, forgetting the reality that Edgar was gone.

He flew by us as though we were nothing, Scott, Sarah and I followed his image with our eyes. We stood there, unmoving and silent. I squeezed my hand around the ring on my neck, smothering it in my sweaty palm. My lungs stung as

I refused to breath, afraid that he would realize me, attacking though I knew he couldn't.

I felt the ring exhale with a sharp pinch of heat. I yelped, dropping it against my chest, feeling bitten. Scott was quick to silence my disruption as Edgar's ghost halted, turning on his heel and glancing back. His eyes were cold and dark, somehow changed as though looking into Hell itself. For a few unbroken moments he stared right through me, the look changing to one of knowing.

My breath choked in my throat and his gaze fell to the ring on my chest, now burning into my skin. Edgar's mouth curled into a half smile as mine fell open in disbelief. Though the exchange had only lasted a split second, it had felt like an eternity. He twisted his gaze back, just in time to avoid dissipating through a large group of students.

I looked down at Margriete, her gaze frightened and confused. "What was that?" I asked.

She let out a frightened meow.

I looked toward Scott and Sarah, both still stunned by the event, their eyes fixed on Edgar's back.

"What was that?" Scott finally exhaled, his remark mirroring mine and his body trembling with suspense and fear.

Since I had told them about Edgar's death, I knew they had felt a certain unease toward the ghost. Sarah had expressed that she'd even noticed a change as though it was acclimating to the human world. It was taking on a personality of its own and forgetting the purpose as to why it had been created.

"I don't know," I breathed, my mind racing to figure out what had just happened. Had his ghost felt the presence of Edgar through the ring? Had he known? My body shuddered at the thought. I wondered if it was a danger I needed to keep in mind.

Margriete hoped off my lap and began to pace before me, her eyes looking back toward the woods, and then me.

"I think I should go." I stood and looked down at Sarah and Scott, standing in suspense. Their eyes questioned me. "I'll try to be back soon, but I'm not sure how long it will be. Something strange is going on here, and it only fuels my need to press forward with my plans." If the stories Margriete had told me were true, then it was uncertain what the gods would do to foil my arrangements. The longer I waited to take action, the more they would succeed in stopping me.

Something about the ghost's eyes felt like a warning, and I couldn't let something like that slide. If there was indeed an inkling of Edgar left inside the hologram, it may have been his way of telling me I needed to make haste. I squeezed my hands together and my stomach lurched.

"Sorry, guys." I leaned down and gave them both a hug. "But thanks for all the work you did."

Scott jumped to his feet. "But keep in mind, Elle, you're safer when you're..." he paused and looked around him, making sure no one was in earshot. "A raven," he whispered. "The armor only works then."

I nodded before turning on my heel and walking toward the woods. Margriete trotted behind me. My arms swung freely at my sides and we entered the trees. "How did his ghost change like that? He's just a holograph, a program. It was as though he saw me." I looked back at Margriete, but she gave me no sign or answer.

"Did you feel it was dangerous?" I looked back toward the trail. "I mean, do you think the gods know about the ghost? Do you think they're using it against me?" My mind could not stop asking this same question, bordering on insanity.

When I glanced back to look at Margriete, she was suddenly standing beside me, human again. "I really don't know, something isn't right, though. My heart was racing, but why? I don't usually have that sort of reaction, and it wasn't the fact of seeing his face, either. I think the gods are getting anxious, scared that if they let you continue to formulate a plan, it could ultimately harm them."

Margriete had been practicing with her new changeling, becoming accustomed to the feeling of the cat, rather than raven. We had both figured out how to keep our clothes now, and had mastered changing without a sound, just a breath of seamless air. My changeling had been a little harder to master, but I was beginning to get used to it. My clumsy nature from growing up human had spoiled my once graceful ability. Even Margriete had commented on the awkwardness of my new body. It still didn't know how to keep up with my mind.

"Strange," I finally answered. "Do you think we need to worry?"

Margriete looked around at the trees that now engulfed us. "I think it's more important to get Edgar back at this point. All the preparations we've made need to be put into action. We can't allow this distraction to sidetrack us. Besides, the best person to deal with the problem is Edgar himself. It's just another reason why saving him is quite crucial."

I exhaled. The notion of saving Edgar seemed unattainable, but the certainty in Margriete's voice was comforting.

There was a large crack from the trees overhead as Sam crashed down before us, the ground collapsing under his weight and shaking the nearby trees.

Margriete released a sigh of annoyance. "Is he always so dramatic?"

I put my hands on my hips in a nonchalant pose. "Unfortunately."

"Hello, ladies." Sam took one step forward, hoisting his large body out of the crater he had made.

He approached Margriete and lifted her in his arms. She groaned with hate. Since she couldn't fly, she had been subjected to the same egotistical teasing that Sam had forced me to endure. I quickly twisted into my changeling, now hovering among the branches, my wings lingering in the thick misty air.

With a nod we both shot skyward, and I caught a glimpse of Margriete as she flipped back into a cat, spitefully digging her claws into Sam's chest. Sam was eyeing her in disgust, allowing her to cling to him though obviously disliking the closeness. If anyone were to see our parade of friends now, they would surely find humor in the awkward alliance. There were two hawks, a white raven, and an angel with a cat grappling at his chest, all flying through the forest.

Sam glanced at me as we entered into the field, his gaze sheepish after the reprimand he had eventually received for what he had done to my car. He was learning the rules of the house, and I was thankful that he was at least attempting to abide by them. He landed in the field with another heavy thud, jolting Margriete. She helplessly clung to his shirt, her back paws dangling free.

She hissed at him as she quickly twisted out of her changeling and then slapped him across the face. With a dramatic toss of her head, she stormed toward the middle of the field, the grasses turning a vibrant red in her wake. I laughed and met Sam's eyes.

"I don't think she'll ever come around, Sam. Sorry." I brushed the dust from my jeans and wool vest.

He snorted, an amused smirk slicing across his white face. "She's sure fun to pick on, though." His eyes followed her as she disappeared into thin air, into the house.

"She's not really your type, anyway," I joked.

He walked toward me and put his face right next to mine. "She's feisty. What more could I want?"

Shocked, I looked at him sideways.

He leaned back. "Just joking."

I chuckled under my breath, bringing my hand to my chest. "You wish."

His eyebrows rose and there was hint of something serious lingering behind his golden eyes.

I quickly looked away, finding this development intriguing but also sensing the awkwardness that had somehow crept between us. We were bonding. I pretended to gag then, stepping away from him. I refused to admit that I found him fun and friendly. I coughed awkwardly, walking toward the house with dignity and poise.

Turning my mind to more productive matters, I thought about our agreed plan. Tonight we would leave, for where, we still weren't certain. Margriete informed me that her golden journal possessed all the tools we would need to find our way, and she was confident as our guide.

I could hear Sam behind me as I walked to the middle of the field. I grabbed at an invisible handle, now acclimated enough to know where to find it. Opening the door for Sam, we both disappeared within, the meadow now returning to its silent beauty as our shoes echoed across the granite entry. Ducking into the library, we found Margriete with her nose in the gold book, her hand tracing the air as she added a few notes to the magical pages.

She didn't look up when we entered, sensing our presence. "So, I made sure to keep track of what I had done last time." She pointed toward the page showing the image of her as a cat, entering the cave.

It had been one of the first pages I had turned to when I first found the book, and I remembered the moment and how enthralled and amazed I had been. Much had happened since that day, and there were now records kept, all magically written into her living book: a piece of her mind.

The words turned to gold as she slid her finger along each line, reacting to her familiar touch. As she sat back, they faded back to black, moving as though suspended on the page like tiny snakes. I felt the familiar twang of envy in my chest, childishly wishing my journals were also so magical.

"I think we should try to align our thoughts as best we

can. If we can think of the same things, I think the cave will reveal itself more readily," she continued.

I nodded, sitting beside her on the couch. "Where do you suppose the cave will appear?"

She took a deep breath and exhaled, twisting her lips in thought. "I think it will be relatively easy, as long as we concentrate. Knowing the cave exists is half the battle." I watched as she expertly navigated the pages of the book, knowing it like the back of her hand. "See here." There was an image of two eyes in the dark. "This was how my journey was. The thing is, they're all figments of your own imagination. No matter how real it seems, you and Sam must remember that it's not real." She sighed. "I'm not sure what the cave will do to Sam. He is different than us. He has a similar thought process and mental structure to that of the gods, so they may not even detect his presence, or his intrusion. It could be a good tool for us."

Sam walked into the room with his hands full of supplies. "Dusk is coming. I think we should think about leaving."

For the first time, Sam had a serious look on his face. It was as though he knew the challenges that faced us, and was now focused on the task. After all, it was his job.

Margriete and I nodded, and she gently shut the book. She then tied a leather strap around it, knotting it in such a way that she could swing it onto her back like a satchel.

"We won't need many supplies, but we're definitely going to need that dagger." She looked at me with a nervous glimmer in her eye.

I looked at Sam, then back at her. I stood and walked

to the kitchen where I opened the drawer, digging toward the back and grabbing the wadded cloth that contained the dagger. I drew back the cloth and exposed the handle, remembering the day it had stolen everything I had cared for. I ran my finger across the engravings as I wondered what they meant. There were three rats and a snake, their eyes made of red rubies and their faces snarling.

The hairs on my arms stood on end, realizing the power of the weapon now in my possession. I quickly wrapped the rag back around the handle and shoved it into my belt. It felt strange to leave, as though the coming quest was still just a dream.

I walked back out into the hall where Henry sat on Margriete's shoulder. Sam stood arbitrarily by her side, his face like a marble statue in the receding light of the day.

"Well, are you ready?" Margriete took a deep breath and exhaled.

I nodded, anxiety crackling through my limbs.

"Let's go."

THE CAVE

I glanced up at the trees as we slowly made our way deep into the woods, heading even farther from the college and up the mountain. A raven landed on a nearby branch, but it no longer evoked the same potent fear as before. It was now merely a bird, and an American breed at that.

Margriete's white hair contrasted sharply in the darkness of the woods, almost like a beacon. Sam's stride was long and heavy as it landed on the forest floor, causing the Earth to tremor. I felt the cold, moist air ripple through my lungs, releasing like a cloud.

As darkness fell, my instincts took over and my eyes adjusted to the nocturnal light with little effort. It was easier for me to see at night, the colors de-saturated and the trees and animals became heavily contrasted. It felt like I was wearing night vision goggles. I remembered how easily Edgar had always found the light switch in the dark, and how weak my vision had once been. A smile crept across my face at the memory, finding it a welcoming motivation.

Margriete seemed to know where we were going, but to me it felt as though we were wandering aimlessly. I still did not understand how the cave would reveal itself, especially when there seemed to be no real hillside for it to appear. As we walked, I analyzed every hill, the sound of summer crickets carrying through the towering evergreens and filling the air with a melodious sound.

Our feet trekked across the damp forest floor, the fertile mud welcoming our fragrant secretions. I clasped my hands together and cracked my knuckles, my mind beginning to drone into nothingness and boredom. The pack on my shoulders was making my back sweat, and I tried to reach around and itch it.

Sam looked back at my struggles. "Giving up already?"

I grumbled as I fought with the pack. "I'm not exactly seeing the relevance of the direction we're going in," I whispered, hoping Margriete wouldn't hear me. "It just seems like we're lost." She was a few paces ahead, her eyes concentrating hard on the scenery around her.

She noticed our disruption and turned to face us, stopping for a moment to catch her breath.

"So, where are we exactly? How do you know we aren't just hiking around in circles?" I asked, my face full of skepticism I was feeling.

Margriete's eyes were still looking around her, glancing sharply from side to side.

"This is about as much nature as I can…"

"Shh," Margriete cut Sam off, her brows furrowed and her hand lifted up to silence us.

"What?" I whispered, but Margriete only became further annoyed by my disobedience.

I tried to listen for what it was that she was sensing, but I heard nothing. In fact, I had heard absolutely nothing. I looked around, finally noticing that the wind had ceased, and the crickets hushed. I looked toward the sky. A robin sat on a branch, its beak moving, but emitting no sound erupting from within.

Suddenly, there was a distinct crackling and I felt a chill roll over us like a quiet fog. My heart began to race, and I continued to scan the forest for anything that could give me a sign as to what was happening. It was then that the ground before me began to grow frost, and it slowly crept its way up the stumps of the trees, halting any subtle movements, freezing it in time and space.

My breath erupted into a warm fog before my face, the air now dramatically colder than that of the deepest winter. Sam twisted in his spot, his body reacting to the sudden change as he readied himself for attack. Sam was the only one of us that did not breathe a cloud of steam, his cold dead body unable to produce the heat.

"It's okay, Sam." Margriete tried to reassure him. "This is good."

The trees were now completely blanketed in a layer of watery glass, and the robin overhead was now frozen, its beak gaping in its last attempt to cry out. The light from the moon sparkled as it hit the frost, lifting the darkness to create a glow.

Margriete's body relaxed. She untied the leather strap containing her book. Steam rose from its golden cover, billowing into the air like a hot cup of tea. She quickly flipped through the pages, her finger following over a paragraph of text that glowed in the dim light.

"According to my last memory, the cave should be very close. If we can just step in the vicinity of it, it will reveal itself to us." She turned the page and read on. "The frost grows in order to freeze all human onlookers from seeing the entrance, and inhibiting them from entering. Only our kind can resist this simple security tactic because we are not of the human world." She pointed toward the frozen robin overhead as an example. "We are the only ones alive here now. Everything else has been suspended."

I blinked rapidly as I watched her. "So, which way now?"

Margriete shrugged. "I'm not sure, but let's continue further. If we get too far away from the entrance, the frost will melt and we'll know."

Sam laughed. "It's like playing hot and cold. Except the closer we get to our target, the colder it becomes."

I snorted. "That's one way to look at it, I suppose." I reached around my back and swung my bag down before me. Rummaging through its contents, I extracted two sweaters and threw one toward Margriete.

She caught it with one hand, her other still cradling the book as she continued to read. "Thanks." Her whole body shook violently, and her teeth began to chatter. "Good to see you were prepared."

Sam cut in, unable to resist. "Oh, come on now, girls. You could have just cuddled up to me." He winked.

Margriete and I looked at each other and rolled our eyes.

"I doubt that's really going to do much, Sam." I looked at his now blue skin.

I repacked my bag and we continued forward, my boots crackling against the frost, sounding like broken glass. We rounded a large evergreen and down a small embankment. At the bottom of the small ravine, a stream had been frozen, along with a small frozen frog leaping from the water with one foot still engulfed in ice.

I leaned down and inspected it with interest. Its eyes were completely iced like shiny marbles and its skin coated with a thin layer of clear glass. As I looked down the stream, there was also a deer, her tongue out as she licked at the water, now perilously stuck until our job here was done.

"This is incredible," I breathed, jumping from one bank to the next. My boots slipped as I landed and fell back, my arms flailing. I hit the frog with one hand and gasped in horror. I turned to watch as its leg snapped like an icicle, and I let out a sorrowful cry.

Sam laughed and pointed as the frog whirled through the air, landing on a nearby log and shattering into pieces.

Margriete gave Sam a disdainful look before turning the glare toward me. "Do try to be careful, Elle. We're not here to harm animals."

I sighed, my heart sinking, but also finding the humor as Sam continued to laugh, despite Margriete's warning. The little frog foot was still stuck in the frozen splash of water, and I tried as hard as I could to stifle a grin. With one last glare, Margriete looked away, pointedly ignoring us.

I looked above me where a flying bird was still elevated above the trees, its wings pinned back as it pumped for air. The world was frozen in suspended animation. Sam jumped over the stream, his wings guiding him. He landed softly on the other side.

Margriete leapt last, like a doe, with a grace and agility I hadn't yet learned. As we walked up the hill, Sam brushed his way through a cloud of gnats, each falling to the ice with a quiet ring. I heard Margriete exhale irritably as she watched him. Sam's face was amused and alive, the remaining gnats crashing helplessly against his cold face.

I tried to change the subject. "I feel like it's getting colder. Do you feel that too, Margriete?" I put my hand out as though feeling for rain, though there were no clouds in the sky.

She hiked toward me, her rubber soled shoes slipping on the ice. "I think you're right. We have to be getting close. Just keep your eyes open for any signs of… well, anything."

I looked through the frost covered branches, the leaves strangled by the cold. "What did you see when you came?"

Margriete crinkled her brow. "It's hard to say. It's like a dream. When it happens it's very vivid, but by the time you wake up, most of it fades. That's what dreams are: your soul's journey into their world. It's there in Heaven that anything happens."

I tilted my head. "So, you're saying I've actually been there?"

Margriete nodded. "Essentially, yes, but not in the flesh. You'll see what I mean when we get there. There are hoards of dreamers filling their world, doing all sorts of things, quite literally, to their heart's desire."

I pursed my lips and considered what she had said. My mind went wild with imagination.

We all pressed forward through a large grove of evergreens, their frozen branches scraping hard against my coat. Sam thrashed through a nearby bush that had hindered his path, his hands bleeding as the sharp ice cut through his skin, but it didn't seem to bother him. The already cold blood froze in small drops on the forest floor almost instantly.

I glanced forward once again, staring at the back of Margriete's head, still trying to remember her. To me, she was like a stranger, but to her, I was a sister and the typical constant conversation between new friends didn't exist, leaving me in the dark. After all I had tried to remember from my journals, I had decided to give up, realizing it was more important to live in the now and let everything else just fall into place.

We traveled another mile before reaching what appeared to be a path, most likely a hiking trail that crossed the Cascades and down into the Columbia valley. We turned on a natural curve and followed the path, hoping it was the right direction. I kept my eyes on the treacherous, frosty dirt, my boots stumbling over piles of solidified summer mud.

As I glanced up, I noticed Margriete had stopped ahead, her head tilted down and watching something that was glowing on the ground. As I approached, I noticed there was a cloud of steam erupting from the source of the glow.

"What is it?" I huffed as I reached her, trying to find the source of the steam. I blinked at the familiar object before me, smiling with recognition. A glowing feather was discarded on the path, burning through the cold frost and leaves.

"It's a Gryphus, or Griffin feather," Margriete replied in an excited tone, suggesting this was something she had encountered before.

"A what?" I tried to recall the creatures I had learned about in Greek history.

She tore her gaze away from the burning feather, her eyes glimmering in the cool air. "A Griffin. Half hawk, half lion, and made of solid iron."

Sam crunched up behind me. "I haven't seen one of those in ages." His eyes were alight with happiness, as though it was a good thing, though something inside me felt it was anything but.

I looked at them both, my eyes blank and my jaw hanging open. "Wait, what's going on? I still don't get it. I thought we were the only creatures out here?"

Sam cleared his throat and stood up straight, narrowing his eyes as he began to recite his rebuttal. "The only mythical creatures, maybe, but surely there are others. Typically, they stay in their world, the god's world. They only come here to hunt for sport from time to time…"

Margriete cut Sam off. "But the most important thing is that a Gryphus is the natural guardian of the divine, meaning we must be reaching the cave. They must be guarding it. They are appointed to watch over the most precious treasures of their world. Surely, the entrance to their world counts!"

I wanted dearly to reach down and touch the feather as it smoldered before me, finding something about it irresistibly mesmerizing. Sam grabbed my arm, sensing my desire and shaking his head. I frowned.

"Trust me, honey. That thing will burn your fingers off before you even know what's happening." Sam released my arm.

It continued to glow as we stepped past it, continuing up the path. The Griffin had left no trail behind it, much like all the creatures of our world. It seemed like we were just shadows, leaving no real trace of our existence among man.

Margriete walked beside me, her hands clenched into anxious fists. "I just wish I could remember what happens next. I can recall what the Griffins looked like: burning coals of death; but I can't recall much else." She let her fists thud against her thighs. "To most, Griffins strike fear into your very soul, but having Sam with us may be a huge advantage. He has no soul."

"So, there's more than just the one?" My fists were also clenched into tight knots at my sides, but more from fear than frustration.

She nodded. "They're sweet animals, really. They're just angry. It's not like I can blame them. Who is there to love something that burns as hot as the sun?"

I nodded slowly, wracking my brain for a good mental image of a Griffin. I cursed myself for not listening in class, or for at least reading more into the 'Mystical Creatures' books that had been stacked endlessly on the second floor of the library. I could have been more prepared for this, for Edgar.

Saying his name in my head sparked the pain of loss. It had been almost eight months since he'd gone, and his memory was fading from my mind though I fought to hold onto it hopelessly. I longed to feel his touch, to energize his eyes to that brilliant blue. Wherever he was, I knew he was weak without me, which was why it was my job to bring my power to him.

A breeze sliced through the frozen trees, blowing the hair away from my face and breaking the still silence in the woods. As the wind continued to blow, it was becoming obvious that it was not about to let up. Margriete and I both leaned hard into the breeze. Sam tucked his wings behind him tightly as he pressed us both forward with a strong hand on our backs.

We walked slowly now, our efforts hindered and our feet slipping backward. The minutes passed, and I felt my muscles finally weaken from the effort, my feet dragging. It was then that it all ceased and we toppled forward into a pile. We frantically scrambled to gain our footing and detangle ourselves. Margriete's golden journal burned through the ice as it lay on the ground.

As we regained our composure and brushed ourselves off, we all looked at the same spot at once, our movements halting. The warm glow that landed upon us revealed two silent Griffins, both commanding their spot before a blocked cave. The ground shook as their feet pawed at the Earth, the ice melting around them and the trees browned and dying.

My eyes were wide and I drew in a heavy breath, watching as one Griffin, nearly three times my size, reared before me.

As it came down, its claws crashed through the ice, water spraying out from beneath his footing and the Earth violently shaking. I saw it all in slow motion, fear arresting my thoughts and channeling them to my senses.

I stepped back as the Griffin leaned its head down close to mine. I put all my weight on my back foot and I leaned even farther away, its burning eyes blinking and my cheeks erupting with heat. The second Griffin was at its flank, and Margriete tumbled back as it swung its head into the first Griffin, nipping at its back playfully.

Sam grabbed us both by the arm and ushered us behind him, reacting to his strong instincts to protect. Margriete and I slammed together as he encircled us with his wings. We grunted with pain as our heads smacked. The pain was brief, though, and I hastily craned my neck for a view over Sam's shoulder. Both Griffins sat calmly now, their tails snaking through the air. Sparks glittered in their wake and floated to the forest floor, sizzling as they melted into the ground.

The first Griffin let out a sharp cry and Sam tilted his head, listening to the tone as if he could understand. What happened next sent chills down my spine as a voice erupted from seemingly nowhere, but not just any voice: it was Edgar's voice.

"And what is your business here?" it boomed, shaking me to my very soul.

I listened to the familiar, perfect tone, reveling in the sound. "He stole his voice," I whispered sharply to Margriete, her eyes scanning my face. "They're tricking us, trying to break us down."

She nodded. "They take whatever voice they find the most effective, and steal it from your memory to use it against you. Try to drown it out. You can do this. You've done great so far."

The voice rang in my ears, somehow more real than that of Edgar's ghost. It was as though he were there, alive and right beside me. I squeezed my eyes shut, willing away the feeling and restraining my hand from reaching toward the sound. I felt the Griffin's heat as it filtered past Sam's cold arm.

"We've come only to pass," Sam finally replied.

I opened my eyes and watched the two Griffins. They analyzed him with burning eyes, their empty souls seeing into all of ours. The lead Griffin tilted its head, the voice again erupting from seemingly nowhere.

"Guardian, we do not sense that you are a threat. You are welcome to pass into the world of your kind, but you cannot bring the two half-hearts."

I felt Sam's muscles flex beneath my anxious grasp.

He leaned toward them. "I am delivering their souls to the gods. They're of no harm to anyone, and their hearts are of no concern to you."

The second Griffin reared haughtily but the head Griffin nipped him back, containing his youthful fervor. They bickered amongst themselves for a moment.

The head Griffin turned back to us, its fiery brows pressed together with irritation. "My brother does not trust your stand, but he is young, and I am certain you are of noble means and will not harm our great land beyond these gates."

I looked past the Griffins toward the cave as the rocks tumbled open and crashed to the ground. Shards of stone and ice sailed into the air. I shielded my eyes as they flew toward us, each hissing angrily as they crashed into the Griffin's skin.

"You may pass." The Griffin stepped back, its wings extended at its sides, the air steaming around him.

Sam stepped forward, pulling us both behind him, his wings protectively ushering us forward and shielding our skin from the searing heat. I saw Sam wince as a spark landed on his arm, the first sign of real pain I had ever seen from him. The Griffin's powers were not of this world and Sam was no longer the invincible man he had been, but just another immortal.

We passed under the rocky eave of the cave, the cool dampness returning as the Griffins stayed behind. Soon, darkness fell on us and the rocks once again formed into a wall at our backs. We were now sealed into the next world, and there was only one way to go: into the cave.

THE CATACOMBS

I stumbled blindly across the ground for a few moments as my sight adjusted to the pitch black. My eyes were attempting to see from what little light still remained, shining from deep within the tunnel. We stopped briefly to check our things and readjust. I slipped the pack off my shoulders, the sweat that had formed now drying to my skin, causing a rash of irritation.

Margriete flipped through her book, her eyes an inch from the page. She, too, struggled to see in the dim light. Sam leaned against the cave wall, his eyes scanning the spot where the spark from the Griffin had burned his skin, his face twisted in a grimace of pain. He was not enjoying his own sudden weakness.

"There is a map in here somewhere, I know it." Margriete flipped through each page hastily. "The caves are large with many tunnels, some leading to dead ends. If we get lost, we could be here for an eternity.

She walked to the wall, her fingers brushing across the rough cut stone. She traced her way toward Sam, shoving him out of the way. She knelt on the floor, the book open in her other hand. I watched as her fingers traced the stone and I drew closer. A rough circle was carved into the rock where she was touching. She then pressed all her weight into the stone, and a loud clank echoed through the cavern. A dim light began to grow from above us.

Satisfied, Margriete stood, a contented sigh escaping her lips and a smile creeping across her face.

"Good job, Grietly!" I stepped toward her. The cavern was now filled with a soft blue light.

Her head snapped in my direction, her smile widening. "Oh, Elle! You remembered!"

I gave her a puzzled look, not realizing what it was I had done. "What do you mean?"

Margriete stepped toward me. "You called me Grietly! All this time you kept calling me Margriete, and I was certain you had forgotten." She wrapped her arms around me and squeezed the breath from my lungs before stepping back. "You never called me Margriete. It's been so different lately. You're not at all like who you used to be." She shrugged. "But that doesn't mean the new you won't also be my best friend. At heart, you'll always be the same, Elle. And you are."

The small bout of excitement cut through the tension of our task, briefly showering us with a small light of happiness. My eyes began to well from Margriete's words, and I looked away toward the source of the new light. There were small jars hanging from the ceiling that were attached to a separate, smaller cave from which glowworms now poured out of.

I gasped, completely forgetting the recollection of Margriete's nickname. "How does it work?" I asked, walking closer to one jar and peering up at it.

Margriete walked up beside me. "They live in the Earth, I suppose. There are these hidden switches all over the caves." She pointed back toward the indented rock circle. "They hold for about thirty minutes before releasing. Then, the caves close off the network of gates that allow the worms to crawl into the jars.

Sam smirked. "The ones left behind eventually disintegrate and die."

I let out a disgusted snort, looking at Sam. "Leave it to you to ruin a beautiful moment."

Margriete laughed. "Seriously, how did you get stuck with a martyr of a guardian? They're typically a lot less sadistic."

"It's my luck, I guess." I winked toward Sam.

He knelt and grabbed my pack off the floor. "At least this idiot of a guardian is willing to carry your things," he retorted.

Margriete rolled her eyes. "We better get going so that we can make it to the next switch. It's rather uncomfortable for me to see in darkness, though the cat eyes do help considerably." Margriete added, slamming her book closed and strapping it to her back, refusing Sam's offer to carry her things.

"How will you know the way without the map?" I asked,

stepping forward.

Margriete walked beside me, the cave large enough to fit four men across, and high enough that a Griffin could probably fly through it without touching the ground. "You'll know, as long as you can trust your heart. Most times, we refuse to believe the notions inside us." She crinkled her brow. "Much like when you take a test and you know the answer right away, but then spend too much time thinking about it and you second guess yourself. I'm sure you can relate to that," she nudged me, "having gone through high school and all." A smirk cut across her fair face as she teased me like a sister.

"Yeah. The good thing is, I always went with my first hunch and I was top of my class," I retorted sassily.

Margriete smiled at the challenging retort. "Well, then, we shouldn't have any troubles." She winked before facing forward, our pace steady, but not fast.

I was deep in thought for a while as Sam whistled, his song echoing down the long chamber. The walls leaked water, and between Sam's breaths of whistling air, you could hear it trickle across the granite and marble. I never really imagined that the human world contained a whole other world, tucked away beneath the surface. I chuckled at the general belief that Heaven was above us, but at the same time, burying our dead in the ground began to make a lot more sense. We were actually getting them closer to Heaven.

I thought about Edgar and how the ground had claimed him. He should be dead because he had been stabbed by the dagger, but something inside me refused to realize it until I knew for sure. My heart ached for his return, longed to feel his velvety touch on my skin. The Griffins knew what would drive my emotions, and they knew how to tangle me in their vicious web of lost souls. Had it not been for my friends, I fear I would have sat there for all eternity, listening to that beautiful voice instead of searching for its owner. There was nothing I longed for more than to feel his face again, his body against mine. I sighed and Sam took notice, eyeing me as he read my thoughts on the matter.

"You really love him, don't you?" He kicked a rock and it skipped through the cavern.

I nodded, holding back tears. I had tried too hard to keep a stalwart exterior, but as we continued to test our will, my armor was crumbling, and I was beginning to feel sad and weak.

Sam sighed. "I guess I didn't understand before. Time usually heals all wounds and we move on."

I fidgeted with my hands.

Sam continued. "If Edgar is dead…"

"He's not," I finally spoke, my hand reaching for the warm ring as it lay against my chest.

Sam pursed his lips. "But you have to consider the possibility that one day you will be like Margriete, eternally lost without him."

I looked up at Margriete walking in an anxious manner a few paces ahead. I found her existence sad and lonely, something I knew I couldn't handle the way she did. "I will never rest. I will continue to find a way."

Sam sighed again, his heart feeling the pain mine did.

"You will forever be his, then. Edgar's girl."

I looked up at him, finding the words a comfort.

He smiled, revealing the soft side I was afraid to embrace, but for which I was nonetheless grateful. I watched him carefully, his thoughts turning away from our conversation to something else. I longed to know what he was thinking, but his face gave no clue as to his emotional state or the past that haunted him.

I looked around the cave, not sure how much time had gone by, but I began to brace myself for the inevitable black-out. Margriete was scanning the walls now, looking for the next switch through the streams of water. Sam seemed relaxed, and even a little content. It was something I rarely sensed from him.

"Ah ha!" Margriete jumped in the air, thrusting her hand toward the ceiling in victory.

Startled, I looked around for the switch I knew she had found. The room went dark around us.

"Great." Margriete cursed under her breath as she fumbled through the darkness, her eyes not yet able to see through the thick shroud of black. I listened to her shuffling. Hopefully she would be able to find the switch again.

My breathing was shallow as I heard familiar velvety clank as she pressed the switch. Light slowly burned back to life, the gentle sound of worms falling against glass filling the air. I watched them tumble from their small caves. It was morbid yet intriguing.

Margriete stood and brushed the dirt from her pants, her knees darkened and wet from the damp floor. "This place certainly isn't glamorous, that's for sure."

"Yeah." I looked around. "Why did the gods give the humans the surface of the Earth? Why not give them the center?"

Margriete chuckled. "Just wait. You'll see why soon."

I marveled at the response and tried to imagine what could be more magnificent than the sun and moon, the clouds and sky.

As we worked our way deeper, the cave arched to the left and then suddenly divided. We all halted and looked at each other, tired of the continued trial of our spirit. Margriete quickly untied the golden book and flipped through its pages. We watched her with anxious eyes as she concentrated on the words, scanning each page with irritated haste. The book seemed to groan under her vicious touch, angry that she was treating it with such carelessness.

Sam became distracted by something and his gaze darted about the cave. He sniffed the air, sensing something was different. Ever since our talk, he had remained distant, as though tangled in his past. His breath became labored as I watched him, now struggling for a breath he didn't need. Rubbing his palms together, he looked down into his hands.

"What's wrong, Sam?" I finally asked, seeing now that something was clearly not right.

"My palms." He paused, pressing them against his jeans. "They're sweating."

I walked up to him and grabbed his hands, the noticeable warmth shocking when it touched my skin. I looked into his eyes. "Sam, you're warm."

176

His breathing was still heavy, his eyes now looking toward the cave on the far left. Margriete and I both followed his gaze, our heart rates quickening. As we stood in the silence, a soft sound began to grow from the cave, approaching like a slow soft echo. We stood like statues as the sound grew. I listened closely, recognizing the subtle tones of a woman's humming.

I looked at Sam, a scared spark now glazing his eyes. Fear was a feeling I never thought he could exhibit. A light grew from within now, approaching us at a steady pace as it began to silhouette the figure that held it. Sam took one step forward, the shadow approaching us. This being either did not sense our presence, or did not care.

The figure emerged then, her humming coming to an abrupt halt. She let out a soft scream, startled to find she was not alone.

Sam gasped.

"Jill?"

THE WAY

"Sam?"

The woman dropped the lantern that she grasped in her hand. "Oh…" she knelt to the ground and tried to grab the handle. Her small hands shook.

We all faced each other, all frozen in either shock or curiosity. The young girl that had emerged was no older than eighteen, but clearly not from the modern time, either. She had long straight hair that fell to her waist, spilling over her back as she stood and flipped it behind her. Her leather bell bottoms were a far cry from stylish, and her beaded necklace was clearly a product of the late sixties.

"Sam? You know this woman?" Margriete finally broke through the thick tension.

Sam turned his head to face Margriete but his eyes remained on the woman. "Yes, I do," he breathed, his mouth moving as though it was not a part of his face.

Jill spoke then. "Sam, I...." She blinked and took one step toward him. "I never thought I'd see you here."

Sam stepped forward as well, but was careful to keep his distance. He was frightened by her presence. "Er...." He tilted his head, finding the words. "How are you?"

Jill looked around her. "Well I... I was just awake a minute ago. I needed some water, but...." She looked around again. "I must be dreaming again." She looked down at her body. "And I'm young again!" she gasped, smiling with childish pleasure. Her mind was clearly in a foggy dream.

"*Dreaming?*" Sam uttered in disbelief.

Margriete and I looked at each other. Her face lit up, remembering something.

"Jill." Margriete took a brave step toward her, placing one hand on the shoulder of her brown and mustard-colored polyester blouse. "You're human, right?"

Jill looked at Margriete sideways. "What do you mean? Of course I'm *human*."

Margriete turned to face us. "She's dreaming." She stared at Sam. "I told you. This is the place humans come to dream. Their perfect world, so to speak."

Sam blinked hard, eyeing the cave around him curiously. "Jill, I..." He froze as Jill finally pressed past Margriete and ran into Sam's arms. He closed his eyes and embraced her. Margriete and I were now both completely confused, our mouths gaping.

"Sam? Who is this?" Margriete finally hissed, her patience wearing thin.

I had known who this was as soon as Sam had said her

name, but I hadn't found it appropriate to fill Margriete in. I watched Margriete's brows furrow, a surprising hint of jealously filling her eyes. I let a sharp breath of amazement pass my lips, finding this moment a revelation into the hearts of all things.

Sam opened his eyes and let go of Jill. "This is Jill. My love."

Margriete rolled her eyes and turned away, pretending not to care, though I knew that for some strange reason, she did.

Jill stared deep into Sam's eyes. "Oh, Sam, you saved me. I never got the chance to thank you, to tell you *I loved you.*" Her face suddenly changed as though she had just forgotten what she had said. In the world of our dreams, things are not always clear.

I continued to gawk even though Margriete had given up. I was too taken by the moment, and the display of love before me, to let myself miss this. It was sad to see Sam in such a state, to see the one thing that could ever make him falter.

He looked back at Jill who was looking around, confused and lost. "How did you come here?"

She took a step back, realizing where she was for the first time. "I am dreaming, aren't I?" She stumbled over a rock, but Sam was quick to grab her arm and steady her.

Sam looked at Margriete for affirmation.

Margriete pulled herself together enough to nod. It didn't seem that Sam was picking up on Margriete's jealousy, but I could understand why. His mind was likely too overwhelmed to even notice or care.

An innocent smile grew across Sam's face, like a teenager in love. "Yes, I think you are."

Jill frowned. "I wish I weren't," she whispered, her voice sounding tired and distant. Her gaze fell to the ground. "Oh, Sam, I think about you all the time."

Sam smiled. "Me too."

I laughed to myself. I had been right. Sam did have the capacity to feel after all, but he had hid it from me in a metal cage within his heart.

"Oh," she cooed again. "I was in the most amazing place before…" her voice trailed off. "It was like *Heaven*."

Margriete grabbed Jill's hand. "Is that where you came from, through that cave?" It seemed she had settled her emotions and was trying to be rational.

Jill slowly turned and looked at her, trying to find her through a thick fog that filled her mind. She worked hard to remember, but dreams were as such. "I think so. But I'm not sure why I entered the cave." She looked at Sam. "But I think I see why now."

The love between Sam and Jill was undeniable. I suddenly realized why he had done what he did, and why he had watched over her, even when she had chosen to love someone else.

Margriete's eyes lit up then. "That's our cave!" She pointed toward where Jill had emerged. "We need to go through there."

Jill looked stunned as she stared off into space. "Oh!" she cried. "I think I'm waking again."

Sam thrust himself toward her, his wings now exposed.

"No, Jill. Don't go."

She gave him a rueful but surprised look. "Oh, Sam. I never stopped loving you. You were always my knight." She finally noticed his wings and gasped. "Oh, Sam! Sam, you're an angel!"

Sam smiled. "All because of you, my love."

Jill's long straight locks blew behind her then, blowing in a vortex not our own. Fear filled her eyes. "I'm falling, Sam!"

Sam wrapped his arms around her, exerting all his strength as he tried to keep her here. "No… I can save you, Jill!" The torn expression on his face struck fear into my heart, and I helplessly watched as the horrors of his past were relived.

Jill began to scream then, her voice fading as her body began to disappear in the wind like particles of sand.

Sweat coated Sam's brow, his body somehow alive and warm in her presence. "Come back, Jill!" he yelled, but she was already gone. Sam fell to the ground and his knees cracked hard against the stone, his face buried in his hands. Margriete and I approached gingerly, placing one comforting hand on his back as we tried to ease his distress.

"She was all I ever wanted." His voice was muffled and sad.

I rubbed his back soothingly in an attempt to help him feel better.

His face twisted to face mine. "I see now, Elle, why you torture yourself. Why you are so determined to find him. I remember the love now, Elle. I remember…" his voice trailed off into sobs, his large body shaking as Margriete and I tried all we could to help him.

I nodded and knelt by his side. "Of course, Sam. I don't blame you for the things you've said." I hugged him hard and I felt our hearts meld closer, our friendship now more than a simple transaction or duty. He was no longer the same annoying Sam I had loathed, but a brother and dearest friend.

Margriete swallowed hard and I saw her eyes begin to well from the corner of my eye. I knew the words we were speaking were like daggers in her own heart, reminding her of her murderous love and the feelings that her heart had been denied.

"We will get through this together, Sam." I brushed the now cold tears from his eyes. "Somehow," I added.

He took one shaky breath and stood, his hands trembling and his eyes rimmed with red. "We need to press on." There was a sudden sense of determination about him. He had realized the importance of this mission beyond his binding agreement to protect me.

Sam let one last warm breath escape his lips before his body fell cold and he stepped forward. Margriete and I steadied each other and regrouped, finding the best way to be supportive was to follow his lead. In his large shadow we all filtered into the cave to the left, following the footsteps Jill had left.

As the archway passed over our heads, the carvings across the top became clear. I smiled, finding it a familiar sight in such a dark world. There was a small raven above each door, and I recalled my dream. It was not the dream alone that brought a smile to my face. It was also Edgar Allan Poe's poem, and the raven that had sat above his chamber door. I wondered if he had been here, if he had referenced these caves.

Margriete noticed my curiosity. "You do remember the importance of the raven, don't you?"

I shook my head as we moved deeper into the cave, the glowworms casting a blue hue across the walls.

"The raven was a symbol of the divine, long before anyone called it a raven. The gods created them in a physical form when the human race began to grow on the surface of the Earth, so that they could watch over them. Wherever ravens congregate is a place that is being watched, a place the gods fear could be a threat to the Earth. Just as the ravens flock to the Tower of London, they flock to all things that secrete true evil and human despair." She paused, thinking to herself. "Like Matthew."

I nodded. "I guess that makes a lot of sense. It almost seems obvious." I began to wonder what else was out there.

Margriete nodded. "There are a lot of things you've yet to learn about yourself." She kicked a stone that lay on the floor. "I can't imagine how this all must be to you."

I shrugged.

She looked at me sideways, almost laughing. "And your friends!" She threw her hands up in the air. "I just can't believe you have real human friends. When we went down to see Scott and Sarah, I must admit, I was a little repulsed."

I pursed my lips, giving her a sour glare. "You too? I don't see what the big deal is. I mean, I was raised by humans. Why wouldn't I like them?"

Margriete snickered. "You're sort of like a human raised by wolves, except, I think it fits better as a wolf raised by humans."

Her analogy was weak, but I got the point. It was something I had thought of myself. My heart sank at the thought of Scott and Sarah. I had all but ditched them in favor of this magical life, but what was I to do? It was clear that I was here for a reason, a mission I did not yet understand. If we were the guardians of their world, then I knew I would be able to make it up to them one day by saving it.

The cave narrowed and curved back to the left. Margriete was again analyzing the walls, searching for the next switch. Sam dodged past her, having been silent until now.

"I got this one, sweetheart." He winked at Margriete, his lecherous personality returning. He slammed the heel of his hand into the rock, the switch giving.

As I looked up, the light beyond began to brighten, like the opening scene at the movies. The narrow caves led forward where they poured out into a large room, about fifteen feet across and ten feet deep. As the worms plinked their way into the jars, I noticed where the rocky cave seemed to give to something strange, something human.

Margriete let out a sharp, amused breath, recognizing what was before. She walked to where the wall ended, running her hand across the stone and wood. Sam stretched his wings in the space, also approaching the strange wall.

"It's..." I paused as I crossed the distance between me and the wall. "It's a wall." But not just any wall, it was like a wall you would see in a house, complete with ugly green wallpaper. In the middle of the wall stood a white door with a gold handle, and to the left hung a painting. I crinkled my brow as I looked at the picture, seeing an exact replica of the wall painted within its frame.

Sam came and stood beside me. "How original," he snorted.

Margriete quickly untied the book from her belt and wrestled with the pages. Her face lit up as she found the right spot and shoved it toward me, pointing at the lithograph on the page. "See here, the painting is important. In order to open that door." She motioned to the life-sized door to our right. "We have to first open this one." She pointed to the same door in the painting.

"Seems simple enough," I said, watching in fascination as the picture in the book glowed gold under Margriete's touch.

"Well, but that's where we hit a snag. I don't really remember how I did it, exactly. There was something…" her voice trailed off. She brought her hand up and pressed her fingers hard against her forehead.

Sam wiggled the handle of the real door, giving it a good yank. It didn't budge. I turned back and looked at the painting, reaching up toward it with an inquiring hand. As my hand fell upon the surface, I gasped as it sank right through. I pulled my hand back, watching as paint dripped from the tips of my fingers.

Sam laughed at me. "Hey, check this out." He motioned for Margriete to look.

Margriete turned and looked back at us. I reached into

the painting as far as I could, up to my shoulder. I wiggled my fingers, seeing that my arm was now painted within the art itself, becoming a part of it. Visually, my reach was hardly long enough to reach the door handle of the painting, as though I were positioned on the other side of the room.

"Of course!" Margriete's mind seemed to flood with memories, making sense of the jumble. "Elle, you need to open it from inside the painting."

I pulled my arm back out, now covered in thick oil paint that pooled on the floor of the cave. "No way!" I cried as I slopped the paint from my arm. "I'll drown in it!"

"Come on, Elle," she urged.

"Why me? Why can't *you* do it?" I walked away from the painting to the other side of the room.

Margriete's body pulsed with excitement and anxiety. "Because you can fly."

A sharp exhale escaped my lips, realizing that my new talent finally had a downside. "Well, so can Sam!" I retorted.

"Sam's too big, Elle. He'll destroy the painting and then we'll be stuck here."

I was pacing now, my nerves alive with fear. "But I'm still not very good at this whole changeling thing. And how will I open the door? With my beak?"

Margriete shook her head in defiance. "No, you must change back once you're in there and open the door. Then change again and fly out. You'll have to take a deep breath and concentrate."

She made it sound so easy, though I knew it was anything but. Clearly she had done this without flying once before.

Clearly she was not willing to do so again, meaning it wasn't easy, and likely perilous. She was just too stubborn to admit that.

I shook the fear from my body, my palms now sweating. "Okay," I mumbled. "I can do this." I was still pacing.

"You *can* do this. This is the only way through. You know it's inevitable," she urged with confidence.

Sam had nothing to say on the matter so he stared at me instead, a glimmer of anxiety in his eyes. He was sworn to protect me, but this task was mine alone. There was nothing he could do to help. I saw his weight shift restlessly from one foot to the other, finally nodding toward me and giving me the okay.

I squeezed my eyes shut as tight as I could, concentrating on flight and wondering what that would feel like in the painting. It was then that I was able to change and I opened my eyes, veering sharply to avoid crashing into the stone wall. Margriete and Sam ducked to avoid me, and I found it close to impossible to control myself.

My feathers glowed in the dim light of the cave, adding a clear white hue to the blue light of the worms. On my second pass, I took a deep breath, aiming now for the painting and preparing for the splash of its thick contents.

I looked at Margriete and Sam once more, both poised and still as stone. Closing my eyes, I tucked my wings and picked up speed. I did not have the time to feel afraid anymore. I blinked one last time as I crashed through the paint, the sound around me instantly muffled. Cool, wet liquid filled my ears, my speed noticeably hindered.

I kept my eyes squeezed shut, but quickly realized that in order to do this, I would have to see at some point. I opened my eyes slowly, finding that my vision worked much like it would in a pool, though everything was blurred and melting. I flapped my wings hard, feeling the paint smear its way through my feathers. I swam as swiftly as I could toward the door, the breath I had held not yet stinging my lungs, but my muscles were burning from the lack of oxygen.

I could just make out the soft, muffled voices of Sam and Margriete behind me, urging me to hold on. As I reached the door, I quickly concentrated on my body, changing with such haste, that I knew I had lost my clothes. Despite the embarrassment, it was easier to move through the paint without the added resistance. I grappled for the handle, feeling my hands slip against its solid mass. After a few tries, I was able to get a good hold and twist the handle. I yanked hard and I felt it finally give. A soft sucking came from beyond and I felt myself being pulled toward it, into a place I was certain I did not want to be.

I turned and pressed hard against the current, changing back into the raven as I tried to tread through the paint. The wings worked better as they pushed me forward, and I made progress. I pressed as hard as I could, my body now weak and tired. My muscles were screaming in agony, desiring rest. I began to doubt itself and my eyes closed in pain and fatigue. Suddenly, Edgar's voice echoed from somewhere next to me. I looked to the sound.

"Darling, I'm here. Don't go."

His voice was clear, as though the paint was no longer

clogging my ears. I looked through the thick streaking rays, barely able to make out his face as he stood in the corner, smiling in a way that made my heart melt.

"Elle, you can't leave me here," he pleaded.

I continued to press forward, opening my mouth to reply, tasting the paint as it gushed in. "You're not real!" I tried to scream, my only breath escaping my lungs. Tears fell from my eyes, washing away in blue streaks. My chest began to sting as my lungs filled and I began to drown.

"But I am, Elle. I am real. I'm right here." Edgar's blurred image reached out to me, his hand just inches away.

My wings began to slow and my mind grew fuzzy from the lack of oxygen, no longer differentiating between what was real or fake. I reached one wing out to him, a smile now blurring across his familiar face as he reached back. I wanted to tell him I loved him, but there was no breath left.

I felt my wings falter and my mind dim when suddenly I felt a cold hand wrap around me, yanking me backwards. I changed back into my human form and another hand then grabbed my arm. Edgar's figure fell away from me and I screamed one last time, my lungs seizing as paint gushed in. Crashing through the painting, I fell hard against the floor of the cave, landing on Sam and Margriete. I coughed in violent spurts, spitting paint all over the walls of the cave. My mouth burned from the oils, the linseed taste unbearable.

As I wiped the paint from my eyes, I saw that Sam and Margriete were both panting furiously, Margriete's head and arm were completely soaked in paint and Sam's face was streaked with blue and green. I let out a hysterical laugh and spit more paint on the floor, realizing how close to death I had come.

Margriete pushed my sopping hair away from my face. "That was close," she breathed, finding no humor in the matter.

Sam had a disgusted look on his face as he stared at his sodden arm and face, also not seeing the humor.

My laugh withered to a frown as my sanity returned. "Edgar was in there," I said as I tried to calm my breathing. "*I saw him.*"

Margriete scanned my eyes, never breaking her stare. "It wasn't real, Elle." She grabbed my hair and rung it out. "He was just in your mind, tricking you. You need to recognize this."

Sam muttered to himself as he slung paint against the wall, pacing in a circle.

I shook my head, my eyes finally welling with tears. "No. It was him this time." My emotions were like a rollercoaster, rising and falling, leaving me dazed and confused. I looked back up at the painting, but there was no one there.

Margriete still had her hand on my head. "It's not real, Elle. It's all in your head."

I sighed. "Well, you saw him, right?"

Margriete and Sam glanced quickly at eachother before she replied. "Er…" her lips became a straight line. "No. We saw nothing but you."

I held her gaze, wondering if she was telling the truth or not. I didn't need them to protect me. I know what I saw, and there was no reason to keep me from feeling the sadness. If they had seen him, I wanted to know. At least then I'd know whether or not I was crazy.

Sam walked toward us and offered us both a hand. My grip slipped through Sam's fingers, paint squeezing out between our linked knuckles. We erupted into laughter as Margriete fell on her butt in a puddle of paint, leaving her with a painful frown of embarrassment.

Re-grouping to try again, she gripped Sam's arm with both hands and managed to stumble to a standing position. I looked down at my body, naked except for the paint that coated it. Margriete walked to my satchel and dug inside, pulling out a change of clothes I had brought, just in case. She tossed them to me and I used them to wipe off some of the paint, and then pulled them on. Letting out a breath of relief, we all simultaneously looked at the now open door, eyeing the opening cautiously. As I approached and my eyes adjusted, I saw that there was a staircase that began just inside the small, dark space. It swirled downward in an endless spiral like a whirlpool, the steps carved from solid stone.

Sam placed his hand on the door knob, leaning his weight against it as he also peered in and down. "Well, I guess it's all downhill from here."

Margriete and I contemplated the journey ahead. My body was screaming for a rest.

"We can't stay here. We must press on," Margriete finally said. The light in the room now fading as the power from the worms began to die. She placed one hand on my drooped shoulders. "We'll rest soon, but not now, Elle."

DOWN AND OUT

The stairs continued to spiral downward. I was dizzy and my head ached from curving endlessly for so long. My thighs burned from exertion, and even Sam was struggling to remain stable, showing his first signs of weakness. Light filled the space from somewhere above, as though the tower of stairs had an open roof to the sky, though that seemed impossible. By now, it was clear that we were deep beneath the Earth's surface, far deeper than any explorer had ever been.

Margriete was breathing evenly, her stride never breaking. She was in a trance. From time to time she flickered into her cat form, seeming to find it easier to travel that way. I tried hard to keep up, though my body begged to take a break.

I was not as lucky as Margriete. To change into a raven would mean spiraling out of control. The stairwell was narrow and tight, and I knew that once I picked up speed, I would only continue downward without a place to land.

I rubbed my palms against my thighs. "Grietly? How much farther?" I whined.

My words startled her, breaking her rhythm. "Almost there," she snapped. "I think." She turned to look at me and I noticed the dark circles under her eyes, her skin pale and drawn.

Sam groaned behind me, obviously bored from the sudden lack of action. The paint had dried on all of us and was now cracking as sweat gathered beneath it, leaving a trail of color down the stairs.

I thought about Edgar as I had seen him then. Despite the blurriness of paint, I was still convinced it had been him. His voice was unmistakable, if not overly seductive. I shuddered, remembering how it felt when he used to touch me, that undeniable feeling that we were one soul, bound for eternity.

One would think it would be easier, that our lives would just go on in a happily ever after. But like most things in life, perfection is too coveted to be easy and free. Contentment can ultimately lead to self-destruction if one is not too careful. Our love had become our demise, and ultimately, would forever hold us in this tumultuous cycle of crisis.

Up ahead, more light poured into the space, as though through a window. I blinked hard, trying to discern the rays that shone against the wall, trying to decide what, at this depth in the Earth could possibly resemble the sun as it did.

"Is that sunlight?" I asked, tilting my head as we continued to descend.

Margriete laughed. "Yes!" She was displaying a sudden burst of excitement and energy.

"But…" I paused, looking toward the top of the tower, now so high that the light there was but a pinhole. "But, we're underground!"

Sam said nothing, but there was an obvious look of curiosity in his eyes.

"Well, your dreams were never without sunlight, were they?" Margriete slowed slightly, allowing herself to catch her breath and speak. "Put it this way, you wouldn't think that the gods would let the humans have the only sun, do you?"

"Well…" I thought for a moment. "No. But there is that little issue called space and gravity. I mean, isn't the sun rather large to fit inside the Earth?"

Margriete snorted and it echoed through the chamber. "You have to think differently, Elle. Anything can happen, and will. Besides, it's not like they're trying to heat the entire universe in here. Think on a smaller scale."

I pursed my lips and lifted my eyebrows, finding that her explanation had clarified my thoughts. "I guess I could understand."

The window was approaching us now, and Margriete slowed even further. Her steps were now landing one at a time, rather than the steady trot she had held for so long.

Sam finally spoke. "Wait, I know this place."

I turned and looked at him, his face now glimmering with the light, whiter than I had seen in what seemed like days.

"This is…"

Margriete cut him off. "Yes, Sam. It is."

The window was right before us now, and I found myself holding my breath in anticipation of what I would see. As I rounded down the last spiral, I could now just barely make out what the window revealed. Exhaling slowly, I stepped in front of the frame, the sunlight pouring across my skin and the sudden warmth sent waves of comfort throughout my body. It was a feeling so much like home, that I couldn't help but forget where I was.

With amazement, I looked out on what appeared to be a lush valley. Wind was blowing through the green leaves on the trees and a fresh fragrance poured from the wind and into my nostrils. The air was sweeter than I had ever smelled, laced with the perfume of a hundred fragrant flowers.

My heart leapt, longing to play within this world, to forget Earth all together and be here, once and for all. This was not just the place of dreams, but it was also my Heaven.

Looking to my left, I saw that there was a river that poured past the tower and down the hillside. We were still about fifty feet in the air, but I could see that we were now close to the bottom. I looked toward the sky, the sun of this world blazing above us. I was amazed that I could look at it directly without the familiar sting in my eyes. It did not seem smaller than the one I had grown used to on Earth, but the fact that it was indeed closer suggested that it was smaller after all. The color that burned from it was blue, slowly radiating out to a warm white.

Clouds began to slowly pass before the light, fluffy and thick with rain. As the light died away, it drew my vision further into the landscape. In the far distance stood a city through the misty air, and it was difficult to recognize much more than the few tall structures. For a moment I was disappointed, seeing that the structures seemed plain, anything but the castles I had imagined.

It was then that there was a yell from below and my head snapped toward the sound, a strange reminder of my past. Margriete placed her hands on the sill of the window, also shocked by the sudden disruption. Sam, feeling left out, came up behind us, placing one hand on each shoulder and peering over our heads.

There was a man below, dragging a canoe across the soft earth toward the river, heaving hard and swearing under his breath. I watched him for a moment, finding something about his physique oddly familiar. The man stumbled and fell on his butt. He swore loudly as the words echoed through the valley, audible over the rushing river. As the man struggled to right himself, and straighten the awkward glasses on his nose, I gasped.

"Scott!" I yelled, my body surging with excitement. I jumped up and down, my hands gripping the sill. I looked around, contemplating flying down to him.

Scott jumped, frightened by my voice. He was frozen, thinking that he had been the only one and now finding he was not alone.

He tilted his head. "Hello?"

"Scott!" I yelled again.

He was now scanning the nearby bushes. "Elle?" he asked, more to himself than the air around him, looking as though he'd thought he'd been hearing things.

"Scott!" I yelled a third time, now waving from the window.

Scott seemed confused as he finally realized there was a giant tower before him. He looked upward, his mouth gaping and his glasses still crooked on his nose. Sweat glistened on his forehead and his eyes met mine.

"Elle?" He repeated himself, but this time it was as though he wasn't sure he was seeing what he had. He paused, a smile creeping across his face as he finally saw that I was real. "Elle!" He ran toward the tower.

"Scott! You're here!" My voice cracked.

"Elle! What are you doing here? This is my dream!" he yelped, now standing directly below us.

"I know, Scott! But we're here!" I turned inside and faced Margriete and Sam. "We have to get down there!" I looked back down at Scott. "Stay right there, we'll be right down!" I yelled.

Sam waved to him. Scott placed his hands on his hips and turned back toward the river to wait, his gaze floating between it and the canoe.

"Come on guys. Let's go!" Adrenaline now pulsed through my veins and I forgot about how tired my muscles had been. I skipped full steps down the last few flights, landing at the bottom with both feet. Arched doors lead out onto the valley where ivy engulfed the opening like a curtain. I pushed the curtain aside, my feet welcoming the soft grass as I bounded through the door.

I halted as the sun streamed across my whole body. I took a deep breath and closed my eyes. When I opened them,

Scott was standing directly in front of me.

"Elle? What are you doing here!" He was surprised, as though he hadn't remembered he'd already seen me. His face re-enacted the same emotion it had just moments ago.

"Scott." I furrowed my brow. "Scott, you already saw me. We went through this. You know, up there?" I pointed toward the tower and the window.

He looked down at the ground, up at the tower, and then back to where his discarded canoe lay near the rivers edge. "Oh," he paused, turning back to me, his beady eyes dilated behind his glasses. "Oh, yeah!" He slapped his leg, finally remembering as the pieces fell together in his head.

I laughed and gave him a big hug. "That's okay, Scott. You're dreaming."

He nodded with wide eyes. "Unfortunately," he replied. "I was studying for this big test in the plant lab, and I must have fallen asleep." He slapped his leg again. "Darn it! I needed that A."

I patted him on the back. "Don't worry about it, Scott. Besides, what's better than being here with me?"

He smiled, now ruefully rubbing his leg where he had slapped it twice. "Yeah, that's true." He pressed his brows together as Sam and Margriete emerged. He looked at them with both fear and interest. "Who are they?" He looked around him, then back up at the tower. "And where are we?"

I followed his gaze as he looked skyward. The tower went on for what seemed an eternity, into the clouds where there was no trace of the outer walls or caves. It was like being on the surface of the Earth, and for a moment, I second guessed myself.

Sam and Margriete approached behind me as Margriete offered an answer to Scott's inquiry. "This is the outlying fields of the City of Angels." Margriete stuck her hand out toward Scott. "Hi, I'm Margriete."

Scott was understandably slow, which could be expected. He was dreaming after all. He hesitated for what felt like minutes before grabbing her hand and giving it a shake. "Hi. I'm Scott."

Margriete choked on a laugh. "Yeah, I know. I've met you before."

I couldn't help but smile. "Yeah, Scott. Margriete is the cat I brought down with me the last time I came and saw you."

Scott lifted one finger and pointed at her, his eyes narrowing. "Oh yeah," he exclaimed, putting the pieces together.

Sam refused to step forward as he crossed his arms against his chest, disgusted with being in the presence of a real human. "So this is it, huh?" he spoke, directing his remark toward Margriete.

"This is it," she replied plainly.

"Hm…" He grunted with a hint of criticism on his breath.

"Well, don't you know this place, Sam?" I was a bit confused, if it was the City of Angels, he should have been here.

Margriete stepped forward and stuck her nose in the air, crossing her arms. She looked just as cold as Sam. "Ha, he wishes." She was arrogantly proud of the fact that she had knowledge over something Sam didn't. "He has to earn his way in." She sneered in Sam's direction. "And he simply isn't good enough yet, so this is his first time seeing it." She childishly stuck her tongue out at him, causing Sam to leap toward her with a hateful glare. Margriete dodged him, laughing.

"Well, what does he have to do to earn coming here?" I asked, speaking for the whole group. I eyed her expectantly.

She continued to back away from Sam's advances with a cool look on her face, and leaned against the tower in a relaxed pose. "This is guardian angel retirement, so to speak. Where the angels come after their mission to protect one soul is fulfilled." Margriete's eyebrows shot into the air as she chuckled and looked at me. "Looks like you're going to be a guardian angel for a long time, Sam. Elle will be alive for eternity, if it all goes right."

Sam growled at her. "Shut up, Margriete."

She let out one explosive laugh. "Oh, take it easy, Sam. It's not that great here, remember? You were just criticizing it a moment ago."

If Sam could turn red with anger, he probably would. His jaw clenched, and he turned and stalked toward the river.

Margriete's face instantly lost all of its humor as she pushed herself off the wall. "He sure is sensitive for someone that pretends to be so tough."

I burst into laughter as Scott stood beside me, completely lost.

"So, wait," he elbowed me gently, trying to follow our conversation through the thick mists of his dream. "That guy, the guy from classes last year..." his face was pursed up as he tried to put the pieces together. "He's a guardian angel?"

I patted him on the back, not realizing my own strength as I nearly knocked his glasses right off his head. "You got it, Scott! I'm so proud of you," I teased.

Margriete rolled her eyes and began down the hill toward Sam.

I urged Scott forward. "Come on, Scott. Let's make the most of this dream of yours." He stumbled before regrouping, straightening his glasses and acting as though he was a renewed man.

INTO THE CITY

"Oh, look!" cried Scott. "A canoe!" He jumped in the air and ran toward it.

Margriete chortled as we all circled the vessel. "Yeah, Scott. I think you've established that already."

He pressed his brows together and rewound his memory. "Oh yeah," he replied in a sheepish manner. He shoved his hands in his pockets and looked at the ground, now embarrassed.

Sam looked at him with disgust. "*Vile creature,*" he hissed under his breath.

"You didn't seem to find Jill *vile,*" Margriete grinned at him.

"Go hug a tree, Margriete," he spat back.

I shook my head at them, feeling their attitude toward each other was turning rather sour and childish. "Would you guys please concentrate? Scott, they didn't mean to be that way."

Scott looked at me and gave me a big smile.

Margriete and Sam glared at me, and I glared right back. We each chose a side and grabbed onto the canoe, hoisting it over our heads and marching it the rest of the way to the water. At the edge, I peered into the river's depths, marveling at how clean it was and also how blue.

I looked down at my feet. My toes were inches from the water when something I hadn't noticed caught my attention. I turned and looked behind me. There in the grass were my very distinct and deep foot prints. We placed the canoe on the ground, and I knelt down and ran my hand around the indent of my footprint, admiring the way they had remained.

Up there, I was something magical, but here, I was finally able to leave my mark. This was a world where I could belong. Aside form the footprints in the mud, there was also a lack of blooming flowers trailing behind us. Like everything in this world, it was already enchanted with eternal beauty and life, and no longer needed to bloom from our presence.

I sighed, loosing myself in the feeling of harmony.

"Come on, Elle!" Margriete yelled, "Push!"

I snapped back to reality as I placed two hands firmly on the edge of the canoe that was resting beside me, shoving the large vessel into the river. As the current pulled at the hull, Sam held the back steady as we all climbed in. Scott was thoroughly lost in his own dumbfounded amazement, and was smiling to himself as Margriete manned the oars.

"Doubt we'll need those," Sam yelled over the roaring current.

Margriete gave him the evil eye and looked away,

pointedly ignoring.

All at once, Sam let go and jumped in. The canoe surged forward. Scott grabbed the sides of the boat, his knuckles white as he held on tightly. We were tossed between boulders as we rapidly picked up speed. Entering the trees, the river dropped over a small collection of rocks, jarring us with a heavy thud and pushing the canoe to the right. Scott began to laugh wildly over the roaring current like a mad man, lost in the mists of his dream and unfazed by the fact that this could possibly kill him.

As we roared down the river, we struggled to keep the canoe facing forward. Margriete was quick to right us with the oars, smirking at Sam every time he looked back at her, proving that the oars had their purpose after all.

I could tell they were both excited by the game and the thrill of the moment. I, on the other hand, couldn't help but feel terror stream through my blood like hot lava. The last thing I needed was to die on my way to save Edgar.

Sam gave in and assisted Margriete as we narrowly dodged a large boulder that split the river. He shoved us away as we got close, grabbing the sides of the vessel and then spreading his wings so to allow a soft, gentle landing. The rapids continued to bump us forward, and soon the river slowed, twisting to the right. The deafening sound of angry water trickled away behind us.

Scott was yelling in triumph as he rocked back and forth in his seat, still lost in the dream. The fact that he had been in harms way hadn't fazed him, as it shouldn't. Dreams were the only place you could die, only to wake in the real world. It was an interesting concept to think of what would happen to me if I had died. Would I wake up from all this? Would I realize that I really am human after all, depressed and alone, abandoned and scared?

The river began to slow to a lazy roll and I could see our adventure was now over.

"Well, that wasn't so bad," I pushed my damp hair from my face.

Margriete kept her keen sight forward. "Yes, but we should probably think of getting out soon." She pointed and I followed her stare.

Just as I had thought, our ride had come to an end. I saw that the gentle flow of the river was just the precursor to what was ahead. I watched in horror as the water ended in a sudden line, giving way to an angry waterfall beyond. I should have known this would happen, it always did.

"Sam, quick. Grab Scott." Margriete threw the oars overboard and they floated away from us. "And, Elle, grab onto me." She climbed past Scott and sat in front of me.

Sam groaned.

"Just do it!" she yelled, her words trailing off as she changed into the cat and climbed in my lap.

"But you'll be too heavy!" I protested, knowing that as a raven, I struggled enough as it was to keep myself afloat, let alone carry a cat as well.

Margriete hissed at me and dug her nails into my legs.

Sam tried to restrain Scott as he continued to flail. I hurried to prepare as I heard the telltale roar of water drawing near. It was hard to concentrate with Margriete clawing at my skin, and I changed just in time to grab onto her tail with one talon. The canoe fell out from under us and down the mountain. The gushing air from below helped to keep me afloat, despite the weight.

Margriete hissed and growled as we watched the canoe splinter against the rocky hillside, the water washing it away in tiny pieces the size of toothpicks. Sam and I circled downward, my grip on Margriete's tail nearly failing as we reached the ground. Exhausted, I dropped her five feet above the grass at the rivers edge. Misty spray matted her fur as she crawled away from the water.

In a flash, she quickly changed back. Sam wrestled Scott to the ground, his hand firmly placed over Scott's mouth. Sam looked at me as Scott's face turned as red as a beet in his attempt to scream. "What is your fascination with this breed? *Really*," he hissed, throwing Scott to the ground.

Scott instantly began to roar with a throaty laughter, like a mad man sent to solitary confinement. "Amazing! Absolutely *wild!*" he yelled, quickly standing and skipping to the river's edge where he inspected the damage. Being as sheltered as he was, this was certainly new to him. I'm sure there was never a time when he thought he'd fly from a waterfall in the abusive hands of a guardian angel.

Sam snorted in disgust, walking to the water's edge where he attempted to wash himself of the human scent. I twisted back to my human form, hastily checking my belt loop to ensure the dagger was still there. I had left it behind when I'd gone into the painting, so I hadn't worried about losing it. In the commotion of the river, though, losing it would have been disastrous to our plans. I would have been left trying to succeed with no weapon.

"Did you have to grab my tail, Elle?" Margriete's voice was full of sass as she shook off the rest of the mist. "I mean, really." She rubbed her hand against the base of her back where her tailbone was.

I shrugged and smiled. "Sorry."

She exhaled as her breath dragged between her lips, causing them to flap with annoyance.

We all took a moment to regroup as I calmed Scott, helping him to realize where he was and hoping he'd find his sanity. After a few minutes, I managed to get him to stop laughing and look at me. Despite my pleading, he proceeded to forget that I had been here the whole time.

"Remember, Scott, we came down from there." I pointed to the top of the waterfall. "From the river, where you first saw me at the tower? Remember?"

He pointed his finger at me like he always did, narrowing his eyes in recognition. "By gosh, Elle. You're right!" The look on his face was priceless, as though he couldn't believe he had been so lucky and adventurous.

Rolling my eyes, I stood, joining Sam and Margriete as they went over what to do next.

"I hope he wakes up soon," Sam muttered under his breath.

I attempted to elbow him, but instead I ended up with a bruise.

"Sam, forget Scott. He's here for now, so get over it." Margriete waved a hand at him and Sam shut up.

"Nice job!" I yelped, giving her a high five for successfully beating Sam at his own game.

"So…" Margriete calmed her laughter as Sam sulked. "Back to business. I think it's safe to say that if we follow the river, it won't be long until we come across the city."

I nodded while Sam refused to give her any acknowledgement. "On our way down, it didn't seem too far off," I added, looking in the general direction.

Smiling to myself, I recalled the works of Jules Verne, remarking at how *The Journey to the Center of the Earth* had been pretty accurate. I wondered if Jules knew, much like Scott would, that this place was real, and I wondered if he had actually indeed been here, as his book would suggest.

Margriete gathered her things. The paint was now washed from all of us, leaving us somewhat presentable, if not a little wrinkled. As we made our way along the river's edge, I watched the colorful fish weave beneath the surface, no longer in need of my life or my attention. For all I knew, this was Heaven, or at least what any man would consider it to be. Everything seemed perfect and healthy, eternally bound to a life of happiness.

It wasn't long before the trees began to thin and we came upon a small cottage with a gated farm. The roof was thatched, much like you might have seen in the colonial era, or perhaps in the country. The fencing was rather tattered, and in spots, completely torn down. A herd of goats was scattered across the landscape, half within the farm gates, half out.

"Is there some sort of currency here?" I asked, to no one in particular.

Margriete nodded her head. "Hmm…" She looked at the worn house and weighed her thoughts. "Yes, I believe there is." She pulled her book from her back and flipped through a few pages, swiftly finding the spot she was looking for. She smiled. "Yes, it seems the angels earn their retirement…" she paused and eyed Sam with an accusing glare. "You are such a money grubber!" she exclaimed, dropping the book to her side and gawking at him.

Sam smirked and looked away from her.

She brought the book back to her face. "It says that guardian angels earn various amounts based on whom they choose to protect in their life of duty. Protecting someone like you…" She pointed toward me, her head still buried in the page. "Fetches the largest bounty, something equivalent to royalty." She snorted, now seeing Sam as greedy, not chivalrous.

I let out a surprised grunt, my mouth gaping as I looked at Sam, wide-eyed. "You little sneak!" I yelped, partially amused. Sam's personality certainly suggested he'd be so mercenary, but I had hoped otherwise. "But why would he get paid so much to protect us when the gods actually want us dead? Doesn't that seem a little strange to you?"

Margriete's brow was creased. "You have a point there, but I don't think I know why." Her mouth curled into a smile. "Maybe there really is more to us than just being a mistake." Her eyes glazed as she turned her thoughts inward, trying to come up with a rational explanation.

Sam stuck his nose in the air. "Before you chastise me, you should know I didn't want the job."

"Yeah right," Margriete choked.

Sam looked at her with a menacing glare, his eyes now blazing a deep gold. "I did it for Edgar, okay?"

My smile sank, seeing the tension in his expression.

"Edgar has done a lot for me in some very hard times. The money is just a bonus." He looked away, his face stung by our hurtful assumptions.

Margriete looked at her toes, somewhat ashamed. "I'm sorry, Sam. I didn't mean to offend you."

Sam said nothing as he crossed his arms.

"What did Edgar do for you?" I pressed, intrigued by his revelation.

Sam turned and looked at me with narrowed vision, the mauve under his eyes darker than I had ever seen. "He helped me get over Jill," he replied plainly.

I gave him an encouraging nod, letting him know that I wasn't the enemy here. "He helped you forget her?"

He nodded. "He said that no man should have to endure that kind of torture for all eternity."

My heart sank at the words, and for the first time, I wondered if Edgar really had gotten over me and moved on in my absence. I never considered the fact that perhaps he had tried to find love elsewhere. I had been gone for three hundred years, and I knew nothing about that time, or what he had done.

Margriete grabbed my arm, seeing my distress. "But not Edgar, honey. He always loved you."

I looked at Sam but he looked away, as though he were hiding something. What if Edgar had been with another woman? What if he had even loved her? Perhaps he didn't love her as much as he'd loved me, but at least enough to make life bearable. Whatever it was that Sam hid, I knew he'd never say.

A sudden feeling of absurdity washed over me, and I felt foolish for being here. Was I crazy for taking the initiative to find him when he obviously hadn't come to find me? Tears welled in my eyes, and I tried to press them back as Scott began to whistle behind me, his feet tracing the edge of the river and dangerously close to falling in.

I placed my hand on the dagger that was snug in my belt, a reminder of the sacrifices I'd made for Edgar, for someone I still felt I didn't know. Suddenly I wasn't sure I could trust him anymore. I had fallen so quickly into the aspects of love and happiness, never questioning his motives, or mine. Was it easier for him to find love and connection when there was no soul to hunger for? Or did it not satisfy that hole inside him, the hole only I could fill?

We were well beyond the small farm now, and another house appeared through the trees. This one had a sturdier tile roof with board and batten siding and a fresh coat of white paint. A plume of white smoke rose from the chimney and a cage of birds was built onto the outside half of the house.

Margriete again opened her book, a look of recognition crossing her face. "I think we're here! I recognize this place. It's just like déjà vu!" She ran her hand across the page and smiled.

"Where are we? I thought we were headed to the city?" I looked down river, then back at the house.

"We will," Margriete replied. "But first we need some rest, don't you agree?"

I nodded with enthusiasm.

"Elle, you're going to love this place, I promise." She winked at me as she slammed the book shut and shoved it into the leather ties on her back.

As we came closer, I was now able to see the birds as they hopped between the branches of the cage, cooing softly. "They're ravens," I gasped. "Why would someone keep ravens?"

Sam rolled his eyes as though he knew.

"You'll see." Margriete nudged me, smiling mischievously.

OLD FRIENDS

"Oh, hi! Come in, come in, dear child!" A man opened the door, his face beaming to the point that it seemed to swallow itself.

We had knocked several times, waiting for what felt like hours as the banging of pots and clanking of dishes crashed behind the door.

Scott smiled with a dumfounded expression on his face, and I could tell he was beginning to fade from this world and back to his own. There he would wake and find himself facing a test for which he was ill-prepared.

"Ah, dear friend." Margriete leaned in and gave the man a hug, as though she had known him like an uncle.

"It's been ages, dear!" He patted her on the back with his withered hands. "I never thought I'd see you again!" The man's smile was so big that his cheeks had pressed his eyes shut, causing him to stumble about like a blind man.

Behind him rested a set of wings, hanging from his back

like tired kites, drawn with age. His smile relaxed and I was finally able to discern his features, seeing that despite the fine lines left from years of happiness, his overall being seemed young and vibrant. Untamed strands of black hair hung down his forehead and it reminded me of Edgar's, tousled and a bit long in the back as it swept to the right and out of his eyes. He had thick eyebrows and a full black mustache that added to his character, making his smile that much more entertaining.

I tilted my head and looked at him with interest, finding something familiar in his overall appearance.

"Where are my manners!" Margriete grabbed both of the man's shoulders, holding him at arms length as she analyzed him. She released one hand from his arm and placed it on mine, suspense now growing as the man looked at me. He was anxiously waiting to know my name, his body shaking. "This is…" she paused and patted my arm, his features about to explode. "This is Elle!" she cried. She jumped up and down, squeezing both our hands tightly.

The man's face became even more animated, if that was even possible, and he unexpectedly rushed into me and gave me the biggest hug I had ever received. Not only did his arms nearly choke me in the embrace, but his wings as well. I gasped for air as he swung me around and around, and I still wondered who it was that could possibly be this excited to see me.

He plopped me down before him. "No! Really? *The* Estella?"

The man looked at Margriete for affirmation and she nodded with wide eyes. He held me at arms length, thoroughly examining me.

I had a shocked expression on my face.

"I have waited all my life for this moment! This is a complete culmination of my life's work!" he announced He looked as though he was witnessing a miracle, and it filled his eyes with immense energy.

"Oh, *please*," Sam uttered under his breath.

Scott was now losing it as he ran around the yard in circles, his odd behavior returning with all the commotion.

"You've done me a great service, Margriete." He patted her hard on the head. "Come, girl, come! We have much to speak of!"

I was still stunned and confused as Margriete laughed beside me.

"But, wait…" Margriete grabbed the man's arm as he turned to lead us into the house. "She has no idea who you are! Tell her!" Margriete urged.

"*Oh*, how clumsy of me." He spun on his heel to face me, the base of his hand thudding hard against his forehead in his forgetfulness.

I smiled, finding his outgoing and cheery attitude nothing like Sam's. I had been convinced that all angels were as cold-hearted, but this simply wasn't true.

"Dear girl, why…" he paused for dramatic effect, and I could tell he had a flair for suspense. "I am *Edgar Allan Poe!*" he exclaimed, throwing his arms out to either side of him with excitement.

I gasped, my hand covering my mouth. I looked to Margriete. "*No…*" I denied in a low voice as my mind raced to believe it was really him.

Margriete nodded with enthusiastically.

Edgar jumped up and down on the threshold, clapping his hands before him. His once cute personality was now a bit nutty. Edgar grabbed my hand and yanked me inside. Margriete followed, watching us with a pleased expression. Sam ushered Scott through the door as he ducked under the threshold, finding it too small for his mammoth height. As they entered the room, Sam hissed at Scott to shut up, and I could tell he was trying his best not to knock him out.

Looking around the room, I saw that he had finery greater than I would have initially imagined. The living area was quite expansive, and two large leather sofas sat facing each other before a roaring fire. There was a large bear rug on the floor between them, and the walls were crammed with books as though the foundation of the house itself was built upon them.

I watched as Edgar rushed around the corner to another room and the banging of pots commenced. Margriete shamelessly threw herself onto the couch, obviously familiar with the place. She must have been here before. I couldn't help but continue to smile. Edgar Allen had been one of the first amazing things I had found out about my Edgar, but now to meet him in the flesh was truly astounding.

Sam pressed Scott into an armchair near a worn black desk in the corner, placing a blank piece of paper before him and shoving a pen into his hand. I laughed at the childish behavior, seeing that Sam was trying to distract him with coloring.

Edgar emerged seconds later, a teapot in one hand and cups teetering on a tray in his other. He placed the tray on the table between the couches, his foot carelessly smashing the head of the bear skin rug. The rug almost seemed to fight back, as though it still had some life in it. Humming, he gave the rug one more fervent smash before hooking the kettle above the fire to warm. Satisfied with both the rug and the kettle, he then sat opposite Margriete, patting the cushion beside him and beckoning me to sit.

"Come, come child. Let me tell you some stories." He smiled widely as his mustache snaked up his cheeks, nearly poking him in the eye.

My eyes stayed fixed on the head of the bear as I approached, nervous it would snap at me. I sat on the edge of the cushion, still quite shocked by the whole thing. Never did I think I would meet the man himself. Certainly I never imagined him to be so odd, either.

Sam pushed Margriete over, claiming his half of the sofa as she whined and leaned her head into her hand against the armrest. Her eyes were too tired to care what was happening around her, so she kept them shut.

Edgar took my hand, rubbing it between his cold grasp. "Darling, you have been my biggest inspiration for love." He couldn't sit still. The words he had to say to me where boiling over in his mind. "Edgar's tales and ongoing pain was so deep, so everlasting." I noticed his teeth were yellowed, suggesting he had chewed tobacco when he was alive.

My grin faded, my head still swimming with my thoughts from earlier, thoughts of infidelity. "How did he seem then?

When you knew him?"

"Well..." he sat back. "I've known him quite some time, even after my human death. I was still his angel." He motioned his hand around the room. "How else could I earn such a lush living?" He laughed, his chest heaving with drama. "But it was all out of friendship and admiration. I found his life so amazing, so different from mine, that I wanted to learn all I could. I wanted to understand how this world came to be."

"So you guarded him." I was shocked to find that my Edgar had needed guarding at all.

"Yes, after your death..." He looked me up and down. "Or rather, disappearance. He was frightened Matthew would come back for him. He confided in me, even as a human. I actually died protecting him. Ha!" He saw the absurdity in it, for it was clear that in any fight, it made sense that Edgar should have been able to defend himself. "That is why, in the human world, my death is still a mystery." He winked.

"So that's how you became a guardian angel? You sacrificed your life for him?" I looked away from Edgar as I took in the strange turn of events.

Edgar smirked and leaned in toward me. "Well, I sort of cheated. I knew that if I died protecting him, then I'd live on forever in the next life." He winked again and leaned back. "Your Edgar told me the stories of how people could live on, even on Earth. This is how I came to be known as a major contributor to the emerging genre of science fiction literature." A chuckle escaped his lips. "Knowing Edgar gave me some great stories, and some of my greatest mysteries." He spread out across the couch in a prideful manner. "I desperately wanted to live forever and continue with my gift, so when the opportunity finally showed itself, I jumped on it. Literally."

I smiled, finding his plan a bit conniving but smart, and I marveled at how he had tricked us all. "But what happened when you died? Who was it that tried to kill Edgar?"

"Oh, my dear, this is where it gets interesting. If you can believe it, it wasn't Matthew. It was an everyday human!"

My eyes got wide. "Just an ordinary man? But then Edgar would have been fine! That man couldn't have hurt him."

Edgar slanted one eye. "You're catching on, dear! *You're a smart one.* I see why Edgar loved you so, dear." He rolled with laughter for a moment before regrouping. "You see, I was sick with tuberculosis and so Edgar angered a man, tried to get him to attack me." He sat up on the couch, adding drama. "He told the poor chap he had slept with his wife! Can you believe that?"

I looked down at my hands. *"I'm really not sure anymore,"* I mumbled under my breath.

Edgar hadn't noticed as he went on. "So, the man made a vendetta and came after him. It was our little secret, to trick the gods into making me immortal." He was leaning close to me again, one finger over his mouth as he whispered. "And to this very day, they still don't know."

I smirked, leaning away from him as I found his breath to be stale and his trickery somewhat discerning, but still brilliant.

"So you see, I owed it to him to protect him after that, and I did!" He looked proud of himself as he stretched his wings out behind him, allowing them to rest on the back of the couch. "Eventually, Matthew planned a vendetta of his own, and that was when I made the ultimate sacrifice and earned my retirement. He pushed his chin in the air. "I'm proud of what I've made of my life, hard earned lies and creativity and all." He smacked his lips together as he stood and grabbed the now boiling pot of water from the fire. He poured four cups of tea, hesitating on the fifth as he turned to look for Scott.

"Looks like your friend has left us," he exclaimed rather plainly, his mouth sinking with disappointment.

I turned and looked at the chair where Scott once was, the pen now carelessly discarded on the paper. The writing ended mid-sentence and the ink dripped into a pool. I frowned as regret washed over me. I hadn't even had the chance to say goodbye.

"Cheers to that! Good to see the little vermin went back to his own world." Sam thrust his teacup in the air before gargling it down rather rudely.

Edgar pulled a flask from his pocket, pouring an amber liquid into his tea as an oak smell rose from the steam. He then guzzled it down in one hot gulp, smacking his lips.

Margriete jolted awake and leaned forward, her hands trembling as she grabbed the cup and brought it to her lips.

I placed mine between my now-chilled hands. Edgar had held them while he was talking, leaving them cold. He hummed to himself and poured the same amber liquid into my own teacup without my permission.

"This will help you sleep, dear." He patted me on the head like a child.

I brought the tea to my nose, allowing the smell to fill my senses before taking a sip. I coughed wildly as the liquid stung my throat and sent an instant wave of sweet dizziness to my head. Edgar watched me as I took another sip, holding one finger on the bottom of the teacup and forcing me to finish it all.

I coughed one last time, my head now clear and my body relaxed. "Thanks," I choked.

I was surprised to find that Edgar drank, or even ate. Perhaps in this world, their hunger was real, where as on the surface they had denied any sort of nourishment, or even comfort. I had never seen Sam eat anything before, but Edgar seemed to enjoy it.

"Ahhh," Edgar sighed. "It was unfortunate that I could not kill Matthew when I finally passed on. It was the dagger I needed to get him, but it was impossible to knock it from his hand."

My eyes perked up, and I placed the teacup gently on the table. I reached into my belt and grasped the dagger from inside its wrapping, pulling it out. I held it in both hands. As it lay upon my palms, the light from the fire shone across the gold blade and Edgar stared at it with frozen eyes.

"Why child, you've found it!" His excitement overtook him as the cup in his hand flew into the air. The cup shattered as it landed in the fire, hissing tea filling the air with steam. His face became grave then. "But you must protect that. There are any number of beings here that would love the chance to own the power that dagger brings upon this world."

He placed his hands across the blade and handle, then

grasped my hands and curled them around it.

My gaze rose from the dagger to his face. "I hope to win Edgar back with it. I do not wish to be powerful. I just wish to be happy and love."

Edgar's eyes seemed to well with tears and he smiled. "That is what the dagger is truly meant for. Its corruption was never meant to be reinforced, and the curse of it dies when someone sacrifices the power before the gods." He held tight to my hands. "You have the heart to destroy this dagger, and in this, no more of your kind will die."

I looked at Margriete then back at Edgar. "I fear there aren't many of us left, at least not that I know of."

Edgar's face sank and he sighed. "This is quite unfortunate." He shook his head. "But if you can achieve this, there will still be hope for you." He smiled. "You will receive what you wish, but for how long, I am uncertain. You must be wary of the bargain you sew with them."

"What do you mean?" I pulled the dagger back toward me, pushing it back into the edge of my belt.

"The gods are tricky, and will find any possible loophole to get what they want. They want to ultimately cause you as much pain as necessary before they feel you deserve your reward of happiness, especially your kind." He sighed. "I fear their discrimination against your perfection has gone further than necessary. I do not understand how or why they still hate you, or rather, fear you. I have come to believe that they created in you the power to overthrow them, with or without the dagger, but how this will come to pass is another question completely." He brought a hand to his face, tapping his chin with one finger.

I looked at Margriete as she dozed once again on the couch.

Edgar seemed to come to a conclusion. "They will stop at nothing to torture you. Though your soul is innocent and though you do not deserve the pain, it will not matter. It is their fault for creating you, not yours, so never feel as though any of this is your doing." His eyes fell to his lap in sorrow and pity.

I placed my hand on his. "Do not pity me, Edgar. I feel I have lived a sufficiently happy enough life, even if most of what I remember was dark. Though I have faced my troubles, it is nothing I do not willingly bear."

He looked me deep in the eyes. "Then you are a better soul than the rest of us: selfless and kind. You will surely face a lovely retirement. I would not be surprised to see you placed in a chair of power one day, and not from greed, but retribution. They will think that it will be punishment, but I fear you will rise to the task and we will see a better day, a day of light and peace with those that inhabit the surface, with what was once mine."

I smiled. "Thank you, Edgar, for all your kindness, for all you have done for my soul, and for my Edgar."

He clapped his hands together. "I will bless your journey, and hope you find your way to that ultimate peace." The wild flash in his eyes returned as he stood suddenly. "But now, child, you must rest." He hastily grabbed the teacups from us all. He then rushed into the kitchen where I heard them crash into what I supposed was a sink.

He ran back out, his socks slouching around his thin ankles. "Rest here, and in the morning, we will get you better equipped for the task." He blew into the air in no exact direction as all the candles in the house were snuffed out.

Still grinning, I watched as he ascended the creaky stairs to his room. I leaned back into the warn couch, my muscles aching but satisfied with myself. I was making progress and my heart was valiant enough to handle the coming challenges. I had no idea what faced me, but I knew I needed to keep a clear, sharp head. Whether Edgar had honored our love or not, my task was heartfelt and true. I would never stray from my morals to persevere.

I allowed myself the comfort of the night as my lids shuttered close. As sleep fell over me, my mind did not wander to dreams. I was already there, in the place where dreams were made and nurtured, in the City of Angels and on the cusp of facing my demons.

COMBING

The sound of loud squawks woke me from a deep sleep. Sunlight streamed through the stained glass window and onto the couches. I rubbed my eyes and turned my head to look for Sam and Margriete. The table between the two couches was now gone, along with the bearskin rug. I raised my eyebrows, looking around to see where it could have possibly escaped to, and wondering who had moved it.

Seeing nothing, and feeling a bit uneasy, I looked back at Sam and Margriete. Both were still in a deep slumber, sprawled across each other on the couch. I let a small quiet laugh escape my lips, finding their unconscious snuggling, ironic when compared to their attitude towards each other during the day.

I pressed my weight forward as I urged my sore body to sit up. The leather squeaked loudly and I cringed, hoping for a few more minutes of solitude before Sam and Margriete woke. I ran my hand through my hair to tame it.

My clothes hadn't felt as grimy as I had expected, but after the swim in the cleanest river I'd ever seen, I figured they had the chance to come clean. My jeans felt tough, as though they had been line dried and I couldn't help but feel travel-worn. Still, I could handle these small inconveniences in honor of our mission.

I stood and tiptoed to the old cottage window, peering through the wavy handmade glass and into the yard. It was there that I finally found the coffee table and bear skin rug, creeping through the grass like a pancake, stalking a goat on the other side of the fence. I tilted my head, finding the phenomenon not only disturbing, but unreal as well.

I shook the image from my thoughts, focusing on something familiar. The surrounding mountains and trees gave it the impression of happy solitude, of retirement. Like the mountains of the North Cascades, their peaks were kissed with snow, and the clouds wrapped them as though drawn to their power.

I looked away from the mountains to the bird cage that was to the right of the window. I could barely make out the ravens rustling within their confines. They pecked at a lump of corn and seeds, held together by what seemed a mixture of peanut butter and grape jelly. Their eyes were a soft gold, and I found beauty where any normal person would only find fear and hate.

Edgar Poe hadn't been anything like I'd always imagined. He had always put on the mask of a tortured sad soul, but in this life, he seemed careless, clumsy, and rather kind. Perhaps the tortures of life had been hard on him, but now, he was free of all his worries and losing his mind to happiness.

I turned from the window toward the room. Everything felt old and eclectic, like the home of a gypsy. There was a clock on the wall and I squinted as I tried to make out the strange icons that encircled it. Where the numbers should have been, there were pictures of food instead. I laughed, seeing the absurdity of keeping track of time in this world. It seemed that the only thing you needed a reminder for was when to eat, especially for someone that had given up food during his time as a guardian.

There was a long side table set in a corner with a cloth laid across it. On top of the cloth sat five items, dusty with age. I approached, still attempting to be as quiet as humanly possible as I tiptoed past the mess of discarded books and papers on the floor.

The first object was an old pen, surely a memory of his past and his great contributions to the literary genre. The second was a small glass marble, its purpose unbeknownst to me, but obviously one of importance. The third was a rolled bit of parchment, tied with a red string, and the fourth a magnifying glass with no handle. It was the fifth that truly perplexed me.

A small brush glittered in the light from the room, unfazed by the dust that had collected everywhere else. It was more delicate than anything I'd ever seen. The handle was made of an iridescent ivory that shown like crystal, but with a milkier haze. The handle was carved in the shape of a feather, but not a feather I was accustomed to seeing. The way the fronds curled was almost whimsical, and the carving so delicate, I feared it would break from the gentlest touch.

As I examined the strange object, I mindlessly touched my hand to the ring around my neck. I had nearly forgotten about it in the turmoil of the journey, but it had also become calm and silent, as though sensing it was in its own world and was drawing closer to Edgar with every step.

It still felt warm to the touch, and it made my heart feel secure knowing that it was still alive. The power of our love was astounding, creating magic out of everyday materials, and creating the turmoil and anger of the war I now led. It seems there are few things that we fight over: possessions, love, and power, but in the end, they are the three pinnacles that drive us to our own self-destruction and torment.

There was a crash from the top of the stairs, and I turned just in time to see a metal pot come tumbling down. Sam jolted awake, rubbing his eyes and inspecting his position beside Margriete. I caught the glimpse of a smile cross his face before he noticed me watching, instantly changing it into a frown.

It hadn't occurred to me until now that I had never seen Sam sleep. The more time we spent here, the more human he became, and the notion of him as a machine of destruction began to fade. He yawned one last time before moving himself away from Margriete, watching me from the corner of his eye as though he'd been caught.

The metal pot spun on the ground before coming to a silent stop. A cursing breath erupted from the top of the stairs.

I heard shuffling as Edgar approached the landing and began to descend. Based on the state of his living room, I could only imagine that his bedroom was even more cluttered with trinkets and junk.

Edgar exhaled and smiled at us as he landed on the ground floor, smoothing his fresh shirt over his not-so fresh pants. Scratching his head, he looked to where the bear skin rug had been, cursing and looking out of the window and into the yard. He mumbled something under his breath but I couldn't make out what he'd said. He then looked to me, noticing the table beside me and letting out a happy hoot.

"You have found my prized possessions, dear!" He scurried toward me, kicking the pot on the floor in his clumsiness. "Whoops!" He glanced down but paid it no mind as he continued forward. He placed one hand on the edge of the cloth where the five trinkets sat. "*Ahh*, yes." He plucked the marble from the table and held it up in the light.

I watched him with curiosity, wondering what tales he had locked away in such a tortured and creative mind.

"*My marble*," he breathed, the light shinning through the rounded glass and showing off the various colorful planes that were locked inside. "This marble is from when I was a kid." He chuckled. "Well, perhaps it's not the *exact* marble, *but it looks just like it*." He placed the marble back on the cloth.

"And this is my magnifying glass." He picked it up in both hands and held it before his eyes. "So that I can actually *see* the marble." He placed it over the marble as a happy chuckle escaped his lips. He urged me to look. "Lovely, isn't it?"

I nodded, finding his strange collection of goods suddenly worthless.

"And this is my *pen*, with which I like to make my lists of chores!" He picked it up and hastily grabbed for the bit of parchment. "And here is where I write them," he added. Leaning into me, he elbowed me lightly. "Obviously, it has been a long time since I did chores." He winked, referencing the dust that had collected on the pen and paper.

"But this!" he announced. "This is quite phenomenal." He delicately pinched the brush between his two pointer fingers. "This is a Pegasus brush!" He held it high in the air, leaning so far back that I feared he'd topple over. He scrunched back into himself, shielding the brush in one hand and pointing at me with narrowed eyes. "One of only three in this world, mind you."

Margriete and Sam were both now staring at the brush with hungry eyes. Margriete's hair was horribly frazzled and her eyes were puffy, as though she'd slept like the dead.

Seeing their expressions made me curious. "Well, what's it for?" I asked.

Edgar began tossing it around in his hands, treating it like nothing more than a regular brush. "It's for taming a Pegasus of course!"

My anxiety rose as I watched him, fearing the delicate material would shatter at any moment. "Won't you break it if you treat it that way?" I asked, feeling suddenly hot with fear.

"Don't be silly, girl! This comb is made from the strongest rock known! It cannot break."

"Well, isn't that diamond?" I asked, my eyes seeing that

the material, though resembling crystal, was not at all clear like a diamond.

"No, no dear. It's made of the same rock as the thrones of the gods! It's *fazonite*."

I flinched at his somewhat abrupt and awkward comment, and naturally, I didn't understand. As far as I knew, there was no such thing as fazonite. Margriete suddenly stepped from around the couch and approached.

"What he's saying, Elle, is that that brush is literally the key into the kingdom of the gods. In order to get to them, we must cross a vast sea. In order to do that, we must ride a Pegasus, the carriers of the gods. And in order to ride a Pegasus, we must tame them with that brush." She took a deep breath, finding her explanation had drained her lungs.

I looked back at the brush and Edgar. He smiled at me, his beady eyes and tangled hair comically benevolent to the games he was trying to play. "And you keep it with your fake childhood marble and list of chores?" I gasped.

Edgar shrugged. "Why not? What's wrong with that?" He looked to Sam and Margriete for some sort of affirmation that he wasn't crazy. "To each their own, right?"

Sam grumbled and shook his head. "*Man's a nut case*," he muttered under his breath.

Margriete smiled, giving me a sly look that told me to play along. She placed one graceful hand on Edgar's back. "And you're going to let us borrow it, aren't you?"

Edgar looked at me with a skeptical glare.

"Please?" I cooed.

Edgar smiled then. "Oh, all right." Giving in, he tossed

it to me.

I stumbled forward in order to catch it, its weight nothing compared to its size. It was as light as the carved feathers its handle would suggest. "It's so light!" I exclaimed, now letting it rest in the palm of my hand.

"Perfect," Margriete exclaimed. "That was just what we needed. Thank you, Edgar."

Edgar nodded and left the room, the pots again clattering in the kitchen. I assumed he was attempting to cook us breakfast.

"So, how did you get across before?" I whispered to Margriete.

She leaned toward me with a smug look on her face. "I borrowed it."

"You mean you stole it," I added.

She shrugged. "The old coot didn't even know it was gone."

"You're terrible!" I cried.

She ruffled my hair. "It's all about survival, honey. Our kind could benefit from being so resourceful."

There was another clamoring noise from outside and a loud thud reverberated against the cabin wall, followed by a painful murmur. Sam quickly went toward the window, his fingers resting on the pane as he looked out into the yard.

"You've got to be kidding me," he grunted.

There was a clumsy knock at the door in a familiar rhythm I couldn't deny recognizing.

"Scott!" I skipped to the door, swinging it open. Scott stood with his hand on his head, looking behind him as though something was hunting him.

"I thought you couldn't hurt yourselves in dreams?" he whined. "I think there's a table trying to attack me out here!"

I laughed as I gave him a big hug and he groaned in agony. "How did you make it back?"

Scott stepped over the threshold, eager to get inside. "How could I forget? I woke up and wrote all about the dream. And then when I fell asleep again, I remembered it and was able to make it back." He was quick to shut the door behind him, looking out the small window and scanning the yard anxiously.

He was much more alert than he had been toward the end of yesterday, and I figured that suggested he was in the beginning of his sleep, in his deepest REM cycle. There, his mind could lend itself to the reality of this world.

"How did your test go?" I asked.

Scott frowned. "Not too good. But I think I'll pass, maybe."

I gave him an encouraging pat on the back and leaned toward him. "That's all right. Sometimes teachers just don't get that perhaps you know more than what a test really looks for. Don't worry," I whispered. The relevance of an education now seemed trivial to me.

He nodded and stepped inside as Edgar jumped in the air.

"Ahh, wonderful! The human is back! How fascinating." He rushed to Scott's side and examined him while Scott gave him a rude glare. "Frank didn't hurt you, did he? He can be a real bear sometimes." Edgar laughed and elbowed Scott.

"Get it? Bear?" He winked.

Scott gave him a strange smile, suggesting he was trying to be nice, but also acknowledging that he was crazy.

Sam was tapping his foot, his arms crossed against his chest. "This is ridiculous. Can we please get going?"

Margriete stifled a snicker as she gathered her things and strapped the book across her back.

Edgar frowned. "Leaving so soon?"

I put one hand on Edgar's frail arm. "I'm sorry, old friend, but we have to go. I have to find Edgar."

Edgar's eyes glittered. "I understand. You love him, just as he always said. You will never find a connection as strong as what you two have. It's beautiful, the essence of the term love." He became lost in a day dream.

I watched him for a moment before answering. "Thank you, Edgar." I leaned in and squeezed his small body against mine, but no matter how hard I hugged, he managed to hug even harder.

"Alright, everyone!" Scott pushed his hand into the air. "We're off!"

Sam walked past Scott, brushing his shoulder and knocking him into the wall. "You don't even know where we're going, idiot."

Scott rubbed his arm with a sour face. Margriete eyed him with a coy stare as she too, brushed past him and out into the yard.

"Thank you again, Edgar. I promise to return your brush." I went back to the couch and gathered my pack.

Edgar sulked. "You didn't even get the chance to try my

235

cooking!" He sighed, trying to guilt us into staying.

"When I return, Edgar. I promise you can fix me an eight course meal." I kissed him on the cheek before heading for the door, fighting my desire to look back at the unbelievable figure in my wake, the greatest poet the world had ever seen, at least on paper.

I shut the door behind me, the clasp grabbing with a gentle click. The magnitude of the outdoor world took my breath away. This place changed more than that of the world I was used to, and it always left me guessing. The clouds in the sky were a deceptive soft white, the sun now somehow orange and the air the perfect temperature.

We quickly gathered in the yard where we all took a moment to assess our next move. I heard a loud roar from the backyard, followed by Edgar's yelling. I laughed to myself, figuring he had finally found Frank and the coffee table.

"So, which way?" I asked Margriete, watching as she licked her finger and held it up, testing the air.

She narrowed her eyes, looking to the tower from where we had come. She then looked at the water fall, and turned to look in the opposite direction.

"Forward," was her only reply, and that was exactly what she did, traipsing past the fence and into the trees.

BLACK AND WHITE

As the morning wore on, the houses that dotted the woods seemed to grow ever smaller and ever drawn by age. From time to time, a curtain would flutter behind the thick panes of glass, suggesting there was someone there to watch us on our journey. The trees had changed as well, as though our travels had taken us to another country and geographical region all together.

The clouds overhead grew dense, and the light around us seemed to suck all the color from the world, leaving it drained of its former luster and rich beauty. It had been nearly an hour since we had passed a house, and I was growing bored.

Sam grabbed a bunch of evergreen bows, pulling them back and then letting go. Scott dodged between trees, a game unfolding in his mind to which only he knew the rules. He was engulfed in its world, mind and soul. The change in atmosphere had been so subtle, it was hard to tell exactly what was happening, but as I looked back at Margriete, she too seemed to analyze the change. I noticed how black and white she looked, the colors now completely gone. We were nothing but a cluster of monochromatic figures, like you'd see in an old movie.

"Margriete? What is this place?" I asked. Her silvery eyes were still as brilliant as ever. She looked at me and they flashed like sharp rays of light.

"We're entering the outer perimeter of their kingdom. Whatever lies around it is literally sucked of its beauty. Their kingdom needs the power of that which surrounds it, and so as you may expect, their castle teems with color and life."

There was a break in the trees up ahead, and as we reached the edge of the forest, all life ceased. My breath struggled to find the relevance of the vast empty space before me. I looked to my right, seeing the line of trees circle widen into a perfect circular perimeter around our final destination, leaving nothing but desert.

The clouds overhead clapped with thunder as they swirled into a distant center point. I craned my view to see what that point was, but the mists were thick and the horizon closer than that of their kingdom.

Scott came to a screeching halt as he emerged from the trees. "Whoa…" his eyes got large and the light that hit his face made his skin turn white with sudden fear.

Sam choked on a laugh, stepping forward onto the dry desert ground. His footprints were washed away by the wind, leaving a perfectly polished surface of fine sand and dust. Margriete also stepped forward, pressing on in her stubborn manner.

I grabbed Scott's hand and we followed, eyeing each other with wonder. The storm overhead clapped again, light flashing through the clouds as a bolt of lightning landed somewhere in the distance.

"Everyone, we need to stay alert. Those thunderclouds are dangerous, and out here, we are likely the only conductors. We need to stay just behind the storm and move fast." Margriete's face was like stone as she yelled over the now howling wind. Angry clouds of dust blew by us, stinging my face.

I nodded, grabbing Scott's hand even tighter as we picked up our pace. Another flash erupted across the sky, this time right overhead. Margriete frowned and looked skyward. Sam's wings sprung from his back, readying himself for disaster. Scott marveled at Sam as we walked behind him, somehow forgetting the danger and now taking in the science of Sam's condition.

I moved faster now, almost breaking into a hurried run as Margriete's long legs widened the distance between us. The skies grumbled and Sam's wings flared, the tips completely splayed. My palms began to sweat as they grasped Scott, his attention now faltering. I saw it was growing time for him to wake. Despite the fact he was leaving us, I continued to drag him along as the rain began to fall, determined to keep him safe, though it hardly mattered.

Sam's wings became heavily matted as the drops fell in fat swollen orbs, cooling my now hot skin and soaking my hair. Rain ran down my face, dripping from my lashes and flooding my mouth as I licked my lips, eyeing the skies once more.

There was another rumble, and like the flash of lightning itself, Sam lunged forward and crashed into Margriete, shoving her to the ground as a giant bolt crashed into the spot where she had been walking. The bolt shattered the earth with a loud crack, leaving my ears ringing painfully.

I skidded to a halt right before the smoking crater, my heart surging and pushing blood through my now trembling limbs. There was another sudden pop as Scott's hand disappeared from inside mine. Squinting through the rain, I saw that he had disappeared back into his world. I pushed my wet hair from my face, slapping it down my back as I looked back to where Sam and Margriete had fallen.

They both scrambled to get off each other, quickly standing, breathing hard. We all looked at each other then, and without a word, began to run. As Margriete's feet began to tangle with haste, I watched her change into the cat. Her soft paws now pounded the Earth with twice her previous speed, leaving me quite literally, in the dust.

Another rumble cracked across the sky, shearing down to Earth right in front of me. I jumped backward, also changing into a raven before my feet hit the ground. I banked back and around the now-smoldering crater and caught up with Sam. He, too, fanned his wings and took flight, ignoring the fact that flying made his body twice his original size, marking him as an obvious target while sparing Margriete and I.

He shielded Margriete below him as I pumped my wings faster than I ever had in order to keep up. The rain pounded hard across my feathers, filtering from my tail and making it hard to navigate through the air. Another crack lit up the sky, hitting the ground beside us as the bolt split, the smaller half-igniting across the sky in slow motion. It nicked the tip of Sam's wing and I heard him cry out in pain. His body jolted down to Earth where he cut through the muddy desert ground, leaving a deep trench about fifteen feet long.

The last rumble filtered into the distance, the clouds now somehow content with the injury they had inflicted. They twisted east and away from us as whiter clouds suddenly filled the skies. I landed on the wet ground right next to Sam. He lay on his side, half grunting and half laughing from the pain. I quickly changed and placed one hand on his smoldering wing, inspecting the spot where the bolt had hit him.

Sam shook his head as Margriete trotted toward us, mud layered in thick clumps to the fur on her feet. She shook the rain off her as she changed, her spine arching up into a standing position.

"*Sam,*" she gasped, falling to her knees as she placed her hand on his wing. She pushed me out of the way.

I couldn't help but gawk at the way she had reacted to the situation, as though Sam had suddenly meant much more to her than she had previously revealed.

"Sam, does it hurt? Will it be okay?" Margriete tried to heal his wound, but in this world, it was no use.

Sam smirked and sat forward. "Oh, stop mothering me. I'm fine. It's nothing more than a battle wound." He grabbed Margriete's hand and pulled it away from his wing, his fingers laced gently around her wrist like a twig.

They stared at each other for a brief moment before Margriete thrust her arm out of Sam's grasp, grumbling and

241

falling back onto her butt.

A sharp exhale rushed from my lungs as I realized what had just happened. Looking away, I hid the smile that was growing on my face despite the somewhat stressful situation. Margriete actually cared for Sam, cared for him in a way I could tell she didn't know how to react to. When I looked back, Margriete was rubbing her wrist as Sam tended to his feathers, tucking his wings back into his back and standing. The tension was now thicker than the clouds.

"I think we should get going," I urged. The wind picked up then, just as it had before.

Margriete looked to the sky and adjusted the pack on her back, turning with an abrupt grumble and walking forward with one arrogant step. Sam looked at me and shrugged, winking as he gave me a partial smile. He had heard everything I had thought about the situation, right down to the thoughts in Margriete's head as well.

We walked forward then, both struggling to keep up with Margriete. The storm was still a ways off, but up ahead I could just make out the edge of what seemed a cliff where the desert floor ended in an abrupt drop-off. As we came closer, it almost seemed as though the world suddenly ended, and all that was beyond this point was swirling clouds and a sea of misty air. Margriete halted just inches from the edge, craning her head and looking both ways. She grabbed the book from her back, her face still painfully twisted as she tried to make sense of the earlier incident.

Distracted, it took her a while to get the book open and flip through the pages. The wind also created an annoying obstacle. Sam walked right up behind her, looking over her shoulder and reading along, antagonizing Margriete even further. She took one angry step to the left, twisting away from Sam and muttering to herself. Her finger was pressed firmly against the glowing paper of the book, causing the gold lettering to sear off the page in her flustered attempt to read.

Sam gave me another wink. I tapped my foot impatiently and narrowed my eyes at him. I looked overhead at the impending clouds, now only minutes from where we stood. I crossed my arms against my chest and inched closer to the edge, looking over and experiencing a rush of vertigo. It dove down through the misty clouds and into nothingness, the world still black and white, only emphasized by the subtle light escaping from the sky. Below, the misty fog sat still like a giant pool of cotton, the wind unable to reach it as the cliffs shielded it from this landscape.

A large drop hit my forehead and I looked away from the crevasse and back toward Margriete. Her eyebrows looked more relaxed and I could tell she had found something helpful. She seemed to weigh the information on the page against that of our surroundings.

"There should be a ladder somewhere here." A drop of fat rain hit the page she was reading. She shut the book.

I looked over the edge. "Where?"

Sam approached the cliff, now squinting and craning his head as well.

The wind was really beginning to pick up, threatening to push us over the edge as I continued to search.

"There!" Sam yelled over a heavy gust and I looked in the

direction he was pointing.

Squinting even harder as the sand began to swirl over the edge, I saw something jut from the cliff. It tangled downward and I struggled to discern how Sam had even seen it to begin with. The clouds clapped in the distance, sending chills down my spine. Margriete motioned us toward the ladder, picking up our pace as we hurried to reach it before the storm. Sam spread his wings and flew out over the edge, his injured wing causing him to struggle, but holding as he spiraled around and downward, inspecting what he had seen.

He flew back up toward us, yelling across the distance. "It seems safe!"

Margriete didn't hesitate as she put one hand on the rough wood that seemed to grow from the Earth, and as I looked closer, that's exactly what it did. She threw herself over the edge and the large root ladder groaned and twisted under her weight, but it was strong enough to hold. I placed one hand on the twisting root, looking skyward once more before ducking below the surface of the cliff, the wind ceasing almost instantly.

Rain began to fall in heavy bands, but as we descended, we were safe from the storm, now shielded by the edge. Sam continued to spiral downward and as we became engulfed by the misty fog. The world was suddenly silent, and Sam was no more than a blurred figure beside us.

THE LAKE

"Sam!" My voice echoed but I was unable to see just what it echoed from. "Sam, are you still there?"

I heard a deep throaty laugh as the fog beside us swirled and Sam flew closer to the ladder. "Still here."

I looked down at Margriete, wondering if she was as tired of climbing as I was. It had been at least an hour since we descended below the ridge of the desert floor, and I wondered if this would ever end or if we'd end up in China. The rooted ladder was bound to the mountain, still creaking under our weight as it grew downward and out of our view.

Margriete looked up at me, her face taxed and tired. The light was slowly growing dim and I knew it meant that the night was coming. I didn't want to be stuck on the ladder in the darkness, though with the thick clouds, it already seemed as though we were.

I tried to think if I had ever seen fog quite so thick, and my mind aimlessly wandered back to Seattle on a crisp fall morning. The fog would often settle between the buildings, creating a sort of blanket that had felt so comforting. The fog choked out all the greed and hate of the city, leaving nothing but silence. It was then that I realized that we must be close to water, for what else could create such a dense fog?

I heard Sam yell from somewhere below us, and I snapped out of my reverie and listened as he repeated himself.

"Not that much farther. I think I see the ground!" he yelled.

I snorted. "See? How can you see anything?"

Margriete allowed herself a chuckle, but it was instantly silenced as she abruptly dropped through the bottom of the fog and everything came clear.

I paused and looked around, the fog floating just above me now as I descended another few rungs. The thick cloud was suspended like dry ice, as though something invisible had been holding it there. I looked down past Margriete, seeing the ground only a few feet below her. In my excitement to get off the ladder, I pushed away from the wall and jumped over her, hitting the ground with surprising softness. Sand gave beneath my feet.

I ruefully rubbed my sore shoulders, holding my arms at my sides as the blood ran to my fingers. It tingled with such discomfort, I found myself shaking my hands to relieve the pain. The fog continued to linger like a house with a low ceiling. Sam's tousled hair was nearly touching the clouds, but as we stood there, they lifted slightly, readjusting themselves after our assured agitation inside it.

Looking away from the cliff wall, I saw that the sand

extended about fifty feet before it gently sloped into a body of water. There were no waves that lapped against the shore and I was amazed by the silence, having become accustomed to the roaring life of this world.

Approaching the water's edge, I looked down into it, seeing my de-saturated reflection look back up at me through the glassy surface.

"Perfect." Margriete came up beside me, a look of satisfaction on her face.

"Perfect?" I gave her a sour look, wrinkling my forehead. *"We're stranded."*

Margriete looked at me with disdain. "Have I led you astray yet? Elle, you've got to trust me. Just wait." She plopped down on the sand, crossing her ankles before her and propping her elbows on her knees.

"We're just going to wait?" I looked down at her, irritated and anxious to move forward.

Margriete nodded and tapped the sand beside me as Sam walked down the beach, assessing the situation.

I plopped down next her, finding myself defeated. A heavy exhale drained the energy from my body as I melted into the soft sand. Despite my desire to go on, I could not deny the fact that I needed a rest.

A few minutes passed before I looked back at Margriete, her eyes closed and her mouth frozen in a half smile. "What are you thinking about?" I broke the silence, my voice carrying over the water.

Margriete slowly opened her eyes, her long silver hair perfectly layered against her back. "I was thinking about

Matthew, and when we were happy."

I looked down into my lap, tracing my finger through the sand and making a circle. Edgar's ring dangled downward like a pendulum, swinging out toward the water as though begging me forward, toward its rightful owner. "You really did love him once, didn't you?"

She nodded, tears welling in her eyes, but I could tell she forced them back out of pride. "I feel cheated, as though I was always set up to fail, always meant to end up alone."

I nodded, remembering what it had been like to be alone. "I can't imagine what that's like, knowing you have no future in love." I expected her to cry, but instead she smirked.

"But then, if I am bound to be alone, as others are, then we aren't so alone anymore." I saw her glance down the beach toward Sam before she turned back to me. "Do you ever think you'd learn to love someone else if Edgar were gone?"

I shrugged, giving the question a lot of thought, as I had already. "I think that over time, I would learn to love again." I tilted my head. "Especially for you because you now know who your true love was, a monster and a murderer."

Pain flashed across her eyes. "It's true. Knowing what Matthew had become made it easier for me to forget him. After all, he had discarded me in his greed, left me to die. I would have never done that to him, and it makes me wonder why we were soul-mates at all. I always figured we shared the same desires, the same morals." She sighed and pressed her brows together. "I could never take an innocent soul as he had so carelessly."

Sam was walking back to us now, a smile on his face. He

had heard our conversation, but it was no secret. It wasn't like Margriete and I had been discreet about it.

"I feel as though I could love again." She searched my eyes. "It's surprising how thrilling it is, to have that feeling light up my soul."

I laughed. "So you do like Sam. *I knew it.*"

The corners of her mouth pressed into her cheeks and her eyes glittered. "He *is* pretty handsome."

I let out a loud hoot, my voice echoing off the water. The sound magnified on its way back toward us. "Grietly! *That's sickening*! This is Sam we're talking about."

"What?" she put her hands in the air and pulled her shoulders up to her ears. "Well, he is! And he's funny. It's hard for me to keep from smiling every time he opens his mouth."

I shook my head and leaned back onto my hands. "I can't believe it."

"What are you two talking about?" Sam loomed over us, his mouth painfully twisted in a comical manner.

"Oh, shut up, Sam." I snorted. Though he knew exactly what Margriete and I were talking about, it was fun to pretend that he hadn't, like it was our little secret.

It was getting dark now, and the only light that lit up the air was the subtle reflections of the calm water. There was something about this place that was eerily calm. It was like the center of your own mind, where nothing lives but silent thoughts. I ran my fingers through the warm sand, feeling how it rubbed my skin and calmed my soul.

I missed Edgar deeply, and despite our separation, I was

certain I would never love anyone more than I loved him. He had not wronged me in my lifetime, nor had I felt he had any beliefs beyond my own. It still bothered me what Edgar Poe had said about the time when I was gone, that Edgar had tried to move on, but failed. I wanted to know whom it was he had tried to love, whom it was that sparked his interest enough for him to try to forget.

The water lapped against the sand and I looked up, startled by the subtle sound that had previously been void from this world. Margriete perked up along with me, sitting forward as the water lapped again, this time harder.

"It's coming," she whispered, motioning me to stand as she was.

"What's coming?" I whispered back, but she gave me no answer. I would find out soon enough.

We stepped back from the water's edge, the water now lapping like a summer's night back on the shores of Puget Sound. I looked to Sam and Margriete, but their eyes were both fixed on the waves. It was then that something erupted from deep within, illuminating the water with a soft blue light, the only thing that had any color in this strange place.

The water pushed toward the beach as the thing approached, disturbed by the movement. As it came close to breaking the surface of the water, I winced, finding the light hard on my eyes. Stepping back once more, my heart began to beat faster, the object now just a few feet in front of us.

It was still silent other than the waves on the shore, but as the light broke the surface, a loud cry filled the air: that of horses. Astonished, I covered my mouth, watching as three sets of giant wings cut through the surface along the waters edge. The water splashed violently up toward the fog layer above us.

The horses reared and crashed through the water, their bodies made of a glowing opaque crystal, like that of the brush Edgar had given me. Their eyes were hollow, as though smoothed out by years of rushing water rolling over their skin. They trotted through the waves now, approaching the beach as their wings remained extended, assisting their advance, yet not quite flying.

Tossing their heads, they gathered before us, their empty stares watching us, waiting.

"What do we do?" I whispered to Margriete under my breath.

"Get the brush," she hissed.

I slowly reached behind me, unhooking the delicate brush from my belt and holding it in my grasp. It, too, was glowing now, and when the horses saw it, they let out another cry.

Margriete nudged me forward, my feet sliding through the sand in my attempt to resist her. One horse stepped forward, its hoof pawing at the sand, nudging me. Its crystal nose felt cold against my skin. I lurched backward, watching as my gaze looked through the beast and into its soul where a large crystal heart beat in its chest.

Margriete again pressed me forward, and as she did so, I thrust the brush toward the animal. The horse lowered its head, its wings retracting against its spine in rueful appreciation. I held the brush out in front of me as far as my reach would allow, inching forward as I placed it on the horse head, moving it in short small circles.

The horse let out a small whinny and pushed forward, nudging me again, but this time with a playful toss of its head. Sam snorted, stepping forward and grabbing the brush from my hand. The horse before me nipped at him, angry that he had made me stop. It pinned its ears back.

Sam gave it a warning glare before bravely approaching the horse to its left. With one fluid stroke, he brushed down the length of the horses flank below his wing. The horse delightedly danced in place as he did so, accepting him despite his rude demeanor.

Sam then turned and tossed the brush to Margriete who caught it. Her face was stunned as she slowly approached the last horse. She ran the brush through the crystal mane, the horse's hairs pinging against each other like bits of glass, filling the air with a soft music. The third horse had been much calmer than the other two, as though sensing Margriete's unease and adjusting in such a way to make her feel comfortable.

We took one step back, waiting for the Pegasi next move as we all stood on edge. All three horses watched us now, suddenly at our service. Their eyes darted between the three of us. It was then that the first horse let out a satisfied snort.

Margriete smiled, the smile turning to a sly look of satisfaction that glowed in her eyes. The ethereal light from the horses reflected within them.

"And now, *we ride*."

CENTER OF THE WORLD

"This is unnatural." Sam adjusted himself atop the Pegasus, the oddity of angel wings and Pegasus wings tangling amongst each other, fighting for control.

"Sam, just tuck your wings. You're fine. You don't need to be so defensive." Margriete pointed to Sam's back as her horse walked in tight circles, anxious to move forward.

I giggled, finding the situation embarrassing for those involved. Sam grumbled under his breath as he loosened his grip on the mane, finally giving up as he submitted himself to a position of inferiority, something I'd never thought I'd see in all our lifetime.

Sam glared at Margriete, and Margriete smiled. I rolled my eyes at the sight, sickness threatening to well in my throat as I thought about the love blooming before me, much as it had with Scott and Sarah. Though I knew my own love story was sappy and filled with personal moments, I had at least refrained from subjecting anyone else to viewing it. My horse reared as Margriete's horse nipped at its tail, becoming restless with our inability to collect ourselves and press forward.

I had never imagined a Pegasus to be so beautiful, like a drop of dew on a spring morning. It felt as though I were sitting on air, the cool crystal smoother than anything I had ever felt. It was like the softest water as it runs through your hands. Their existence within the ocean before us was mystical. They were the air of that world, moving with such grace and silence that it made the mermaids jealous.

My horse stepped out toward the water, its hooves clapping against the surface like crystal goblets smacking together. Its wings were extended, allowing the simple rules of gravity to fall away as though the water were no longer a passable element, but a glass stage. I looked below me and then to Margriete, with fascination.

"Cool, huh?" she yelled, her voice echoing. "They walk on water." She pointed toward the horizon. "This is the only way across. That's why we needed that brush, to tame them, so that they would lend us their backs."

I looked up at the layer of fog above me, now grazing the top of my head. Margriete was right: Sam would have never been able to fly through such a narrow space without disturbing the fog. If that were to happen, we would surely lose our way like a boat in a storm.

"Just lay low," Margriete said it more to Sam than me as

she saw that his head was engulfed by the fog, making him appear headless.

I snickered and leaned close to the horses glowing mane. I looked down through its withers to its heart. All three horse's reared as they lurched forward, bucking themselves into a gallop as the sharp clanging of hooves became so intense, that it was like shattering glass. Each step caused the water to ripple, droplets flying up behind us as I looked back over the horse's rump. Its tail was ringing like bells as the strands crashed together, flowing in the wind like a stream of water.

Up ahead, a glowing crescent rose from the water like a moon, its light casting long rays directly toward us, leading our way. As we continued closer, the moon-like orb continued to rise until it rose up and into the fog, the bottom half now peaking from below, still lighting our way.

As I winced from the light, I noticed the color around us was seeping back into the landscape, the light from the moon now spraying bright rainbow rays through the horse's crystal bones. It was then that an island rose from the horizon as though pulled by the moonlike orb, glowing in a color I had never seen in the human world.

I could not look away as we swiftly descended onto the mass of land, the misty air clearing and the water now a vibrant aquamarine. A bright white light began to grow from the center of the large island, its outlines slowly forming into that of a city that was surrounded by a large wall, and guarded by its own atmosphere. The horses approached the other bank without hesitation. As their hooves landed on the sand, they skidded to a halt, their rumps dipping to the ground and their front legs becoming buried in the sand.

I lurched forward, the sudden halt threatening to launch me off and onto the ground. The horses stood, their wings flapping as we all assessed our new surroundings. I tried to blink away the colors and shield my eyes from the sudden clarity of light. As I looked up, I saw that the swirling clouds I had seen in the desert all converged at this point, twisting in a circle like the eye of a hurricane. There were bright flashes of lightning as the storm above still raged on, threatening any whom dared to come here.

"What is this place?" I gasped, looking to Margriete. My heart knew where we were, but my nerves had not been ready to accept that this was it, that this was what I had been working toward all this time. I anxiously grabbed the handle of the dagger in my belt, feeling as the ring around my neck seemed to sink into my chest with searing warmth. I was so close now. Edgar was practically within my grasp. I could feel it.

"It's the nucleus of all things: the gods' kingdom." Margriete looked at me with terrified eyes, her face remembering her last trip here, remembering the fate that had befallen her.

Sam dismounted, his feet sinking into the sand. His horse suddenly reared, taking off toward the water as it crashed below the surface, its light slowly fading as it descended into the depths. I, too, dismounted as my horse was now anxious to follow its friend back home. Once we were all standing on the sand, we watched the last horse disappear, and then our attention turned to the large gates that split the wall.

The rungs of the gate were thick and bright, made of the same rock as the horses, but somehow more brilliant. There were levers and locks covering each rung, glimmering in the light from the Earth and sparkling like diamonds. I looked down at my feet, finding that the sand below the place where I stood felt like pudding. It melted in such a way that you felt you could not stand still for too long, fearing you would sink below the surface.

The overall mood of this new world was ominous, as though stuck in a glass jar that had been placed in the sun. Though there was no one in sight, the overwhelming feeling that someone was watching filled my body with tension. The only sound was that of the waves behind us, crashing to the shore as though pulled by the energy of the island, threatening to engulf it.

Margriete reached over her back and grabbed the book. I continued to analyze the peacefulness of this place, listening for anything and everything. I stepped toward the gates as Sam hung over Margriete's shoulder. Placing my hands on the bars, I tried to look through the clear rungs to the world beyond, but they seemed to blur my vision, refusing anyone to spy in but giving the notion that you could.

The wall itself was made of a cool, grey stone, unlike anything I'd seen before, but perfectly shaped and mortared, as though freshly laid. I took a step to the right, realizing my feet had sunk into the sand up to my ankles. I gave each foot a shake as sand collected in the arches of my shoes. The clouds above crashed and the thunder continued to rumble, my bones shaking with each growl.

"Hey, Elle." Margriete broke my attention.

I looked back to them.

"Come look at this." Margriete summoned me forward, pointing at something in the book.

As I rounded to look at the page, I saw the book now glowed with a replica of the gate. Each gear was in place and each lever locked. Margriete touched her hand to each gear and the ink twisted under her touch, attempting to unravel each catch as the door began to twist. Just as the doors were about to open, the movement began to slow, finishing with a crashing halt. Margriete sighed.

"Well, it's not that one." She looked up at the gate as it loomed before us. "We can test the levers with my drawing." She turned her gaze back to the page, "We only get one chance to get this right on the real thing, so my drawing is a major help. Otherwise, we'd be stuck here, sinking into the Earth forever."

I crinkled my brow. "But there must be hundreds of levers!" I looked at the fifty foot door again, feeling overwhelmed.

Margriete chuckled under her breath. "Exactly. That's why I made the drawing, so that we don't screw this up," she reiterated.

I grunted, feeling defeated and dumb. "Well, don't you remember which one it is?" I shot back.

Margriete glared at me. "If I remembered, then we'd be inside by now. Besides, who knows if they've changed the locks or not." There was a distinct tartness to her tone.

Sam pressed his long finger onto the page. "What about this one?" The gear turned beneath his touch, quickly locking and refusing to budge faster than Margriete's attempt had. He frowned, feeling foolish.

Margriete let out a sharp laugh. "Nice try, Sam."

I glared at the page, attempting to redeem myself. I hesitated at first, but as I looked back at the gate, I saw that there was one lever that seemed to stand out. It wasn't particularly large, but the shape was somehow different than the rest. Most levers were fashioned into round shapes with swirl vine-like handles, but this one was solid and square.

Looking back at the page again, I raised my hand and brought it to the paper. The ink writhed under my soft touch, as if disliking the fact that I wasn't Margriete but still succumbing to my wishes. The gears began to move, one at a time, starting from the far right corner of the gate and twisting each gear until they unlocked another, creating a chain reaction of silent motion within the ink.

Margriete's mouth began to twist into a smile. She watched with hungry eyes, Sam looming over our shoulders. The gears now spread into an overall rest as the latches simultaneously lifted. There was a clean, open line between the two gates, suggesting it had unlocked. We all looked away from the book and toward the bright glowing gates at the same time. Our eyes rested on the square knob, our minds alive with hope.

Sam was the first to lunge forward, an excited grin on his face. His wings sprung from his back, and he gracefully jumped up toward the lever, pulling it down as hard as he could. He let the loft in his feathers drop as he put his whole weight into it, finally landing on the ground with a solid crash as sand sprayed across my face.

Margriete elbowed me. "Show off."

The doors lurched to life then, creaking like rusty iron. Each gear scratched hard against the next, announcing our arrival in a less than secretive way. I put my hand on my stomach, feeling my insides twist into the heart of me, filling it with cold fear. This was the moment I had been waiting for all this time, but I was not yet ready to face whatever was beyond.

Each gear now rested on the next, exactly the way it had in the image. The latches that had previously locked together across the middle of the gates now lifted one at a time, like unzipping a sweater. Light poured through the opening, even brighter than the light of the island itself, and it beat down on us in an array of colors.

I felt Margriete grab my hand and squeeze it. The last latch lifted from its notch and the doors slowly opened inward. At first, it was hard for my nocturnal eyes to focus, but as the lights evened, I was struck by a scene straight from a distant dream. I hadn't been sure what to expect, but as my eyes fell upon the golden valleys of this new world, the nerves in my stomach subsided as though doused in serenity.

A part of me had thought that when we reached the gates, we had reached the end, but now it was evident that there was still more traveling to do. The golden hills rolled before us, the sky a deep blue that contrasted with the hills. A soft wind worked its way through the land, pushing over the golden grasses that grew in perfect rows across the ground.

Walking forward, the grass met me like a wave, engulfing

my legs and covering all of my lower body. I put my hands out to either side, letting the strands of wheat lace into my fingers. The seeds popped off as the tops became locked at my knuckles. The breeze was warm and sweet, and as we passed under the arches of the gate, the world behind us disappeared. There was nothing left but the gate itself, open to more field beyond.

Margriete sighed. "Well, this is it."

I let some seeds fall from my hand. "This is what? Are we here?"

She smiled and laughed. "Of course we're here. We're in the gods' land."

I thought for a moment as I looked around the simple landscape. "Does it have a name?"

Sam stepped in. "Of course it has a name." He let out a snort. "It has many names, but to you, you may better relate to the term Heaven."

I laughed under my breath. "So, this is it, huh? This is where we all go when we die?"

Sam grunted. "Maybe, depends on what you are. Humans all make their way into some future life, or job, such as me. It all depends on who you were in your life on Earth. That determines who you are now."

I nodded and pressed my lips together, finding the logical notion of it easy to digest. It made sense that we all worked toward a future, but that future depends on the life we had lived. "What happens to those who believe in other religions?"

We began walking forward now, more out of habit than

determination.

"They're all recognized here, even those that don't include believing in anything at all. It was all part of the human project, to determine what happens when people are placed in various geographical regions of this world," Sam continued. "All this is one big experiment, and it's true that we are all the same, or rather, we all believe in the same thing, though it's different." He chuckled. "If that makes sense."

Margriete was humming now, and I looked down at my feet, noting that my pants were covered in wheat dust. "I think I get what you're saying. It's just so hard to believe. There is so much pain and suffering that has been caused by this, all over the world."

Margriete stopped humming. "Well, honey, that's the test. Who you are on Earth determines who you are here, your place. It's like a giant college up there." She pointed to the sky. "And this is real life."

Looking up, I found it hard to believe that we were in the center of the Earth. The skies here were so clear, so believable that it was hard to think that if I flew high enough, there would be a ceiling.

As we crested a hill, something bright caught my eye. In the distance a white tower rose from the ground. It was still so far away that it seemed like no more than a dot on the horizon, somehow further than it had been on the beach. It was as though the island continued to grow the closer we got.

As we worked our way through the fields, the golden wheat slowly turned to green and the terrain began to change. The soft earth gave way to rock and dirt, and the air around us grew humid. We dropped down a hill and the tower again disappeared on the horizon. Wildflowers now dominated the view before me, reminding me of the meadow back home. The sweet smell of wheat was replaced with the scent of nectar, far more potent than I had ever smelled on Earth.

We walked slowly over a few more hills before I was able to associate the fruity smell with that of a forest of pear trees that was now surrounding us. Their fruit was perfectly ripened and plump, begging to be picked. The speed with which we changed from one season to the next was magical, like a tiny ecosystem.

Sam looked at the fruit with wary eyes, thoughts swimming before his gaze. "It's like the forbidden apple tree, except there are hundreds."

Margriete giggled. "I just hope we don't run into Adam and Eve. I'm not into nudity in the middle of the afternoon."

I couldn't help but smile as I thought of all the stories there are about forbidden fruit: the poisonous apple, the Garden of Eden. Fruit was a symbol of life, the process the world takes to grow, over and over again. When I thought I was no more than a sad abandoned orphan, I had vowed to never abandon my own children. Now it seemed I'd never be able to have children of my own, and I'd never know the joys of being a mother, or the cycle of life.

I had always figured I'd have time to think about those things, but when you know that having a baby will never happen, it's like having an option ripped away from you before you even get the chance to know it. I was certain my eternal life and our lethal attraction would prevent Edgar and me from ever having that small joy that seemingly every other thing on Earth had.

I sighed, attracting the attention of Sam as he listened in on my thoughts. There was a look of pain on his face, a look I knew meant he was relating to me. I was certain that seeing Jill made him think of the same things. Surely there was a day when he was young where he had dreamed of having his own offspring, of passing on his family name. I saw him glance toward Margriete, his love for her seeming to grow with each step we took.

I was happy for them, happy that they both seemed to want to move on, to find more to this life than the suffering pasts they had observed. Life had dealt them a difficult hand, and I didn't blame them. I knew how it felt to want happiness. If I could have found something to make me smile as a young child, I would have welcomed it into my life with a strong embrace.

Edgar's face flashed across my memories. His awkward smile filled my soul with warmth, and I grasped at the ring at my neck. Edgar was a strong man though his heart was so cold, but when he looked at me, it was as though all that had changed and his heart had found warmth and love. I remembered the way his face would twist into a smile, a smile that was reserved for me alone.

There was a movement between the trees, and I quickly halted in the orchard grass, losing the image of Edgar. Sam had seen it, too, halting just beside me and grabbing Margriete's arm. She winced and cursed at him, but Sam snatched her from her stand and twisted her into his arms. He covered her mouth with his giant hand and narrowed his eyes at her, willing her to stay quiet and calm.

As we listened, the only sound was the soft wind through the trees. My chest rose and fell in measured breaths. Just as I was about to dismiss the disturbance, there was another movement, followed by a young melodic round of laughter. I twisted my head in the direction of the noise, the three of us now back to back in a defensive circle.

Something white skipped through the trees, closer to us than before. Another giggle reverberated off the thick trunks, and I felt the heat from Margriete as her blood pressure rose. She grabbed my hand and Sam grabbed hers. It was then that a small head popped out from behind the tree directly before me. I gasped, dropping Margriete's hand and grasping my chest as my heart threatened to stop.

The small face smiled at me, followed by another giggle. I relaxed a bit, finding the incident less terrifying than I had initially imagined. I blinked and dropped my hand to my side. It was no more than a child, dressed in white with a face like porcelain. She blinked her eyes ruefully and slowly stepped out from behind the tree. Margriete and Sam twisted beside me, now gawking at her the same way I had.

"Hello," I cooed. My muscles relaxed and I let my body hunch down to her level.

The girl gave me another sweet smile. "Hello," she replied, her eyes full of wonder and life.

Margriete grabbed my hand, cautioning me as I took one step toward her. The girl mimicked me, stepping closer as well.

"What are you doing out here?" I asked, watching her as she clasped her hands behind her back and twisted in place.

"Hunting for june bugs," she replied plainly, shrugging her tiny shoulders. Her white dress fluttered at her knees as a soft wind circled through the trees.

Her skin was much like Sam's, but held a more youthful glow. There was something about her that seemed so innocent and strange, as though forever hidden away from the world's troubles and unaware of its evils.

Margriete made a strange noise of recognition. I looked back at her. Her eyes were wide and a smile crept across her face.

"I know what she is…" Her voice tailed of as she began to nod, now holding our attention, even that of the young girl.

"This child died young in her time on Earth." Margriete watched as the young girl reacted to the comment, her face sinking. "Because of this, she is forever bound as a carefree child in this world, since she never got the chance to live out her life on Earth. She lives it now, almost like a 're-do' of sorts."

I pressed my brows together in disbelief. "A re-do? You mean the gods basically said 'whoops,' and they are now attempting to make up for it?"

Sam laughed at my simplistic conclusions.

Margriete smiled along with him. "For lack of a better explanation, yes."

The girl giggled at us as we took a moment to mull over the fact. I watched her as she knelt down in the grass and began to hum, picking at the blades and making a tiny bouquet of apple blossom flowers.

"She's so beautiful," I uttered under my breath. Her soft blonde hair blew in wisps. There was something about her that reminded me of myself as a child, the child I had dreamed I could have been. When I was a young girl, I would sit and stare for hours, wondering why I could not find happiness.

I was suddenly jealous of the girl, enjoying the childhood I never had. I wanted to be able to live that life, and know what it was like to feel that everything was safe, that each day was just another opportunity to play and explore. I sighed, wishing on the fact that maybe one day, I could be granted this opportunity.

Sam patted the young girl on the head. She looked up at him with loving eyes, like those of a doe. She ran her tiny hand through her hair, rearranging what Sam had tousled. She then handed the tiny bouquet to him, his hands crushing the stems as he tried to take them.

There was a sudden call that twisted its way across the orchard. The girl turned her head, her smile even bigger. "Coming, Mama!" she yelled back.

My heart melted as she turned back to us and rose to her feet, the grass twisting between her toes. "It was lovely to meet you folks." She gave a delicate and polite bow before turning with her bouquet and running in the opposite direction toward home.

I forced back tears as I watched her disappear between the trees in her own kingdom of Heaven. I was certain I would never be granted such asylum in the next life, and I began to wonder if our kind even had a future here. If we had already made our place in this land, surely we would crumble away and become a part of the Earth itself, no more than dust.

THE INNER CIRCLE

As we finally emerged from the orchard, I saw a small cottage at the end of the acreage and I figured that was where the girl had lived. The orchard grass instantly gave way to another field, but this time the white towers I had spotted earlier were much closer, close enough to cause my nerves to crumble.

The land before me wended its way down to a city that crowded toward the center. The white towers were smooth and sharp, piercing the sky in their grandeur. Through the field before us was a road, and we made our way to it. The road was rough and cracked, showing signs of heavy wear and travel. I was suddenly reminded of The Wizard of Oz as I felt myself relating with Dorothy, feeling the same fear and hopes of going home.

There was movement around the castle, a bustle resembling that of a street fair. Flags blew in the wind, each one brandishing their own unique design and color. There were a few clouds of smoke that blew toward us from the wagons, each laced with a different smell: meats, flowers and bread. My mouth began to water at the smell, though my stomach rebelled at the thought of food.

Sam cursed as he stumbled through the rivets in the road where water had carved a deep crevice. Arborvitae began to spring up on either side of our path as though rows of soldiers, watching our arrival. My heart was pounding in my chest and my palms began to sweat as I allowed them to filter through the cool spring air.

Crickets were singing from amidst the field. I tried to pretend I was home on a summer day, in the meadow where I knew I was safe and where I knew I could still find Edgar, if not in body, than at least in soul. I closed my eyes as the first sounds of the market met my ears like a tickling song. It had been a long time since I was faced with a crowd, and the subtle noise awakened memories I had suppressed for so long.

Seattle had its own beat, a drum that ached on day after day, thriving with life. I had hated the mediocrity of it, but the sound now felt like a triumph because I knew I was above that, and could handle the pain it welled deep inside.

I struggled to catch my breath as I opened my eyes, stifling my need to break down right here and turn back. I had to be strong not only for Margriete and Sam, but for Edgar and my future. A man approached us on the path, pulling a small goat on a tattered cotton rope. The goat bleated with each step, defying the pull of its master and longing to chew on the fields beyond.

As we approached, the man gave me a terrified glance, followed by a shaken smile and a tip of his hat as though he knew me. I grasped at the dagger in my belt, remembering my destiny and wondering if he had known. The fact of the matter was that I was not here to challenge the gods, I was here to compromise. They had little to fear from me: I would never rule them.

Sweet smells still flooded my nostrils, laced with cinnamon and oil that was now stronger than before. As we came upon the fair, I took in the parade of carts that lined the streets and fields beyond. The gathering was so large I wondered how one could find what they were looking for, let alone find their way back to the road.

I jumped as a clown dove in front of me, his mouth grotesquely stained and his eyes whirling like rolling marbles. Sam grabbed the clown and shoved him aside out of instinct. He threw him into a cart of small animals, each one a mix of many species I'd known from the world above.

I felt like everyone was staring at me, like everyone knew why I was here. Each face I met looked at me with either fear or hate, and I couldn't understand why. The circus of visitors was frightening and dark, obviously the product of a tormented human life of bad decisions.

We walked past continuous rows of street vendors, all peddling their goods in a desperate manner, much like bums. My attention was grabbed by one cart in particular. A cage held an animal that seemed to be made of solid steel. As we came closer, I was able to read the sign, seeing that they were griffins, too young to possess the heat they eventually would.

It was then that I noticed a young girl, much like the girl we had met in the orchard, walking through the crowd toward us. Her head was down and her hands clasped together out of fear. A vendor in tattered clothing approached her, heckling her in a frightening manner. She winced away from him, her eyes remaining fixed on the ground, making it obvious that she didn't belong here. As we approached, I noticed Sam clenching his fists, his back becoming rigid with anger.

The vendor looked up, surprised by our sudden proximity. His grotesque smile sunk to a frown and he quickly backed away from the girl as he saw Sam's wings tighten around his shoulders. The young girl shook before us now, and I knelt to the ground, placing my hand on her arm to comfort her.

"Are you alright, dear?" I asked quietly, the noise around me fading as I listened to her quick and frightened breaths. My heart sank as I remembered my own childhood fear. I was never able to understand my abilities, and the rejection that always surrounded me had left me crippled. Her blond hair fell around her face, shielding her from the rest of the world in a veil of safety.

The cuffs of her white dress were stained with mud, and her bare feet were worn and dry. Her breathing was still fast as she tilted her head up, her piercing blue eyes meeting mine like a wave of electricity. She blinked, fidgeting with her hands.

"Are you Estella?" She whispered, an innocent fear swimming in her eyes.

Shock overcame me as she uttered my name. I struggled

to find my voice but instead I nodded, the lump in my throat making speech impossible.

The girl continued to breathe in long, laborious drawls, and I wondered what had been done to such an innocent being. She was a true vessel of happiness that was now forever stained by this world. People began to gather around us, some watching me with vindictive stares, faltered in their thoughts only by the presence of Sam.

"You…" the girl stuttered, eyeing the sudden crowd. "You are to follow me."

I looked at Margriete, pure fear and sorrow filling her eyes. Margriete nodded to me, placing one hand on my back and urging me to stand. I took the girl's hand in mine, and she looked at me with an adoring stare, as though relieved I was here to comfort her. She turned and led me back toward the direction she had come, back toward the white towers. The crowd around us parted, keeping a safe distance.

Her tiny hand grasped mine with eager force as she pulled me forward. Her tiny palm was sweating, but she refused to let go. She stumbled ahead, a mirror of myself at her age. The ring on my chest was pounding with life, in time with my own heart as the gravel crunched beneath our feet. The girl took two steps for every one of mine.

As we approached the gates, I saw that two guards were flanking each side. Their bodies were rigid like statues and their heads were that of wolves. I watched as their sharp yellow eyes followed me in, their mouths salivating with hatred.

Margriete leaned in toward me. "Be still, as long as we stay calm, there should be no trouble."

The wolves growled at the sounds of Margriete's whispers, and she instantly backed away from me. The girl squeezed my hand even tighter until I could feel her own blood pouring through her veins. One guard let out a wild roar and the gates instantly came to life, the gears grinding as they forced open what looked like pure limestone doors.

I had never seen a structure so amazing in my entire life, so beautiful and yet ominous. The gates were at least forty feet tall and about two feet wide. As they opened, the dirt pressed hard behind the doors and swept inward. Once the doors came to a halt, the girl pulled me forward with dutiful bravery, licking her lips as she concentrated on her task.

As we passed under the gateway, the doors behind us began to close. I turned my gaze to the road ahead. The path before us was made of pure white gravel with grass on either side, cut so short that it reminded me of a golf course. Against the walls were rows of cages, filled with black ravens, an entire army of evil ready to be unleashed upon the world. The ravens began to move about as they saw me, discomforted by my presence in their kingdom. I looked one directly in the eye, shocked to find nothing more than a blank white stare, their souls completely gone.

At the end of the path were large stone steps that led up to another set of mahogany doors, studded with iron. The girl clamored up the steps and ruefully laid her knuckles against the wood, rapping softly as she released her stubborn grasp on my hand. She looked up at me and the doors slowly opened. Her face relaxed as though released from the fear that had bound her. She blinked once, smiling in a manner that tickled my soul in a familiar way.

"This is where my time with you ends." She blinked again, a tear rolling from her cheek. The girl's voice was now full of authority and age, changing from that of the innocent child, to that of a woman who had seen a long life.

She smiled, her body now fading as though filtering away piece by piece. "I always knew my daughter would return to me, and fulfill the prophecies." Her child-like features aged quickly, revealing a face not unlike my own.

My mouth fell as I kept my gaze locked on hers, realizing who she was.

"I have always been proud of you, Elle. Though you never knew me, I have always been there, always watching over you." She reached up and placed her hand on my heart. "Right here."

"I…" I tried to reply, but before I could even muster the words, she had changed into a white raven. She flew up and out of the courtyard as her body faded into the sky, blowing into the clouds as though nothing more than a ghost.

I fell to my knees, tears running down my face. The emotion had been so sudden, that there was little I could do to prevent it. I knew there had been something about her that had felt close. The way she grasped my hand was more than fear, but love and pride, the pride of a mother. I wiped a tear from my eyes as I tried to calm the overwhelming emotions that now knotted me. I did have a mother after all.

Sam wrapped his arms around me and lifted me to my feet. Without words, Margriete and Sam wrapped me in their comforting arms.

"It surprised me, too, once." Margriete whispered into my ear. "It was here that I also met my own mother, but not the same way you have. I would have told you, Elle, but I didn't want to make a promise. Not everyone is allowed to know of them. They are a forgotten generation."

I took a deep breath and leaned out of the embrace. I wiped the tears from my eyes, finding my life unpredictably sweet in the worst of times. "But why did I never know of her?"

Margriete shrugged. "I don't think they ever existed the way we have. We are still the first of our kind, created through breeding, a breeding for perfection."

The sting of reality was still sinking in as Sam urged me forward. I wanted so badly to press rewind, to relish that small, sacred moment once again. It had happened so fast that it now felt like nothing more than a dream, a lost moment that I would struggle to remember all my life.

Margriete grabbed the book from her back and flipped to the last page and smiled. "Here, Elle." she thrust the book toward me. "I'll remember it for you."

As my eyes fell on the page I saw the image of two ravens being drawn across the page. They were together in harmonious reunion, forever remembered in the journals of Margriete's mind. I smiled at Margriete as we passed under the threshold and into the dark rooms beyond. "Thank you, Grietly."

UNGODLY

As the doors shut behind us, the hall burst to life with a hundred or more candles, hanging from iron chandeliers on the vaulted ceiling that were nearly eighty feet tall. The hall itself was large, almost so large that it was hard to see the other side. Our steps echoed across the marble floors that were so black, it was as though you were walking on the night sky. The candles behind us smothered out as new ones before us crackled to life, surrounding us with a halo of light.

Curtains hung from the ceiling, each one a sheer wall as we stepped through them. We followed the long, black marble path and made our way toward a dim light at the back of the hall. Sam fought with the curtains, cursing to himself as he pressed each one aside.

Margriete laughed as she pressed back the last curtain, unveiling a door that had been cracked open as though expecting our arrival. Laughter and music erupted from inside and I found myself full of curiosity, not fear. We all looked at each other one last time, taking a deep breath as I pressed my hand against the old door. I applied gentle pressure and the hinges creaked, opening into a large room beyond. A bright light poured down over us, warming my skin.

The laughter I had heard instantly faded as we entered. My eyes adjusted and a scene formed before me. We had entered into a large room. There was a long table that spanned the length of it, fitting in the space almost perfectly. Curtains hung from the walls on large wooden rods, filling the room with warmth and dulling the echoes. Smoke from the thousands of candles billowed toward the ceiling, acrid as it wafted into my nostrils.

"Ahhh..."

A voice echoed through the room toward me, causing me to shudder. The tone held a frightening resemblance to that of Matthew's. My breaths were short and measured as I scanned for the source of the voice, prepared to face my fate. Roots grew from the ceiling as though suspended from the Earth above, and it made it hard to determine where the voice had come from. Items were tangled amongst their branches, from swords to goblets. All matters of things both precious and trivial.

"We've been expecting you, my dear!" another voice rumbled toward me over the long table, this time full of happiness and humor. "Come, have a drink!"

A goblet scratched its way across the table toward me, weaving between the roots as though a puppet on a string. Sam snatched the glass before it tumbled to the floor, bringing it to his nose and inspecting the contents. He took one deep breath and winced away from the goblet. He then threw it against the wall to the left and shook his head, suggesting that whatever filled the glass was either foul or poisoned.

The laughter of five souls now filled the room, followed by the same deep voice. "I see you have brought protection. You are wise." The voice sighed as I tried to pinpoint the source. "It was worth a try. That trick usually works on someone."

I took a bold step forward and around the table. I pressed back the roots as I went, still searching for the source of the voice. Sam followed me, a hand on my back as though ready to snatch me away at a moment's notice. I pulled back a curtain that the roots had gathered into a knot, and it was then I finally saw them.

With a stern face, I focused on the five figures that were gathered around the end of the table, my eyes doubting what they indeed saw. At the head of the table was a short, chubby and bald man with gold rings piercing through every bit of his body. He was smiling widely, his large belly exposed through his purple vest.

To his right sat a lady, her hair a pure white and her skin even whiter. She was glowing with an ethereal light as though she herself was the sun. She smiled sweetly, but her eyes were a sinister grey that cautioned me. My first instinct was to trust her, but her eyes shook me to the core.

"State your purpose, child." An old man to the left of the man with the gold piercings hissed at me. Though he was not seated at the head of the table, I could tell he was the leader. The air about him seemed to freeze in his presence, striking fear in my soul.

I suddenly felt infinitesimal beside them, these ancient souls of creation. "You…" I began, my voice catching in my throat. "You have stolen something from me." I jumped right to the point, feeling that my nerves would only last a short time before I would surely falter.

The old man chuckled, the room now colder than before. "I believe it is you whom have stolen from us, girl." He laughed with vicious disregard and looked down his nose at me. A small man beside him pressed his glasses up to his eyes like a scientist. I focused on the small man, unable to bear looking into the eyes of their leader. He had a small bowler hat and a cane. He was no taller than a five year old child, though I doubted that he was as weak.

I looked away from the man to the last god that was directly across the table from the small scientist. She was beautiful and young, her eyes a deep blue and her skin like silk. She blinked and narrowed her eyes at me as though comparing herself to me, deducing she was far superior. Judging by her sour face, however, she knew better. As I held the stare, I felt a part of her enter my soul, a part that was afraid of me. She knew we had some sort of future prophecy I did not yet know.

I looked away from her, finally gathering myself and looking back to the leader. "I…" I stuttered. "I am not here to challenge you." I placed my hand on the dagger and all five gods shifted nervously in their seats. It was obvious that they were as anxious as I, and just as curious about what would happen next.

For a moment I let my mind daydream, allowing it to see what it would be like to challenge the gods, and take their seat in this whole world. There was a part of me that longed to save it, to steal it from their clutches so that what had happened to me could never happen again. Edgar Poe had said that by willingly giving up the dagger, all its power of death would drain from it, leaving nothing more than a sharp trinket. My soul longed to believe this was true.

The old man at the head of the table must have sensed the evil thoughts inside me, because the roots above us began to twist. A knot of them fell slowly from the ceiling. My thoughts instantly ceased as the ring around my neck burned into my chest, the root's contents causing the world around me to swirl and fall away. Edgar was wrapped in the branches like a bundle of hay, lifeless and frozen as though suspended in slumber.

The old lady in white now spoke, her voice almost a whisper, but her words justifying her dark sinister stare. "I believe you cannot afford such thoughts, child. You are at our mercy."

I let go of the dagger in my belt and dropped my hands to my waist. I could feel Sam behind me, his body rigid and uneasy. Margriete quickly whispered in his ear, keeping him calm. I forced back tears as I urged myself to look away from Edgar's lifeless body.

"Why do you hate us?" I hissed through clenched teeth. Fixing my jaw was the only thing I could do to keep my teeth from chattering and giving away the fact that I was terrified.

The young woman laughed under her breath. "You act

as though you think you are better than us, child."

I pressed my brows together. "I do not," I retorted with anger trailing in my words.

"Liar," she hissed.

The old man raised his hand to calm the woman's jealous outbreak. "Please excuse her. She does not understand with whom she is dealing."

The woman crossed her arms before her, pouting like a spoiled child.

"I will make a trade, then." I tried to remain composed, but the presence of Edgar felt intoxicating, my soul surging with a love I hadn't felt in months.

The old man laughed once with a soft exhale. "You owe us more than just the dagger, girl. You owe us your life, as well." He folded his hands in his lap and leaned back in the chair. "I will allow you to trade your life and the dagger in sacrifice for Edgar, but that is all."

I felt the anger inside me begin to well. "That is hardly a fair trade, my lord. You forget that I still have the dagger, and I would rather die here and sacrifice us both than allow Edgar to live without me once again." I placed my hand on the handle of the knife, the gods squirming in their chairs, unable to risk taking my words lightly.

The old man leaned against the table, placing his head in his hand and running his fingers through his long beard in thought. The young woman whispered something to him across the table, her voice low and quick. The old man nodded slightly, acknowledging her remark and leaning back.

He raised the roots that cradled Edgar back toward the

ceiling. I felt my heart breaking. "I will make a deal then, child," he paused and adjusted himself in the chair. The small scientist kept his eyes fixed on my hand and the dagger, his mouth gaping. "Give us the dagger and walk away from here. I will grant you your life, and we will think on the matter." He ran his hand across the table. "You see... We need you, so we cannot afford to have you dead."

I smiled to myself, knowing that there was more to what they had been saying. I was more than just a soul. I was a valuable tool, perhaps just as valuable as the dagger. "I will do nothing for you unless you give me his life." I pointed toward the ceiling where Edgar hung.

The old man laughed. "I will promise you. I will give Edgar back, but you must leave now, without the dagger, and without him."

I narrowed my eyes at the man, realizing there was no other way I could twist this. The gods were offering me their word, but I knew better than to trust them. "I will leave." I grabbed the dagger and pulled it out of my belt in one swift movement. "But I will not hesitate to kill all that roam Earth if you do not uphold your end of this bargain. I will destroy your prized creation and there will be nothing to stop me, because without Edgar, I do not fear death."

The old man smiled. He saw the truth of my words, and the heart of the lion that would stop at nothing to honor the man I loved. The young woman leaned across the table with a frantic face and whispered something to the old man, but he hushed her. It was obvious that they had been planning to trick me, but they had not planned on my own vicious attack in return. I was not like Margriete. I was not afraid of these mere beings before me, and I was not afraid to do what it took to avenge my lost life.

I slowly lowered the dagger to the table and placed it on the wood, then stepped back.

"What are you doing?" Sam hissed behind me. "You cannot trust them, Elle."

I gave Sam no reply, but instead watched as the old man hungrily grabbed the dagger. He grasped it in his greedy hand and pulled it toward him. I had given up my best bargaining chip, but something inside me told me to trust them.

I exhaled and closed my eyes, looking up toward Edgar. "I love you," I whispered.

"You've made the right choice, my child. Now leave." He was abrupt.

Sam placed a hand on my shoulder, urging me back. My body did not want to move, the emotion inside me growing thick. I wanted to scream and cry, but I knew I could not show such weakness. I gave into Sam's hand and backed away from the table, never breaking my gaze as we backed out of the room. As the doors slammed behind me, I felt my heart sink. The future was uncertain, but I felt it was not time to rest just yet. I took a deep breath and exhaled, regrouping myself. Hastily, we exited the white towers and made our way back toward the gate. I was anxious to get out of here, my body begging to find a place of comfort.

My hands filtered through the wheat of the fields. I licked my lips, watching as my hands trembled. My steps grew labored, the journey home an uphill climb. Giving in, I fell to my knees and began to cry. Sam and Margriete stopped, coming to my side to comfort me. The wind blew over my tear-stained face, and within the whispers I heard the voice of my mother.

"Be strong," she said.

I sobbed once more before breathing deeply. I would do as I was told. I would go home and wait. I knew that my threat had not fallen on deaf ears, and the sooner I could get home, the better.

I did not wish to destroy the only world I had known, but should it come to that, I would free all humans from the vicious experiment they had been subjected to. The gods could command the world here, but I was in command of the world above. In time, what the gods have created would kill them, and it will be me that would be the leader of this crusade, the last stand of all human kind.

HOME

"Oh, Elle, I'm so happy you did all this for us, I don't know how I've come to deserve such a great friend." Sarah winked at me as her hair blew in the warm meadow wind like a wave of chocolate. There were flowers in her hair, and the dress she wore was simple, blowing like a sheet of silk behind her.

I smiled and gave Sarah a hug. Margriete purred and rubbed up against her leg, her white fur so bright she nearly blended with Sarah's white dress. Margriete had chosen to remain in disguise for the event. Scott walked toward me, dressed in a beautiful black suit I had lent him from Edgar's closet.

I straightened the lapel on his coat as he studied my face.

"Did you find him, Elle?" He put one hand on either shoulder, squeezing me in a way that broke down my emotional guard.

I nodded, feeling the tears begin to gather in my eyes as I looked away from him.

"Will he come back?" Scott pressed. He had grown from the boy he had once been. The time he had spent with us in his dreams had changed his views on life, making him realize how important life is and how much a part of everything he truly was.

I shrugged, pressing my lips together. "When the time comes, Scott, will you be there to help me?"

Scott smiled. "I would follow you to the ends of the Earth if I had to, Elle, and you know that."

I nodded. "You did."

He laughed.

"Thank you, Scott," I added. "I owe you everything for that."

"Aw, it was nothing. I never knew sleeping could be so fun!" He was acting as though it were no big deal, like it was all just a dream, which to him, it had been.

Scott knelt down and rubbed Margriete on the head. As he stood, he looked over my shoulder and laughed, causing me to turn to see what he had seen. Sam had appeared in the meadow, his face covered in an uncomfortable grimace as he fought with the suit he had succumbed to wearing. Despite his initial hatred for Scott, he had come to respect him, and this was his way of showing it.

I laughed as Margriete let out a long meow, her jowls chattering at the end like a chuckle. Sam gave me a reproachful glare as he came up beside us, picking up Margriete in one swift movement and cradling her in his arms.

"You better not say anything about this ever again," he grumbled into her ear, nuzzling her fur and making her purr.

I smiled. Since we'd been back, Margriete and Sam had managed to find love again. It brought warmth to my heart to know that I had been responsible for so much happiness. I had challenged the rules enough that it gave them the strength to embrace their love and live it everyday.

We made our way toward the aisle I had set up in the meadow. Scott and Sarah's entire family had come, even Scott's mother. I chuckled as she wiped a spot of something from his cheek.

His mother had been confused as to why and how we had managed to get so much furniture into a meadow that was so far from the college, but the concept was too complicated for her to ponder over for too long. I was sure Scott had kept my existence a secret, knowing that his scientifically-minded mother would never be able to believe in anything but the facts.

My smile began to hurt as I watched Sam carry Margriete toward the front and take a seat. I lingered toward the back with Sarah, finding that the wedding had begun to wear on my emotions. The ring around my neck had remained there, never faltering to breathe. From time to time it would provide false hope and burn into my skin, as though he was finally here, but he never came.

Sarah was shaking with both fear and happiness, grasping my hand with the same eager strength my mother had. The fact that she had been real was all I ever needed, all I had ever wanted. It was hard to be an orphan, wondering why your mother had abandoned you, but now it was clear that she had no choice, and her devotion to me was undeniable.

The music started. "Go, Sarah," I whispered, placing my hand on her back and urging her forward down the aisle. She walked alone, her father long gone although here in spirit. A soft breath escaped my lips and I took my seat, content with all I had accomplished. I had done my best to find Edgar. I had given it my all and now I would wait. The violinist's music rang across the grass, the flowers around us blooming from the fragrance of so much love and so much life.

I leaned back in my chair and closed my eyes, taking in the scent of it all as the subtle sounds and the feeling of life surrounded me in a vortex of acceptance. Edgar's face was close at mind, always the same and never fading. I thought about his scent, remembering every bit of our short time together as though it were a movie I could play over and over. I inhaled, the sharp ping of longing fluttering in my heart like wings, fluttering around me as though he were here.

Grasping the ring around my neck, I slowly opened my eyes, relishing the true feeling. Startled, I let out a soft cry and jumped. The fluttering I had felt had been real. A black raven now sat in the chair beside me, its head tilted and its opal eyes glimmering in the sun. It had come without a sound, as though a ghost, the ring in my grasp now burning. I dropped it to my chest in shock.

Tears fell silently from my eyes as the raven stood there, quiet and calm, the wind fluttering through its feathers. My chest began to sting and I realized I had forgotten to breathe. I brought my hand to my mouth and exhaled through my fingers. I closed my eyes and told myself it was just a dream, an illusion created by my tired mind. I faced the front, unwilling to allow myself such childish behavior.

Opening them, the raven was now gone, replaced by a dark figure that flooded my peripherals. It was then that the figure took my hand and my soul burst open with more life than it ever had, affirming that this moment was real. I could not move to look at the figure, afraid it would leave as swiftly as it had come.

Sam looked over his shoulder, smiling at me as though he, too, saw what was happening, as though he'd known all along. He winked and nodded, and I found it hard to deny any longer that this was really happening. This figure beside me was no longer in my imagination.

The figure leaned toward me and spoke. "Thank you."

I exhaled as Edgar's quiet breath fell across my ears, sending chills down my spine. His soft fragrance surrounded me in a cloud of smoke, and my head began to feel faint.

I took a deep breath before turning to face him. His eyes were a deep, cloudy blue, crashing like thunderclouds across the sky. The lump in my throat rendered me speechless as Edgar brought his other hand to my face. He cupped my cheek and leaned in, never once breaking our stare as his soft lips met mine. I closed my eyes and grasped onto his arms, refusing to ever let go, but as always, Edgar gently pushed me away. There was a smirk on his face, and his eyes were black.

Still want more?

Log onto

www.featherbookseries.com

or

www.featherbookseries.wordpress.com

for more info.

Also, Check out Abra Ebner's newest book

Parallel: The Life of Patient 32185

Available at Amazon!

Raven Coming January 2010!

Preview on Next Page!

RAVEN
Book Three

Some say that God leaves our world from time to time, giving us weeks, years, decades, millenniums to rule on our own, only returning when things are at their worst; the next Apocalypse. Could we handle this power on our own and thrive? Or would we simple destroy it, polluting this planet beyond what is reversible and pump from it resources we use only to cause further harm. If God is leaving us, then will he return? Do we deserve to be saved once more? Or will this be the last time…

RETURN
Edgar

"You cannot do that to her and you know it." Sam's voice crashed through the trees of the forest.

"I can, I have to see her," The anger inside me was so deep that I wanted to rip Sam to pieces, and I could. I slammed my hand into my palm, angry that I could think of such things.

Sam looked at me with a skeptical face, "I doubt you could actually go through with it. You could never kill me."

"Stay out of my head, Sam. I've warned you." I growled, pacing from one tree to the next. "And I don't care, Sam. I need to know that she's alright."

Sam shook his head, "She needs to grow, Edgar. You know what she is as well as I do. You can't cage her like a wild animal."

I clenched my fists at my sides. What did Sam know anyway? He had no idea how it felt to be me, to feel the hatred and anger of the whole world weighing on my soul everyday. Elle was the only thing that could calm me, the only thing that could make my mind clear.

"Coming to find you was enough of a burden for her. She needs another month to recover. She needs to grow the strength she needs if she is to do as is prophesized. Then…" He laughed. "Then you can come back and tell her what she needs to know. If you know what I mean." He glared at me.

Sam's words of wisdom were far too chivalrous for me to handle, and my nerves ripped apart. I stopped pacing, halting as the dirt gathered under my heels. "I know what she needs, but that's not my concern."

Sam continued to glare. "If you won't tell her about it, then don't come back at all." He crossed his arms against his chest, making a stand against me.

I shook my head. "What is this, Sam? Are you in love with her?"

Sam threw both his hands in the air and laughed in a mocking tone. "Hardly. She's all yours cowboy."

I was looking for a fight, but he was playing it smart. He knew just what to say to keep my emotions at bay, just enough courtesy to justify peace. But, peace was the last thing I wanted.

"Look, Edgar. She needs a little more time. I knew you were coming back. I came to the forest to stop you because I don't want you to barge in on the process that's going on. Right now she still needs to be away from you, so that she can feed on the power independence gives her. But soon enough, she's going to need you. I realize how weak you are right now, but you have to wait." He laughed under his breath. "And by the way, you look like hell."

I narrowed my eyes at him, still hoping that he would give me a reason to slash his throat.

"This is one of those times where you need to be a civilized gentleman, though I know you lack the ability. If you rush to see her now, it is likely you will end up becoming overwhelmed and kill her." Sam took one step toward me and I felt my will to stop myself begin to falter. "I'm thinking in her best interest. Apparently you're not."

I lunged at him, but before I even got close, he managed to spring up and into a nearby tree.

A deep laugh grew in his throat. "I told you, Edgar. You are weak."

I shook my head, feeling the whole world whirl around me like an angry cloud.

"Her friends are getting married soon, that will be a good time for you to show up, if not a little sappy. It will give you a month to regain some strength, and pull yourself together." Sam lowered himself from the tree with one hand. "Besides, you have a problem that needs to be addressed."

I took a deep breath, looking at him with hate in my eyes. "What is that?" I asked through clenched teeth.

Sam crossed his arms against his chest. "You left that holograph of yours behind, down at the college, and its beginning to cause problems. I've found it lurking in the woods out here, looking to find Elle and take the soul for his own. It thinks it can live!"

I let out an annoyed sigh. "Piece of junk."

"Well you created it," Sam retorted.

"Shut up, Sam. It's not a big deal." My jaw was fixed. What was that thing thinking? A red hot feeling of murder rose in my chest. The desire to kill so sweet, that it made my bones ache.

I tried to calm the feeling, remembering that I had declared never to do it unless it was a righteous cause. But this was, I thought. I laughed to myself, remembering the day I had vowed to uphold the code, laughed as I saw Matthew beside me, making the same vow.

I sighed and let the anger roll off my chest. Killing this ghost would help me. Murder was always the quickest way to regain my strength and quench the thirst that burrowed in my heart. Sam rolled his eyes, and I shot my gaze to meet his. His face sunk into a frown, his mind unable to ignore my angry thoughts.

"I'll warn you one more time, Sam. Stay out of my head." I lifted one brow, eyeing him.

Sam smiled and turned away from me, saying something under his breath as he walked back toward the meadow.

"Where are you going?" I snapped, following after him as my feet pounded the earth, threatening to crack it open.

Sam's wings erupted from his back as he jumped into the trees in time to avoid my angry swing. My arm sliced through nothing but air, knocking me off balance as I fell to the ground.

"I'm going home, Edgar. If you know what's good for you, you'll get your act together before attempting to see her. I'll be watching you." Sam hovered over my head before landing and placing both feet on my wrists. He trapped me against the earth, taking advantage of my weakened state. "After all, she is mine to protect, and I will do whatever it takes to do so. If I so much as sniff one ounce of danger from you, I will not hesitate to sacrifice all I have."

I struggled to get free as he once again took to the air. "Edgar, heed my words. I will be back in a day, so I suggest you set up camp and get comfortable. There's not much more you can do." He smiled at me. "Oh and… you're going to need to acclimate yourself to those." He pointed behind me, and I looked to where he had. Shocked, I grabbed at my shoulders, seeing I had wings.

Sam's laughter echoed through the trees. "You should have known, Edgar. Though you still retain all your previous abilities, you still died saving her. You're an angel now, and a raven."

I snarled as I righted myself, sitting in a puddle of mud. I watched Sam disappear between the trees before exhaling. As much as I didn't want to hear it, Sam was right. I had saved her but had also forgotten what sacrifice means. I still felt the raven inside me, but now this? What more did I need to endure to test myself? Was this another way to protect her?

Elle was something special, something different. I had been warned of the consequences of being her mate, but what could I do? Leave her alone? Leave her empty? I had done that for far too long, I was done. I had always thought that I was put here to protect her. Never did I expect that one day she would come to save me. Never. I thought it was my job to remind her of who she was, to bring her back, but now

I was no longer certain.

Why had she forgotten everything about our life before, and everything she knew about herself? Why, if she was so important to us all, had she forgotten what she was destined for? I was beginning to think that this whole thing was what the universe had planned. Perhaps they wanted to see what she would do when placed in these painful situations, tricking her into falling in love with the human race in the hopes of making her feel sorry for them. It was no secret that the universe always hated the rule the Gods had over us. They wanted her to want to save us, and destroy them. They wanted her to have enough anger in her heart so that she would grow strong. Still, the essence of the plan we had made, before Elle had forgotten it all, was finally unfolding. Whatever their reasons, we were still going to take back what was rightfully ours. We would save all those that had been tortured as we had, and torture those that deserve it.

I smiled as excitement filled my heart. Finally, it was time. Finally, the end of the reign of the Gods was coming. But if this was going to work, then Sam was right. I needed to be smart. And right now, smart was to wait.

RECHARGE
Edgar

I threw a log on the fire as I grumbled under my breath, hating every minute of this little camp out. The fire crackled as the wet log worked to heat up, sending sparks into the air and landing dangerously close to my hand. I reached over my back and grabbed a feather from the wings that still protruded, yanking one out and bringing it to my face where I inspected it.

I wasn't surprised that they were black, like a raven. And in fact, I was insulted by it, as though the Gods were making it obvious that I had an evil heart. I drew in a deep breath, exhaling as the smell of smoke made me nauseous. The light from the fire lit a small circle around me, barely flickering enough to reach a nearby tree, but I didn't care; I wasn't afraid of anything.

I began to think back on what Sam had told me earlier, about the hologram gone wrong. It wasn't the first time I had seen it happen, and it made me laugh as I thought back on my old friend Edgar Poe. We had made a hologram of him once, as a sort of joke. We used it to thwart off a needy love affair gone bad. She was a fan of his work, fanatic really, and everyday she would wait for him outside his door, no matter what the weather. The hologram served as a sort of distraction, allowing him to escape when needed, leaving her with nothing but air. Soon though, the woman fell in love with the air, and the hologram in return, fell in love with her, too. The stalker became the stalked, and eventually we had to kill it before a real murder came about. The good thing is, she stopped.

I was happy that Edgar had found his happiness in Heaven, and I looked forward to the day when I'd see him again. He was a true friend. I sighed, admitting to myself that Sam was a true friend as well, though at this moment, I wanted nothing more than to rip him limb from limb. He knew what was best, he always knew, and that's what bothered me most. I hated when people took a position above me, and though I tried to be strong enough to never allow that to happen, I was who I was, and at times I needed help.

I drew my watch from the lapel of my coat, opening the shiny silver cover and tilting the face of the watch toward the fire. It was nearing midnight, but it wasn't the time that had made me look at the watch, it was the engraving from Elle. I ran my thumb across the scratched letters, feeling the indentation rattle across the ridges of my finger. I was close enough to feel her warmth inside my soul, close enough to feel the emotion she held at any given moment; darting from happiness to tension in a heartbeat. She was anxious and afraid, wondering if I'd ever return. I wanted to hold her and tell her it was all right, but I knew there was also that part of me that held the desire to suck that very same life from her bones, ripping her heart apart like a cannibal.

I shuddered at the thought, feeling like a monster as I forced my wings back and away from me. I hid them in the shadows with shame, feeling as though I didn't deserve something so holy. I snapped the watch shut with one hand, still holding the feather in the other. My body tingled with a strength I hadn't felt before. Though I was already strong, I wondered what becoming an angel had really done and what sort of power it had granted me. I could already fly, so getting wings seemed useless. I thought I was already strong, but perhaps stronger? I knew that Sam could read minds, but could I? I tried to think back to when I had seen Sam earlier, but could not recall hearing any thoughts, but then again, maybe he had the power to hide them from me as well.

Feeling bored, I tried to amuse my mind with the memories of Matthew's death. I smiled, but it was short lived as the memories quickly turned depressing, knowing that my own death had followed. Finding there was nothing else left to distract me from the task that was at hand, I finally faced the facts and began to think of a plan. Tomorrow I would set out and hunt down the hologram. Surely then things would begin to fall into place, and I would become more like myself again. I looked up at the trees as they swirled overhead in a gust of spring air, distracting me for a moment. Next, I would build myself a suitable camp, something with all the comforts of home.

A sneer grew across my face, thinking of how lucky I was to be a part of Elle's life and her grand existence. If it wasn't for the prophecies, I would have been killed and thrown away by the Gods like a lump of trash, useless as Matthew was. Elle and I had worked hard to nurture the strength she needed to combat her fate, and luckily for me, her years spent alone and gone had granted me the time to make a plan for the future.

I tried again to tuck my wings into the bones of my back, succeeding as I felt each feather being sucked in and under my skin like an old Chinese fan, now resting along the length of my spine on either side. I smiled, finally content that I had achieved the feat, and relieved the wings were gone, at least for now. I cracked my neck, feeling as though something was out of alignment, but figuring I had a lot of time to practice.

I looked at a nearby tree, feeling it stare down on me with both fear and hope. The whole forest felt anxious, and it should. They knew what was coming, a smell of trepidation secreting from their very shell, filling the air with a sour mist. Other than the sounds of the fire, I also noticed the silence. It was as though every animal also knew, also tried to hide, but there was nothing they could do, and nowhere they could hide.

The long journey was finally over, and we had arrived at the end. All we had worked for was now coming to pass. When I look back, I see that everything had its purpose, all those years I spent alone, all the time Elle spent in darkness and sleep. Elle had been groomed by a force even the God's could not understand, so there was no one we could look to but her. What was coming was unstoppable, inevitable and sealed. Only one could fix this, but only she could decide whether it was worth fixing.

Though Elle's fate was to be this Chosen One, she still held the option to choose, and that's what the God's feared most. Her fate did not include an ending because it was undecided, but it made no matter to me. I found that not knowing the end was what I preferred. If I knew we would die, then why try, why hope? No matter what her decisions, I would stand by her, revel in the fact that she was my other half; the great one, the one.

I dropped my head into my hands, running my fingers through my hair and locking my hands behind my neck. The dirt below my feet seemed to team with power, the whole world of Heaven in an uproar. It was times like this that I admired our race, the human race. For as smart as they claimed to be, they were still too involved with their lives to notice what was coming. I knew that they would be the last to sense the end, and I found it relieving. At least this way they wouldn't waste days with worry and fear, or at least not over this.

I felt my limbs tingle with a familiar emotion. Envy, the sweetest feeling, and one I seemed to wallow in like an endless abyss. What was I kidding? Of course I wished that I were The One and not Elle, but it was never meant for me. That kind of responsibility could never be trusted to a heart like mine, corrupt and black, all but for one small piece that belonged to her. I struggled with this feeling all my life, knowing that I was less of a being, allowing Elle to prosper. It was this emotion that made holding myself back hard. Envy was powerful and bitter, a feeling that all the other ravens never had to deal with, but in this I knew I was stronger than them.

Like Sam had always said, I needed to rise to the task of being her soul mate, and be proud. Become the one thing in the world that could hold her up, and keep her going. I sat up straight on the log. Another gust of wind blew hard at my back, my wings extending as my arms erupted with goose bumps. There was a scent in the breeze that I recognized, even from this distance. I closed my eyes and breathed deep, my wings relaxing to the ground. "Estella," I whispered. The corners of my mouth curled and I exhaled, blinking a few times.

It was getting late and I knew that tomorrow was going to be a big day. I slid from the log to the ground, propping my wings behind my head and allowing them to finally come of some use. I yawned, thinking that soon my love would come back to me, soon the fun would begin.

Stay Ahead Of the Game...

Log into:

www.FeatherBookSeries.com

Or her Blog at:

www.FeatherBookSeries.Wordpress.com

ABOUT THE AUTHOR

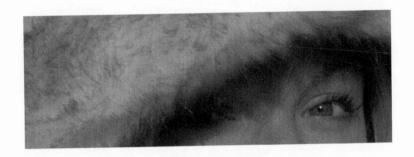

Obra Ebner was born in Seattle where she still lives. Growing up in the city, as well as the mountains of the North Cascades at her family cabin, has granted her the experience of a life full of creativity and magic. Her craving for adventure has taken her into the many reaches of the forest, instilling in her the beauty of a world not our own, in a place where anything can happen and will. Her studies in Australia, as well as travels to England, Scotland, Germany, and Switzerland, have also played as a colorful backdrop to her characters, experiences, and knowledge. Come visit the untouched world of Feather, a place where eternal love, magic, beauty, and adventure are just the beginning.

4838417